WONDERLAND WITH THE BEAST

A STEAMY PARANORMAL ROMANCE SPIN ON BEAUTY AND THE BEAST

CONNER KRESSLEY

REBECCA HAMILTON

EVERSCORCH

DEDICATION

This book is dedicated to Heather Marie Adkins.
Without her support, this story wouldn't be possible.

CHAPTER 1

FIVE YEARS AGO, the only swirling vortex I was familiar with was the curtain separating me from backstage chaos and the runway. Walking through that particular "portal" had meant glitz, glitter, and fawning fashionistas who wanted to see my thick, bootylicious curves wearing that year's spring line. The only downside to that life had been a few blisters from shoes not properly fitted to my feet.

This giant swirling vortex of doom wasn't my idea of a good time. Nowadays, death and destruction were a more likely endgame than blisters from my Christian Louboutins. I'd traded the gowns and stilettos for jeans and Chucks, and in the intervening time, I'd learned to embrace the weird and woolly world of magic.

That didn't mean I had to like it.

I stumbled out of the magic portal that had popped up in my living room with a string of curse words that probably made my mother roll over in her grave. Sparks of electricity traveled along the skin on my arms, and an inadvertent shiver ran down my spine, as if I'd passed through a veil that was never meant for human passage. My feet kicked up dust, and I tripped over my own toes, barreling towards the dirt before I even knew what was happening.

Before I could fall face first and dirty up my Gucci t-shirt—okay, so I hadn't *completely* given up on my prior life as a model—a strong hand wrapped around my bicep and halted my forward momentum.

Dangling over the ground, I flipped my long dark hair aside and glanced back at my savior.

Abram held me with a single hand, in a delicious display of his beastly strength, and his eyebrow had risen somewhere south of his hairline. My heart launched into a fast waltz as I stared at his beautiful face and recognized the look of affection in those dark eyes. It had been more than a year since that look had been focused on me.

"Magic is hard, okay?" I griped as I navigated my feet back beneath me and stood on my own again, turning to face him, though he didn't release my arm.

Abram's dark hair was mussed from my hands, and a look of satisfaction had settled on his face. We'd been dragged out of our lovemaking by our friends, only to be whisked through a magic portal by a twenty year old who claimed to be my best friend's toddler son from the future. What did it say about the current state of my life that I'd just blindly followed him?

"Jack!" I said, suddenly remembering he'd gone through the portal before us. I looked around for the kid's blond head and spotted it bobbing through the shadows up ahead.

"You were too busy falling to hear him say 'Stay here,'" Abram said, his plump, pink lips smirking. "I imagine he's scouting ahead."

"Where are we?" I took a step away from the scorched ground where the portal had been only moments before and finally took a good look at what we'd walked into.

We'd left my New York City behind, it seemed. Gone were the lights, the traffic and constant honking, and even the pedestrians. But I didn't need all those things to recognize that we hadn't left the city at all, because I recognized the thick woods around us and the skyscrapers jutting up on all sides.

We were in Central Park.

Trees lined a narrow, overgrown path that stretched to either side, angling through thick undergrowth on a course for the edge of the park. My Central Park had been beautifully groomed: flat plains mowed for picnickers, paths maintained for the hundreds of walkers and runners getting their steps in. All of that gentle care had been stripped away, leaving a wickedly dark forest of semi-dead trees that wouldn't have beckoned even the hardiest of explorers to step inside.

And the buildings...

"Jesus," I breathed as my gaze landed on two familiar, yet utterly changed, towers poking up above the dead branches. "Is that the San Remo?"

Abram followed my gaze but shrugged. "I do not know the city like you do."

I pointed at the two towers, confusion and horror warring inside me. "There were Corinthian temples at the top of those towers," I whispered. Where the temples had once sat, majestic and shining in the sunlight, there were only broken stones and debris. Even from here, I could tell many of the windows in the towers were broken, leaving the luxury apartments inside open to the elements. "I guess Bono doesn't live there anymore."

"Bono?" Abram glanced at me. "Is that a company?"

Despite our dire situation, I couldn't help but roll my eyes. We could be a couple until the world fell into ruin—which by the looks of it, maybe it already had—and my pop culture references would still go right over his head.

When I opened my mouth to complain about his lack of connection to the modern world, he silenced me with a pointed glance and motioned to the line of trees off to our right. Though the trunks were as dead and dried as the rest of the trees around us, there were thick bushes beneath covered in a mix of green and brown leaves. The bushes rustled and danced on the chill air, but not because there was any sort of breeze.

Something was inside them. Something...spying on us?

Abram held out an arm, motioning for me to stay where I was as he moved off toward the undergrowth.

I wanted to tell him to be careful, and in the same breath, I wanted to tell him off for being so damn overprotective. I'd survived an entire year without him as back up. Granted, I had Ramsey helping me hone my powers, but the fact of the matter was, I didn't need Abram to protect me, no matter how much he thought I did.

Not anymore.

But I remained mute and let him do his White Knight thing, simply watching him stalk toward the tree line and being grateful to have him back. He crept off the path, his footsteps eerily silent even with twigs and debris on the ground. I guessed that was the predator in him, the beast that had control of his body for half of his daily life.

If I'd been the one tramping off to check out the threat, I'd have stepped on every twig with the ferocity of a rifle crack, and whatever was hiding would have scampered away. The curves on my body that I loved so much didn't make it easy to creep around, though it could be argued that Abram weighed a whole heck of a lot more than me with those massive muscles and height that towered even over my own. That thought sent me off on a daydream about Abram without all the clothes, and Abram without all the clothes on top of me.

Dead, ruined, post-apocalyptic Central Park or not, my libido couldn't be dampened. I had no idea what was coming next, but I damn sure knew I wasn't going to wait out another magical disaster without making sweet, *sweet* love to that man. And *soon*.

Abram crouched down so slowly, he appeared as nothing

more than a shadow. Then his arm shot out and he stuck his hand into the bush. My heart leapt in my throat as he pulled out the softest, whitest rabbit I'd ever seen by its ears.

Horrified, I stomped off the path toward him and snapped, "Don't grab that bunny like that! They're delicate!"

Abram raised that infernal eyebrow again, but obeyed, dropping the rabbit back into the bushes.

I stopped a few feet away and crossed my arms over my chest, appalled. "You could have been a little gentler."

Abram stood and brushed his hands together, little white hairs falling delicately towards the dead grass. "It's a wild rabbit in a world that's clearly not in the right state. He's facing a lot worse than being dropped into the brambles, I reckon."

I sighed, because I knew he was right even though I still wanted to be mad at the rough way he'd handled that poor baby. But I had to consider the time he grew up in and the beast that he'd been in the centuries since. Abram didn't look at bunnies and coo over the cuteness as a potential pet. His beast only saw a potential meal.

We were interrupted by a flash of light from deeper through the trees. I turned, catching sight of Jack using his broadsword in the fading sunlight as a beacon to call us over. When neither of us moved right away, he pulled a face and motioned impatiently with his hand.

That expression on his face struck me like a wrecking ball —I'd seen that exact expression on my best friend's face every day since we were kids. Damned if he wasn't his mother's son through and through.

I know I'd blindly followed him here and believed what he said, but that look cemented my belief that Jack really was Lulu's son. That, and the ruined San Remo and desolate park, neither of which could have happened in only a matter of minutes.

We really had gone forward in time.

I brushed past Abram, still salty about the rabbit, and walked farther into the trees toward Jack, leaving the love of my life no other option but to follow.

Jack waited until I'd closed some distance between us, then he skulked away into the darkness of the forest. I followed, picking up the pace so I wouldn't lose him as we set off through the park.

Jack moved with the nimble quickness of a boy who'd learned early to stay quiet and move unseen. He reminded me a bit of Abram's beastly instincts, though of course Jack was a lot thinner and boyish, on the cusp of being a grown adult but still the little boy who I'd once pulled out of a creek bed after he ran off right under my nose.

He was stealthy back then, too.

We reached the edge of the park in the shadow of the San Remo, but Jack didn't leave the cover of the dead trees. He kept us inside the line of protection, his hand resting on the hilt of his broadsword as if ready to draw it at any moment.

Without the trees in the way, I could better see the devastation that had been wrought on the city. The buildings that lined Central Park had once been some of the most upper crust residential homes in the city. Now, they were half-decayed, full of broken windows covered uselessly by sheets or tarps that flapped in the wind that always whipped up high between the buildings. Every surface, from the walls to the fences to the steps, were covered in vines, and in some places, it looked as if the earth were trying to take back the land where trees and plants popped up in places they shouldn't have been able to.

Abram's voice was low and tense when he broke the silence. "I don't think I've ever seen decay this terrible before, and I lived during a time when construction materials were mostly comprised of mud and clay. These buildings should have been built to last lifetimes."

"But Jack said fifteen years have passed," I replied.

"There's no way this level of damage could have been done in so little time."

"Unless it was magical in nature," Abram said grimly.

My heart seized as I struggled to understand the implications, and I came to a dead stop. "The Brothers?"

"The Brother, singular," Abram reminded me as he halted beside me. "Unless Huntsman decided to turncoat in the intervening years, he is our friend, not our enemy."

If magic had done this to the city I loved, I figured I'd be able to feel it or sense it with my own powers. So I shut my eyes and reached out with the magic flowing through my veins, prodding at the nearby buildings and digging my metaphysical fingers deep into the ground and the trees flanking me. But no matter how hard I pressed, I felt nothing of a magical nature. Just the silent, dilapidated city and the eerie howl of the wind above.

Opening my eyes, I resisted the urge to stomp my foot like a toddler. "My powers are acting up again. I hate when they do that."

I'd fought so hard to get control of my two natures: Conduit and Supplicant. And with Ramsey tutoring me, I'd made serious progress, to the point where I could protect myself and the people I cared about. So why were my powers not sensing anything? Either this place was utterly dead of magic, or I was. Neither option gave me any comfort, and hot tears touched my eyes.

"Your powers are fine," Abram said stoically. "It's *this place* that's wrong."

I nodded, brushing away a traitorous tear that dared to crest over the corner of my eye. The urge to move, to get out of this godforsaken forest of dead trees and get shit done, propelled me forward. "Let's go. Jack's waiting."

"Char." Abram reached out and twirled me back into his warmth. His palms slid gently up my bare arms, leaving a trail of fire on my cold skin.

I wasn't an idiot—he'd seen the tear before I could wipe it away. His arms moved around my back, pressing me into his body. Looking up at him this way, staring into his eyes, made everything else fade away. There was passion there in those dark depths. A love that shone only for me.

My heart raced, pounding against my chest in anticipation of his lips on mine. So much time had passed since I put the second curse on him. In the aftermath, he'd turned away from me to protect me from the beast within. For a full year that had felt like a lifetime, I didn't have him in my arms. I didn't have these secret glances and the excitement of his body against mine. I'd thought he would never look at me this way again.

Now, everything was falling back into place. But it wasn't there quite yet... Even the sex we'd had before Jack appeared wasn't at the level of intimacy we'd had in the past. We were patching up the broken walls of our love, and I'd work forever to make it whole again.

Abram's lips finally touched mine, hesitant and seeking. A thrill raced through me, and I pressed harder against him, winding my arms around his neck. My lips parted, allowing him entrance, and the first flick of his tongue on mine sent fire licking through my core.

The kiss deepened into a reckless thing, my hands gripping his shirt, my knees weak. When we finally broke apart, both of us were breathing hard, and desire rode the air between us. I leaned against his chest and held on with all of my strength.

"I missed you." The words came out hoarse, as though they'd been torn from my very soul.

"Look at me, Charisse."

When my eyes finally met his, none of the time apart mattered. None of the hours I'd spent searching for him, hoping to see him alive one more time. Nothing that had happened between the last time we'd been together and this new beginning mattered at all.

"You are my everything," Abram said, gruff emotion in his deep voice. He leaned in for another kiss, but we were interrupted by someone clearing their throat beside us.

Startled, I leapt away from Abram and nearly fell over again, catching myself on a nearby tree trunk. I was starting to think I'd had better balance in my goddamn Jimmy Choos. The Chucks were more appropriate for running for my life, and I definitely preferred to not ruin nine hundred dollar heels, but getting used to life on flat ground wasn't one of my strong points.

Jack stood watching us, a hint of amusement touching his blue eyes and the broadsword back in his hand. "If you're done? We've got to go. There's not much time until the next patrol," he added darkly.

The next patrol? I wondered, but he didn't give me a chance to ask. Jack turned and stalked off through the trees, leading us toward the end of the park without another word.

When we reached the far corner and stood just inside the last of the trees' protection, Jack scanned the street corner, his lips set into a worried line. As we were standing there, a chunk of plaster broke off the side of a nearby building and crashed to the sidewalk, shattering into powder. I clutched at Abram's arm, my heart rate skyrocketing at the sudden intense crash in the eerie silence.

"Not everything is like this," Jack murmured. "There are other places where the destruction isn't as bad. But here, at the epicenter…"

I opened my mouth to ask what he meant by that when the thud of boots hitting pavement thrummed through the air.

Both Abram and Jack froze as still as statues. Jack crept back into the shadows of the forest, motioning for us to follow. Silently, we did, hiding deeper in the darkness and crouching in the undergrowth as the sounds grew closer.

Voices were raised on the chill air, a mixture of laughter and cursing, mostly masculine. Metal clanged, and the unmistakable stomp of marching boots sent apprehensive chills dripping down my spine.

Dozens of men dressed in dark gray coveralls, carrying weapons that ranged from swords to guns. They chatted amicably as they walked, but their footsteps remained eerily in time, and their gazes never left their surroundings. A militia, I realized. Out on patrol?

None of us spoke or moved an inch while we waited for them to pass by on the road beyond the park. Jack clutched his sword, though he kept it tucked out of sight in the dense tangle of weeds beneath us so that the fire of the evening sun didn't reflect off it. Abram crouched on my other side, his body a live wire of tension that sent my own nerves running for cover.

But the militia passed without incident. Jack let out a breath, as if he'd been holding it, and tilted his chin towards us. "Come on. Time to show you what you're here for."

Oh, thank God, I thought, falling into step behind him. I had a mental list of questions as long as the park we'd just traversed, and I was dying for answers. Why was NYC in crumbling ruins? Where were all the people? Why was there a militia walking down the deserted street as if they were looking for people to lock up? And most importantly—why the hell had Jack brought us here?

At least I'd get an answer to that last question sooner rather than later.

I'd expected Jack to lead us away from the park and into the city. Last I knew, Lulu and her husband still lived in New Haven, but if we were fifteen years in the future, maybe they'd moved here for some reason. I was just assuming he was taking us to Lulu, but for all I knew, Lulu in this timeline was dead.

The thought sent me into a lightheaded terror, nausea rolling in my stomach. Lulu and I hadn't kept in touch in recent years, with my life being a buffet of dangerous supernatural terrors and her life being wrapped up in the wife and mother role. But no matter how far apart we'd gone, we never stopped loving one another. She would always be my best friend.

I couldn't wait to ask this particular question. If Lulu was dead, I needed to know. I skipped forward to draw up beside Jack's long, loping strides, but I didn't get a chance to utter a single word. I was distracted by the group of people milling about at the head of the park.

Fresh off the sight of militia men with guns, I braced myself to run in the other direction. But Jack shook his head at the tension in my body and kept walking resolutely toward the small crowd.

There were only five people, all of them dressed in ratty, tattered clothes, all of them thin and haunted as they stood before a line of trees that looked different from the rest of the forest in the park. Considering the militia had marched right by them without carting them off to jail, they weren't trespassing. But what *were* they doing?

As we drew closer, a woman stepped forward and reached up into the closest tree. She wrapped a single yellow ribbon around a low-hanging branch, tying a pristine bow before she lowered her hands to wipe the tears from her face. My skin grew cold as I noticed stuffed animals tucked into the exposed roots and signs hanging on trunks. Dozens of ribbons dangled from above, a forest of color that was anything but cheerful.

In New York, before the chaos and destruction that the discovery of magic brought to my life, there'd been a fire in the apartment building next to mine. It had gutted the entire complex and killed upwards of fifty people. In the hours and days after the fire, the neighborhood, survivors, and families had come together and created an altar to remember those who'd been lost. Friends, family, and even strangers were there to light candles, hang photos, and write notes to loved ones who had died.

Now, staring at the people we were approaching, it was more than clear they were mourning.

"Please come home," I read out loud from a sign on the first tree.

There were dozens more, stretching for fifty yards, maybe even farther. Every tree was decorated with odes to someone else's sadness. Stepping closer, I realized something was carved into the tree, too. Not a sign nailed to the trunk, but an actual carved name.

"Margot Rose," I murmured.

The next tree had another name: Samuel Corwin. I moved quicker now, my gaze scanning each trunk as I passed in front of the quiet mourners, earning irritated glances for my intrusion. I paused, my eyes warming with tears at the sight of a photograph of a young woman with deep black hair, no more than fourteen.

Jack joined me, Abram at his heels. The boy who looked so much like a blond Lulu took my arm and steered me down the line of trees, his blue-eyed gaze roaming the street.

"We need to keep going," Jack said. "You're not licensed. Either of you. If you're caught here, with the militia patrolling, you won't like what happens."

"Jack, what is this?" I asked, jerking my arm from his tight grasp.

He didn't slow down, continuing his journey down the edge of the park, but he did speak. "Every tree has the name of one of the children that's disappeared."

"A memorial, then. For children that were lost?" I clarified, hurrying to keep up with him.

"No," Jack said. "These names all appeared *before* the children vanished. Almost like the trees are an oracle for what's to come."

His words brought back the chill, the one that had been a constant companion since we'd stepped through the portal.

Something was *very* wrong here. Beyond the decaying city and the militia.

"I'm confused." I snatched at his arm to try to get him to slow down and talk to me, but he dodged my grasp. "The person who takes the children carves their name into the trees as a warning?"

"No," Jack said wearily. "The trees carve the names. They're sentient... We think, anyway."

He kept walking, the end of the memorial trees coming up swiftly. I followed, staying as close as possible without impaling myself on the broadsword hanging in the holster over his back.

The few people mourning steered clear of Jack as if they were afraid of him. He finally halted, turning around so quickly I had to backpedal to keep from running into him. From behind, Abram steadied me with a firm hand on my lower back.

Jack cut his gaze to the tree at his side.

Alice Carroll.

The icy chill turned to a slicing knife along my spine.

"Th-that's why you said we needed to save her," I said.

The pieces were finally clicking together.

Jack had come back in time to help save his sister. *That's* why he'd brought us here.

"I need your help, Char," Jack said, turning his pleading gaze to me. He looked so young now, so scared. A boy stuck in a nightmare. "To save Alice. And to save all the rest."

CHAPTER 2

ALICE. The last time I saw that sweet little girl, she was only a tiny infant with hands no bigger than a pair of Cartier diamonds. She had to be a teenager now—God, she probably looked *just* like the Lulu I grew up with, all long limbs and dark hair that seemed to have a mind of its own.

And someone had *kidnapped* her?

Horrified and struggling to process what was happening in this timeline, I couldn't come up with anything to say. All the questions I'd had before came to a complete halt with this revelation.

Lulu must have been beside herself.

Abram spoke up. "How many were taken?" he said in that calm, measured tone I'd come to recognize as his information gathering voice. He was inspecting the other trees in the grove, his eyes narrowed and his mind working over the details we'd been given. Leveling his dark gaze on Jack, he added, "How many and for how long has this been going on?"

Jack let out a huff of air and ran his hand through his messy blond hair. "A lot, man. Thirty, maybe? Thirty-five? It started a year ago."

"A year," Abram mused, his gaze sliding back to the trees. "So why come for us now?"

I pulled my best Vanna White, adding a bit of irritation to the display, and presented Alice's name carved into the tree as evidence. "He came for us to save his sister. Clearly."

"That's not the full story," Abram countered. There was no condemnation in his voice—just an observation. "That's not the only reason."

Ready to leap down Abram's throat to defend Jack's good honor, I opened my mouth to speak, but then noticed movement from the corner of my eye. Jack, nodding slowly beneath Abram's knowing gaze.

"There's more," Jack agreed, subdued. "But now's not the time or place. Come on. We need to get in by curfew."

"Where are we going?" I asked as I fell into step beside him. The sun was setting over the city's skyline overhead, and with every lost inch of daylight, a deeper chill settled into my bones. I wished I'd thought to grab a jacket before I jumped through a magic portal in my living room.

"Our place," Jack replied, cutting down an alley.

"You live in New York now?" I asked, aghast. Jack moved like the shadows, silent and stealthy. Meanwhile, my Chucks clapped along the cracked, concrete road like heels on a runway. "*Lulu* moved to New York?"

Lulu cried for days when I told her I was leaving for the city, because she planned on spending the rest of her life in our hometown. My bestie always wanted the American dream: the big house, the white picket fence, two-point-five kids, and a minivan. She had that, last I saw her.

Jack cut me a glance over his shoulder. "We didn't have an option. New Haven's gone. Like so many other places."

My heart stuttered to a stop and then sluggishly resumed pumping. "New Haven's *gone?*"

"There's a lot you don't know, Char," Jack said simply, his gaze on the silent road ahead. We made another turn onto a wider road, and kept walking. "We'll tell you everything we know once you're out of sight and safe inside."

The idea of a world without New Haven made my heart ache. I thought of my mother's house and Abram's nightclub, The Castle, where I'd worked for several weeks leading up to the beginning of our relationship. The movie theater and the mall and all the other places that had been such a large part of my formative years...gone.

Thank God Lulu was still here.

We walked for some time, leaving Central Park behind us as we headed north into the city. Upper Manhattan was a ghost town, though foot traffic picked up modestly the farther we got from midtown. The few people we passed kept their heads down and their eyes on the sidewalk, moving as fast as we were on their way to their destinations. Like Jack, they wore tattered clothes, clearly patched by hand, and carried a sense of desolation that even the rare smile and nod couldn't cover.

Though many businesses appeared to be abandoned, most of the residential housing was occupied. Lights burned in windows, and every once in a while, toys decorated sidewalks outside art deco apartment buildings. But between those lived-in spaces, there were signs of war and destruction in bullet holes and blast marks and piles of building debris that had been left to grow over where they fell.

We were deep in Harlem, in a neighborhood I'd never seen, when Jack stopped in front of a non-descript red-brick apartment building. The red door was faded and cracked, and a dirty tricycle lay on its side by the front steps. Every window in the place looked as if they'd long ago been broken and boarded up. This pile of rubble covered in invasive ivy was a far cry from Lulu's New Haven dream house.

Jack led us up the four narrow, shallow stairs to the front door as he extracted a chain from beneath his shirt. An old key dangled from the rusty necklace, and I watched him insert the key into the lock, my brain melting down over a world where it wasn't safe to carry your house key on a keychain like a normal person.

The door creaked open like something out of a horror movie. He hit a snag on the warped linoleum floor and shoved against the panel with his shoulder, forcing it open the rest of the way.

My knees shook as I stepped into an interior that didn't look any nicer than the outside. Water had clearly flowed through the dim hallway recently, leaving dirt and trash in piles. Jack walked resolutely past the first few numbered doors, then took the stairs to the second floor.

Everything seemed warped and sideways up here, as if water damage had put a permanent ten degree angle on everything. We stopped at a door that was missing its brass number, though a 2-C had been etched into the wood by time. Jack picked another key off his necklace, tossing me a nervous look as he leaned to unlock the door.

I don't know why he was nervous. As if I might judge them for the state of their apartment or the state of their clothes.

I could fully admit I'd always liked the finer things in life, and I could be a snob about expensive clothes and luxury. But that didn't mean I judged people for their circumstances.

And this…? This wasn't a life Lulu would have ever chosen for her kids. Only a major disaster could have driven her from New Haven. There was no judgment inside me right now. Only a desperate, burning need to gather my best friend in my arms and tell her I loved her and promise to fix every broken thing.

"Ma? I'm back!" Jack called, tugging his key out of the lock as he pushed the door open.

The scent of cooking meat redolent with spices met us at the threshold, and it was just so *normal*, that I immediately let out a breath of relief. Everything in the city had smelled sterile

—strangely acidic and acrid—but not Lulu's apartment. It smelled like her meatloaf with an undercurrent of citrus spritz.

The door opened onto a small living room and dining room combo, and flickering light spilled from a nearby archway beyond which I could see an ancient yellow fridge and white tile counters. All of Lulu's designer furniture was gone, replaced with sturdy, serviceable pieces that mismatched so wildly they must have decorated the entire place off Craigslist.

Jack hung his sword on a rack by the door, clearly meant for holding a weapon, and then crossed to the coffee table, where he lit a match and set it to the wick of an oil lamp. By the time he'd coaxed a bit more light into the room, Lulu arrived from the dark hallway that led farther into the house.

I stood frozen just inside the front door, staring across the room at my best friend. We locked gazes, studying each other. Her dark hair had become speckled with silver over the years, and there were delicate lines at the corners of her eyes and mouth that spoke of the passage of time and hardship.

But there was no doubt this was my Lulu.

"Oh, Char," she murmured, tears sparkling in her eyes. "It's been so long."

Her words were an unspoken green light, and we both rushed forward, crashing together in the center of the living room. She was so thin, almost skeletal, as if food had been hard to come by, but she still smelled like Lulu and she still hugged like her, too.

"You haven't changed a bit," she whispered tearfully as we clutched one another. "Not like my old ass."

I laughed, the sound coming out watery and half-way to a sob. "You're not old. You're aged like a vintage Pinot Noir, and beautiful as the day I last saw you."

"Now I know you're lying," she joked, releasing me. "But I'm so glad to see you." She looked after her son, who had disappeared into the kitchen. Typical teenager—foraging for food while his mother had a meltdown. "Jack, how far back did you have to go?"

"Fifteen and some change," he called back to the sound of the oven opening. "When's dinner? Christ, this smells good, Ma."

Lulu rolled her eyes, and for a moment, all the years fell away. "He's going to eat me out of house and home at this rate."

But I was still stuck on the piece of information I'd gleaned from her question. "You knew he went back in time to get us?"

Lulu's grin fell off her face, and she grimaced. "Yes. I knew."

Abram, who'd stayed silent through our teary reunion, finally spoke up. "You sent him back for us?"

She shook her head, avoiding his gaze...and mine. "Not exactly. Why don't you two freshen up, and I'll put on a pot of coffee? Then we'll chat about why you're here."

Before either of us had a chance to protest, Lulu shuffled off toward the kitchen. In the moment of silence after she left, her voice filtered back to us, low but still audible. "Fifteen years, Jack? God, I'd hoped he was wrong, but I guess I should have believed him, considering the source."

Abram and I exchanged glances. *Him who?*

When they switched to the topic of something that had happened in the building earlier that morning, Abram motioned me to follow him down the long, dark hall. Three doors were closed, but a third stood open, spilling light into the hallway. The bathroom. An oil lamp was already lit on the short, narrow sink, so he took me by the elbow and pressed me into the tiny room, closing the door behind us.

"I don't like this," he said bluntly. "Something is amiss."

I couldn't even argue the point. "Yeah, she's hiding something. I can't tell if she *can't* talk about it or *won't* talk about it. Not to mention, how did Jack end up with the knowledge and magic necessary to travel back in time? I'm at a loss."

"Do you think she'll be forthcoming with the truth?"

I mulled over his question, studying his face in the lamp light. Sometimes, I found myself forgetting that Abram lived hundreds of years ago, before electric lights and all the amenities of modern day conveniences. Standing here now with the firelight flickering over his strong features, I realized he had a face made for flames. The play of shadow and fire turned him into a work of art, more darkly beautiful than anything I'd ever seen before.

Stepping into him, I trailed my thumb down his cheek, his five o'clock shadow tickling my skin. "I don't know. Fifteen years have passed. I don't even know this Lulu, not like I knew her before."

His eyes drifted to my lips, and he palmed my shoulders, hands skimming over my arms. I was reminded yet again of just how long I'd gone without his hands on me. I wanted to be back in my apartment, naked with him beneath my Egyptian cotton sheets, in a world I knew how to navigate.

But I wasn't even sure we'd ever be able to go back there.

I settled for a kiss, tiptoeing to meet his lips. His mouth was hot, satin-smooth, and I relished the taste of him, trying to put all of my emotions into that one, simple kiss. It was a promise that no matter what happened, we weren't done yet. Not by half.

I broke away, my lips brushing against his as I murmured, "If we don't get out there and start questioning, we won't find anything out."

He held me against him a moment longer before grunting his agreement and letting me go.

Back in the kitchen, we found Lulu heating up water over a gas stove, the flame flickering beneath her kettle. There were three more oil lamps here, too, making the kitchen the brightest room in the apartment. I'd almost think the firelight made everything cozy, if we weren't standing in a shell of a building at the edge of some kind of apocalypse.

Lulu glanced at us, then motioned to the small, scratched table tucked into the corner. "Have a seat."

Jack already occupied one of the four chairs, his long legs stretched out and a sandwich in his hands. Four mismatched coffee mugs waited on the table top, along with a few packets of fake sweetener. I sat in the chair to Jack's left, and Abram took the chair beside me.

"Peanut butter and jelly?" I asked Jack, thoroughly tickled.

He shrugged, a flush rising in his cheeks. "It's my favorite."

"Yeah, I know," I said. "I made you a few in my day, though I'm sure you don't remember. Or...do you?" I added, confused. "Is there a me in this timeline? Did you grow up knowing who I am?"

Jack made a face, shoving his sandwich in his mouth so he didn't have to answer.

"Lu?" I asked, turning towards my best friend.

She rotated the dial on the stove, turning the flame off, her shoulders tensing under my gaze.

"Lu, you acted like you haven't seen me in years. What happened to me?" My voice trembled as I asked the question. Jesus, what if I *died*? Being a supplicant and conduit didn't make for a healthy, sustainable lifestyle. I lived with the idea in the back of my mind, that I might not live a full life. But to be faced with the prospect...

"Nobody has seen you since the night you set the genie free," Lulu said softly, picking the kettle up off the cooling burner. "Fifteen years ago."

Confusion warred with disbelief inside me. "But we were with Briar and Ramsey that night. Briar had just announced she was pregnant when Jack showed up, and we followed him through the portal."

"So that's what happened, then." She carried both the kettle and a plastic container of coffee grounds to the table. "Briar and Ramsey couldn't recall anything about that night. They remembered saying good night to you, and you being gone the next morning. We weren't sure… Well, we'd hoped you ran away together…"

"Christ, Lu," I said as she poured water in my mug. "I went missing fifteen years ago, and you never even tried to look for me?"

Lulu's hand shook as she moved on to Abram's mug, but her voice was tight as she said, "Two days later, the world ended, Charisse. I couldn't focus on you. I had to focus on keeping my kids alive." She went on in a lighter tone, as if she hadn't just dropped a bomb on the table. "I know you hate instant, but it's all I can afford. Real coffee is hard to come by, and when we *can* find it, there are other things we need more."

"And that's all the sweetener we have, so go easy," Jack added, earning a light tap on the head from his mother.

"They're guests," Lulu told him warningly. "If they want to use every last packet, they're allowed."

"I can go without," Abram said politely, reaching for the container of instant grounds. There was an undercurrent to his tone that said he was tired of all the beating around the bush, but for my sake, he was reigning in his beastly abruptness.

"I don't need sweetener," I assured Jack, shoving my mug towards Abram. "Load me up. I need all the caffeine I can get for this conversation."

By the time we were all filled up and seated, Jack had polished off his sandwich, and Lulu looked exceedingly uncomfortable. The secrets they were keeping lay between us like land mines—more bombs to explode, more horrifying things to learn.

I took a fortifying drink of the bitter coffee, wishing I hadn't foregone the sweetener. "Tell me everything." My fingers tightened around the cup, and I coaxed my hand to chill before the mug crumbled in my grip. "All of it. From the moment I 'disappeared.'"

Lulu nodded and then looked down at the cup in her hands. She launched right into the story without any preamble. "The night you freed the genie, as I said, Briar and Ramsey left you at bedtime and found you were missing the next morning. No note, no sign of violence. After everything you'd been through, and reuniting as you had, we considered that you'd slipped out in the night to go have a proper vacation and some alone time."

"That's what we should have done," I griped.

"Two days later, Darcus launched a magical attack on the world."

"Darcus!" I leapt to my feet, my fists clenching and my gut turning over inside me. "That son of a— If I'd have been there," I said pitifully, glancing at Abram. "We could have stopped him."

"Nobody could have stopped him," Lulu said firmly. "He had an army of conduits at his back and a systematic plan to destroy anybody who opposed him. New Haven was decimated in a matter of hours."

I sank back to my seat. "Your house?"

Lulu nodded. "And my husband. Edwin died during the first wave of attacks," Lulu said, clearing her throat as if stopping her tears before they started. Even fifteen years later, his loss obviously still weighed heavily on her.

"What did you do then?" I asked, horrified at the thought of Lulu, absolutely alone with a toddler and an infant.

She shrugged helplessly. "We survived. Any way we could. We ended up following the crowd of survivors into the city where there was the promise of food and necessities for those misplaced. We've been here ever since, doing what's necessary to get by in a world led by conduits."

Her statement shook me to my core. "Y-you know about magic now," I stammered. "About conduits and supplicants."

Lulu nodded once. "The whole world knows. The conduits have ruined everything. Not just New Haven. In fifteen years, they've created this world. This destruction all around us. This post-apocalyptic place is our reality now. We need you, Char. We're losing the war."

"What war?" I whispered, even though I didn't want to know.

"The rest of the world against the conduits," Lulu said desolately.

Abram grunted, leaning against the low back of the chair and crossing his arms over his chest. His face had settled into an enigmatic, placid expression that spoke volumes of how he thought she was holding back. "Why Char? If Alice was taken, and you're used to surviving in this world, it seems as if Jack could handle tracking her down."

"The young people...the ones being taken," Lulu said softly, wrapping her hands around the mug. "They aren't just anyone. They're supplicants."

A dull throb had begun behind my right eye. "All of them?"

Lulu shrugged. "Most of them. There are two places they could be going. The first, and the option I hope Alice chose on her own recognizance, is Wonderland. It's an uprising, an underground movement against Darcus and the conduits. They're supposed to be fighting for good, for those who can't. They're the only ones making any headway in the battle. At least, that's what we've heard. I've yet to see anything they've done that might be responsible for helping our cause."

So it sounded like Wonderland was a real life version of the Hunger Games resistance. If dystopian movies taught me anything, the resistance was generally the right side to be fighting for. "This is good, though. Right? If Alice really did go to join

Wonderland, she's *your* daughter, which means she probably has your stubborn, independent attitude. If she thinks something's wrong there, she's not going to stand by and let it happen."

"Alice is seventeen now. She's as close to an adult as a child can get, and I trust her to make sound judgments," Lulu agreed. "The problem is that Wonderland is a shadow movement, spreading propaganda that these kids follow without question. Many of them weren't old enough to understand what was happening in the beginning of the conduit takeover. All they know is that life sucks, and they're willing to believe anybody who tells them they can fight this to make it better. Wonderland is turning these kids against us. Against their parents. Once they join Wonderland, it's like a cult. There's no communication. None. It's like they're gone, forever."

"Okay. That's...less good," I said, blanching. "Is the second option any better?"

"It's not," Lulu murmured, looking down into her coffee instead of in my eyes. "Darcus and the other conduits are taking supplicants and harvesting them for their magic. I've learned a lot, Char. About magic, and how it works. But one thing has never changed. You." She looked up, and there was a fervor in her gaze that hadn't been there before. "You're the only one who has both supplicant and conduit magic. You're the only person Darcus fears. Which means you're the only one who can stop him."

Her words flashed me back to the moment when Darcus tried to destroy my world. I'd stood before him alone with no way of winning, no way of destroying him or ending the havoc he wanted to bring to our world. Now...here we were. He'd won. In fifteen years, Darcus had completely destroyed New Haven and turned New York City into a dystopian wasteland.

He'd been right after all. I lost. And there was nothing I

could do about it. So how could I do anything about the current situation?

As if she could sense my dire thoughts, Lulu spoke up again. "It's not the end," she said, using her stern mom voice on me. "We're not giving up, not ever. 'Til the death, we will fight this. That's why Jack came for you. Back to the last time anyone knew exactly where you were. To bring you here and help us end this. And to help us keep Alice from Darcus's clutches."

Something about her question hit a warning alarm in my head. "If Alice isn't with Wonderland, why would Darcus want her? She's just a kid."

"She's not just a kid, Char," Lulu said, voice breaking on my name. "She's a supplicant. And if we don't bring her home, it's only a matter of time before Darcus gets his hands on her."

CHAPTER 3

THE SUDDEN RUSHING in my ears made me wonder if I'd been harboring a tumor that decided to rupture at an inopportune time. Because surely I'd misheard Lulu. She most definitely had *not* said Alice was a supplicant. That would be insane. Impossible, even, and impossible things just could not exist. Maybe jumping through a magic portal had messed with my head, rattled my brain, or limited my hearing. I could have been imagining all of this, really.

"Alice...your daughter," I said, as if there might be some other Alice in question, "is a supplicant? Like an actual one?"

Lulu rolled her eyes, then leveled a gaze on me that said, in no uncertain terms, *Are you high right now?* "Yes, Char. My daughter Alice is a supplicant."

I sat forward in my chair and let my weight rest on my elbows before every bone in my body turned to jelly and I oozed off the seat. When I'd found out that I was a supplicant, I hadn't been able to fathom it. First of all, even accepting that magic was real was an "out there" situation, but to be told that your entire being could fuel another person's magic...

"Sorry, I just... How?" I asked, motioning to Lulu.

"You're normal! Your husband was an accountant! You shop at JCPenney!"

Lulu chuckled, and I couldn't even be upset that she was laughing at my expense since the woman clearly needed a reason to laugh. "Firstly, there's nothing wrong with JCPenney. I like comfort, and I like deals. Secondly, they don't exist anymore." She said the last bit dramatically, missing only the pearl-clutching faint to go along with the statement. "From what I've gathered, being a supplicant isn't always based on a family line like yours."

My magic had come from my father, a man I remembered only in childhood memories. I'd grown up hating him as much as I loved and missed him, because he'd abandoned us. Walked out of the house one day and never came back. But then Abram came along. He knew my father, and he told me the man left to protect us. To protect me, specifically. Too bad he died before I could find him and thank him.

I looked to my boyfriend in question for confirmation that supplicants could, in fact, develop outside of family lines. He shrugged. "Such a thing is not unheard of."

Turning back to Lulu, I asked, "How long have you known?"

"I found out after your disappearance," she assured me. She knew, in that telepathic bestie way, that the idea she would have kept something so monumental from me hurt my feelings. "We'd already moved here. Barely settled in, even. I was sitting outside with the kids, letting them get some sunshine, when a conduit came looking for her." She paused and rolled up the sleeve of her thin cotton shirt, revealing a jagged scar. The vicious red, puckered skin ran from the inside of her elbow to her wrist.

"Holy shit." I reached out, tracing a finger down the mutilated skin. "This could have killed you."

"It almost did." She pulled her sleeve back into place, as if even looking at the scar was too strong a reminder. "I didn't have a choice. He tried to take her, and the gun was useless against him. He transformed into a beast, and the bullets just…" She shook her head, looking a little dazed from the memory. "I did what I had to until help arrived."

"Did you kill him?" I asked, riveted by the idea. Conduits were notoriously hard to kill. Lulu's own brother had become a conduit—*made* himself a conduit, really—when he learned he was dying of a brain tumor. Taking him down hadn't been easy, and Abram had died in the process. Temporarily, of course. We weren't currently sharing a table with a zombie.

Not to mention, Lulu still didn't know exactly what had gone down between me and her brother. The whole "he tried to kill me so I killed him" thing.

Lulu shook her head. "No. He disappeared when a group of good Samaritans ran to our aid. But I would have, if I could have. He was going to hurt Alice."

"As you should," I said firmly. "And if the guy ever shows up again, you better point him out to me so I can separate his insides from his outsides."

Lulu laughed again, and a little more tension slipped away from her hunched shoulders. "After that, we hardly left the house. I supported us on my husband's savings for several years, until Jack was old enough to babysit. Then I took an office position working for a lawyer. Then I bounced around a few times, working odd jobs here and there until recently." She looked at her son, affection plain on her pretty face. "Jack took over. He's been working at a factory and supporting us for the last year."

When Abram and I both turned to look at the kid, his cheeks flushed red, and he shrugged. "Yeah, whatever. It's my turn to take care of her, you know?"

"And Alice?" I prompted. "What was her state of mind through all of this?"

Lulu sighed. "Boredom. Petulance. She couldn't use her

powers or a conduit might find her. I might have gone a tad overboard with protection—"

"You never let her leave the house," Jack cut in.

"It was for her own good." A long breath escaped her, teasing a lock of her gray-streaked hair away from her face. "She took it all so personally. The fact that she couldn't be a normal kid but couldn't practice her powers, either. Wonderland would have looked like a Promised Land to her— somewhere she could be herself and learn to use her powers for the good of all."

"We have to address the elephant in the room," Jack said, shoving his empty coffee mug away. "Alice's name on the tree. That's not Wonderland, Ma."

"We don't know that for sure," Lulu admonished, though the wiggle between her eyebrows spoke volumes in her uncertainty.

Jack slouched deeper in his chair, the front legs raising off the ground as he gazed at his mother with a mixture of pity and irritation. "We know that the trees are trying to tell us something. We know that every name they've shown us is a kid who's disappeared."

"But that doesn't mean those teenagers didn't run off to join Wonderland," Lulu snapped. "Nobody can trace all the dozens of other young people who've done the same thing."

Jack's chair hit the floor with a startling *bang*, and he sat forward, his expression taking on a new level of zeal. "Ma, I love you, but we didn't go back for Char because Alice took off to Wonderland." His vivid blue gaze darted to me. "Darcus' henchmen took my sister, and we need to find her before they drain her of every last drop of blood."

In the billowing silence after his heated declaration, I could hear a clock ticking in another room. *Tick, tock, tick, tock.* Counting the seconds just as time had done fifteen years ago, a hundred years ago, three hundred.

Every second that could mean Alice's death.

"All right," I said, straightening my shoulders and going for conviction, even as fear settled firmly inside me. "What do we do?"

~

WE WENT to bed before nightfall. I slept fitfully, my limbs as squirrelly as a five-year-old walking in stilettos on Berber carpet. Abram took a few blows and would gently shove my offending arm or leg back onto my side of the bed, but to his credit, he did his best to soothe my nightmares with cuddles.

Darcus's face made multiple appearances in my dreams. Nothing that made any sense or seemed to be any sort of "premonition." I'd only met the man once. Tall, muscular, and imposing but with a total narcissistic arrogance that turned him as unattractive as a gargoyle. Darcus's great taste in designer clothes was nowhere near large enough to overshadow the evil. He'd been so powerful, waves of it shifting off him like cologne, and even though I didn't get a chance to test my own strength against his, I knew it wouldn't have been enough.

I wouldn't have been enough.

After the third time I woke with a shriek, absolutely certain I'd find him at the foot of the bed ready to turn my skin inside out, Abram rolled me into his arms and told me stories. Stories of his life before, of two hundred years before and one hundred years before. We were somewhere in nineteenth century France when I finally floated into a peaceful rest. I guess at some point after that, Abram slipped from the room as his beast came to call, and for the rest of the night, I was alone.

Jack rolled us out of bed before dawn, citing the need to travel across town under the cover of darkness was greater than my need for beauty sleep. I traded my Gucci tee for one of Lulu's non-descript gray hooded sweatshirts and hoped my jeans didn't smell as rank as they felt against my skin.

A dense, heavy fog had settled over upper Manhattan as we left the apartment building and took the empty road heading north. The air was cold and heavy with unshed rain, making me thankful for Lulu's sweatshirt.

"Where are we going?" I asked Jack, throwing up the hood to cover my tingling ears.

"Deeper into Harlem," Jack replied. He'd fallen into a quick pace two steps ahead of me, while Abram kept pace behind me. I was a Char sandwich, protected on both sides by men that thought I needed them to hold my hand.

"Okay, but why?" I amended, since the damn kid couldn't give me the answer I was looking for without me spelling it out for him.

"In order for you to walk around unharassed, you need licenses. If we're out and a militiaman stops us and asks for ID, you have to provide it. Otherwise, they'll lock you up."

"I'm assuming these aren't *legal* IDs," Abram spoke up from behind him, his low, gruff voice broadcasting just how little he cared for the idea.

"Not unless you want Char discovered as a supplicant and carted off to Darcus's compound," Jack said coolly.

"Nope, can't have that!" I said brightly, tossing a glare over my shoulder at my boyfriend. "We like Char alive."

"He wouldn't kill you," Jack said. "Not right away."

"Because that's *so* helpful to know," I muttered. I was beginning to question whether I actually needed either of these two men, or if I should just suit up Lulu and we could have a girls' day out, killing-Darcus style.

Just like yesterday, we passed very few pedestrians, though I did notice more faces in windows than previous. We were clearly in a more residential area, with evidence of residents found in the toys scattered before apartment buildings and laundry hanging on the lines hovering over darkened alleyways.

Jack took us off the main road and down a side street where the buildings grew closer together and hovered over the two lane street, blocking out any semblance of sunshine trying to cut through the fog. We took two more right-hand turns, making what felt like a complete circle before we ended up in a dead-end alley.

Trash cans lined one wall, rank with rotting organic matter. On the opposite wall, a single rusted black metal door was set into the bricks about a foot-and-a-half off the ground. In the wash of sickly yellow light from the globe on the wall, I could see a faint outline beneath the door that proved at some point in the recent past there had been stairs there. As it was now, I'd need a cherry picker to climb inside the building.

Jack reached up and pressed a button beside the door handle. Somewhere deep within the walls, a grating buzzer announced our presence, and only stopped when Jack let his finger off the key.

"Dogs heard that in Milwaukee," I griped, shuddering.

Nobody replied, though Abram gave me an indulgent smile. I appreciated the effort, but I was going to need a little more than a smile to face this head on.

Before I could tell him that, the door flung open with a harrowing shriek of unoiled hinges, and a skeleton glared out at us.

I clutched Abram's arm, a scream strangling in my throat. In all our time fighting supernatural baddies, I'd never seen a walking skeleton, and quite frankly, I could have gone my whole life without. The sunken eyes...the protruding clavicle...the stringy, unwashed hair...

Wait.

The figure stepped to the edge of the threshold and narrowed his eyes at Jack. "What do you want?"

Not a skeleton. Just an extremely emaciated man in a tracksuit.

Eesh.

Jack cleared his throat and rested his hand on his holster. His broadsword was firmly in place in the sheath on his back, and I was starting to think he'd sleep with the thing if Lulu would let him. "We need to see Alan."

"What for?" Skeleton Man snapped.

"For legitimacy."

Jack and the skeleton faced off beneath the garish yellow light, but then the latter man nodded and stepped back into the shadows, disappearing entirely.

"That's not creepy at all," I murmured, still clinging to Abram's arm. "I think this is a bad idea."

Abram patted my hand. "As the kids say today—*same.*"

It would have been hysterical, if I weren't so close to running away like I was about to miss a sale at Oscar de la Renta.

Jack leveraged himself on the edge of the open door and hauled his lanky frame inside, then he reached back out for my hand. Against my better judgment, I accepted. His long fingers were clammy in mine, and Abram braced a hand against my back so that the two of them could boost my curvy ass into the building.

My eyes adjusted to the light to find Skeleton Man hovering just beyond the glow of the lamp outside. As the door crashed shut behind Abram with another wrenching screech, I inched behind Jack but kept my gaze firmly mounted on the stranger.

I'd lived a decade in New York without getting shivved in an alley. I wasn't keen to change that now.

Skeleton Man headed down the narrow hallway with a strange, loping gait, and Jack followed. I took one look at his Slenderman walking style and whirled around, ready to toss myself dramatically out the door. Abram caught me by the sweatshirt and turned me back around, but not before I caught the amused smirk touching his lips.

At least I could amuse him before we all died at the hands of an imaginary supernatural killer.

The hallway stayed in pitch darkness for the duration, until it ended at another similar metal door. This one didn't protest quite as much when opened, but a waft of sour cigar smoke rolled out the minute Skeleton Man yanked it open.

I coughed, waving a hand in front of my face to try to get my nose some fresh air. But no matter how fast I waved, the smoke didn't part. Shoulders slumped, I gave up the battle and followed Jack into the billowing clouds of white. The smoke was so thick that when I passed Skeleton Man, he appeared from nowhere, grinning like a madman. Then he disappeared just as fast, and a moment later, the door slammed shut behind us.

Jack took the lead, and I gripped the back of his shirt so I wouldn't lose him in the white noise.

I peered around Jack as we walked, trying to make out anything from the clouds. What the hell were we walking into? I'd been certain that first wave of clouds had smelled like cigar smoke, but now that we were completely ensconced, the scent was almost sweet and fruity, like we'd entered an orchard or a tropical forest.

Suddenly, a dark shape loomed from the smoke ahead. A head emerged first—large and lumpy, with a mane of wild dark curls coiled tightly at the crown of his head. Light glinted off one of his eyes; then I realized he wore an honest-to-God monocle, like Mr. Peanut. A large, thick cigar the shape and width of a fat caterpillar dangled from his overly plump lips.

"Jack Carroll," the man intoned, his cigar bouncing with every syllable. He sucked deeply on the cigar, the tip flaring hot orange, and leaned forward on his elbows. Clouds danced away from him to reveal a counter before his great bulk.

"Alan. Nice to see you," Jack said politely, though there was an edge to his voice.

The man let out a giant lungful of smoke, and the whole cloud curled around Jack's head. Alan wore a thick purple cardigan and entirely too many gold rings on his sausage-like fingers. "Back so soon?"

Jack shoved a hand in his pocket and emerged with a wad of bills. He slapped it to the desk in front of Alan. "Two chips."

"Chips?" The word slipped from me before I could stop it. "Jack, we aren't here to gamble." Or eat—though I had a feeling he wasn't tossing hundreds of dollars on a shady booking agent's desk for a bag of Lay's.

"Microchips," Alan said, letting the *S* disappear into a feral hiss. How he could talk with that giant dildo in his mouth was beyond me. He looked at Jack, his dark eyes calculating, though the left was nothing but a round window of silver in the light. "They don't know?"

"They're not from here," Jack said shortly.

Alan grinned around his cigar, his smile disappearing into pudgy cheeks. "Ah. Not from when, then."

I was too stuck on the word "microchips" to really pay too much attention to their exchange. Microchips. Like the little computers the size of a grain of rice that they inserted into dogs' necks to track ownership?

Abram reached past me, his bulky hand wrapping around Jack's bicep. "Jack. A word."

I was caught between their two bodies as Abram twirled Jack away from the cigar-smoking deviant. As one unit, we shuffled into the clouds of smoke until we could no longer see Alan, and then Abram finally released the kid's poor, probably mangled arm.

"Microchips?" Abram hissed in an equally beastly way.

Jack sighed. "This is why I didn't say anything. It sounds worse than it is."

"It's not implanting a mini computer in our bodies, then?" I asked.

"It is that," Jack admitted. "But it's not a tracking device. It holds all your personal information—name, date of birth, address, whether or not you carry supplicant or conduit powers. The militia carry scanners that can read them to ensure you're legal."

"Not happening," Abram said.

They argued for a minute longer. I tuned it out, because the bottom line boiled down to we had to have these chips. We needed to be able to move about this fucked up, dystopian version of New York without getting arrested, and if that meant letting Mr. Peanut implant me with a microchip, well, I'd had worse things in my body before.

"Guys." I spoke quietly, but both of them immediately shut up at the sound of my voice. I was slightly impressed—had I discovered a new superpower? "We have to do this," I told Abram, reaching up to touch his cheek. My hand displaced the steadily moving clouds of smoke, and tendrils danced and swayed around my wrist. "It's necessary. I know it's scary. But we have no choice."

We trooped back to Alan, Jack and I sharing a kind of stoic resolution while Abram did his broody thing behind us. The smoking man remained where we'd left him, but the table was no longer empty. Two sterile wrapped syringes sat on the surface before him, and he'd opened a laptop computer. The blue light filtered through the smoke, making him look as if his head were floating.

"All settled?" Alan asked with another horrendous grin.

"All settled," Jack agreed. "Do you have identities drawn up?"

Alan flipped the computer around.

Jack stepped forward, his gaze scanning the bright screen before he picked up the plastic wrapped syringes and studied the text printed on their sides. Finally, he nodded and put them back down. "Submit it."

Reaching around the computer, Alan pressed a button, and a check mark appeared on the screen. Then he slammed the lid shut and motioned me forward.

Abram threw an arm out to barricade me from moving forward. "I'll go first," he snapped, clearly still harboring his misgivings. He stalked up to the counter and offered his right arm.

"Left, s'il vous plaît," Alan caroled.

I had the distinct impression he got a kick out of Abram's discomfort.

Then he opened one of the syringes, shoved the giant needle in Abram's wrist, and depressed the plunger.

Abram didn't even flinch, despite that the needle was as big around as one of Kate Moss's thighs. He turned his arm over and back a few times, as if testing whether or not he could feel the chip beneath his skin, and then stepped away to make room for me.

I was not as chill about giant horse needles as my beastly boyfriend. I placed my left arm on the cool glass counter, then gritted my teeth and turned my face away from both the syringe and Alan's sickly-sweet smoke.

A sharp twinge heralded the needle sliding in, and then I felt a strange little plop as Alan pressed the chip into my arm. He removed the needle, then pressed a cotton ball soaked in something that smelled like alcohol to the entry wound.

"See? Easy as pie," Alan murmured, his monocle flashing.

I didn't get a chance to respond. My body raged hot, skin flushing with heat from the point of entry. Magic sparkled at my fingertips, glinting off that infernal monocle, and then I succumbed to darkness.

CHAPTER 4

WHEN I OPENED MY EYES, I experienced a brief moment where I thought I'd died and was floating somewhere in heaven among the clouds. Fluffy white drifts twisted and turned all around me, cutting me off from everything so that I thought, *Is this the day I get my wings?* A peaceful calm washed over me, and I braced myself to sit up and take this afterlife by the balls.

But then I felt the rapid throb of my heartbeat inside my chest. I was *pretty* certain dead people didn't still have a pulse. Especially a pulse rapid enough to power a small country like a waterwheel.

I lay on my back atop hard concrete, though something soft supported my head. I'd initially thought the clouds were embracing me, but when Abram's face slid into view from above, it became clear I was laying on his lap. I recognized at the same time that he was testing my pulse in one wrist and clutching the other.

"Char?" he said sharply. "Can you hear me?"

I blinked. Could I even form words around the heartbeat in my throat? Better yet, did I even want to try? My body was as hot as if someone had dipped me in lava and left me hung out to dry, and my arm itched viciously around Abram's grasp. The same arm that Alan had recently shoved a microchip in.

Shock buoyed me, and I popped up from Abram's legs, tugging both my hands from his grasp. I'd fainted! I could remember the sharp jab of the needle, and then a flare of heat before everything went dark. My sleeve was still pushed up to my elbow from where I'd offered it to Alan for the insertion. The arm was covered from knuckles to sleeve in itchy red hives that were hot to the touch. A great complement to the heartbeat still trying to dropkick a hole in my chest.

"Ow," I said, rubbing my fingernails lightly over the rash. "What the hell happened?"

Jack, who was sitting at my feet, replied, "You passed out after the insertion. Would have slammed your head into the counter if not for your boy's quick reflexes."

I stared at the rumpled blond teenager, amused that he'd referenced Abram as a "boy." My hulking beast of a love machine was anything but, though I supposed that was neither here nor there at this point.

Shaking my arm around like a loaded gun, I asked, "And this? What's this?"

Abram caught my flailing arm and pressed it back to my lap. "You appear to have had a reaction. Of some kind. We aren't certain of the cause."

Okay. A reaction. I could wrap my head around that. The thing I couldn't quite wrap my head around was that my body had had what amounted to an allergic reaction to an innocuous piece of plastic no bigger than a grain of rice. Was there something more nefarious about the chips than Jack or Alan had let on? Some kind of mineral additive that could turn people into mindless zombies to do the conduits' bidding?

I looked around the thick, viscous smoke for the shady guy in the monocle so I could shake more information out of him, but he was nowhere to be found. At least, not within the four feet of area I could see through the ever-present smoke.

"Where's Alan?" I asked.

Jack made a face. "I might have punched him."

"Might have?" I asked with a grin. I was used to Abram doing White Knight things like punching anybody who dared harm me, but that was just my beast being overly protective. Jack had punched a man for me, and I knew he'd done it for his mom.

That was way too adorable.

"I thought he hurt you," Jack griped. "He's fine. It didn't even knock him out."

"He went to get some Benadryl," Abram added. "And ibuprofen for himself. Our companion throws a mean fist. The man's bell will ring for days."

I caught Jack's eye and smiled my thanks, but then said, "Could there have been something in the chip that caused the reaction? Something Alan added to it?"

"I don't think so," Jack said, though he didn't sound too sure of his answer.

I twisted around and lifted up the sleeve on Abram's long-sleeved shirt—no rash. Honestly, I couldn't even see the injection site anymore, which was probably a testament to the beast's healing powers.

"You didn't have a reaction?" I asked, voice small.

Abram looked grave as he shook his head, but before he could speak and either soothe my fears or give me something to really be nervous about, we were interrupted by the shuffling of approaching footsteps.

Clouds of sweetly acrid cigar smoke undulated and flowed out of the way as Alan appeared holding a bottle of water and a smaller bottle with a familiar pink label. Now that I could see him outside his counter, the man was massive—legs like baobab trunks covered in green sweatpants and a round, bulbous stomach that strained at the buttons on his purple cardigan.

He offered me both bottles. "Unopened water. And I figured you'd feel safer pulling the pills out yourself."

I side-eyed him as I removed the child-proof lid. "You keep Benadryl in the office. So does that mean reactions to the microchips are normal?"

"I have a wheat allergy," Alan replied with a sheepish shrug. "As for the chips, nobody's ever had a reaction to an insertion before. Not that I'm aware."

I poured two pink capsules into the palm of my hand, and then passed the bottle to Abram. "So why me?" I asked before tossing the pills in my mouth and washing them down with a swig of room temperature water.

Alan shrugged, puffing on his cigar in lieu of answering. Abram capped the Benadryl and shoved the bottle in his pocket, silencing Alan's protests with a look.

"I don't know why it happened," Abram said, meeting my gaze as smoke curled around his head, making him look ethereal. "But it makes me nervous."

Scratching the scores of hives still raw and red on my skin, I couldn't help but agree. How was I supposed to defeat Darcus if my own immune system killed me first?

OUR NEXT STOP didn't take us far from Alan's smoky, alleyway shop. Jack led the way back out onto the small side street, where we made a few zig-zag turns before coming out on a larger road that had once housed a shopping district. Now it looked as if most stores were closed, and the buildings converted to living spaces, but for a small grocery and a bigger liquor store that seemed to be doing brisk business.

"I could see how alcohol would be an essential business

during the apocalypse," I quipped as we passed the open doors. "But why are they all hoarding toilet paper?"

A line of patrons waited to pay at the Plexiglas-covered counter, most of them looking as if they'd already started their daily bender and had come in for seconds.

Abram chuckled. "People do strange things when they are afraid. We certainly cannot blame them."

Jack rolled to a stop in front of a boarded up pawn shop and beat on the door—a musical rhythm that must have been some kind of code.

"This place looks closed," I said, shooting him a glance.

"On purpose," Jack said darkly.

As if to punctuate his cryptic statement, the sound of a bolt being thrown on the other side of the board-covered glass door cut like a gunshot through the street's silence. The door cracked several inches, and a rheumy gray eye peered out at us.

Either the eye belonged to a child, or the person in question was the shortest human adult I'd ever seen. The eye hovered somewhere near just north of Jack's belly button.

"What?" a voice croaked irritably.

Leaning into Abram, I stage whispered, "Not a lot of good humor in this timeline."

"Again, we can hardly blame them," Abram whispered back.

Besides during the few moments that had seen me ass down, nose up on the concrete, he seemed in a better mood today. I chalked that up to being on the move and putting plans into action. To be honest, though, I was dying for some genuine alone time with him that didn't include passing out or walking into dangerous situations.

Plus, Jack hadn't exactly explained where our next step would take us. After the fun adventure at Alan's House of Smoke, I didn't expect this visit to be any better.

Jack squared his shoulders and met the woman's gaze.

"Slithy."

I blinked at the kid, and then at Abram. "Is he having a stroke? That's not a word."

But the eye just winked as if in recognition, and a second lock was thrown that clanged and rattled a bit like a heavy duty chain. The door opened, revealing the eye-holder in full.

The woman was barely over three feet tall with mousy brown hair shot through with white and skin that puckered with age and frown lines. She wore a red muumuu and ratty slippers, and her pointed nose and beady eyes gave her a rodent-y air.

"Maisy," Jack greeted the woman kindly. "How's things?"

"Dismal," the woman spat. "Cats got into my garden and ruined everything. Fucking hate cats."

She waved the three of us into the building with an old lady's impatience, like if we stood on the threshold a moment longer, death would come to claim her. By the look of her, that probably wasn't too far from the truth.

At least the pawn shop isn't filled with smoke, I thought as I followed Jack's broadsword into the dark interior. Like Alan, Maisy had been lucky enough to land a place that had electric lights. A fixture high overhead hummed audibly, pumping an amber glow over the small front room that didn't quite illuminate all the shadows.

I'd expected an empty retail store, maybe with industrial carpet dented where the racks and shelves once sat, and an old counter that hadn't held a cash register in years. Instead, the pawn shop looked, well, like a pawn shop.

Racks and bins and shelves lined every square inch of the rectangular space, piled high with goods I couldn't make out in the shadowy light. There was, in fact, a cash register on the counter at the front of the store, though it looked like it was probably older than the storekeeper, which was saying a lot at this point.

I wasn't given a chance to investigate what the store had to offer, either, because Maisy led us down a central corridor and through a curtain to the back of the store.

The old woman kept walking, past an obvious living area equipped with a recliner, a couch pulled out into a bed, and a small kitchenette. An office area on the other side of the room held an old metal desk and chair as well as an ancient Dell computer I had doubts actually worked.

At a metal door in the back corner, Maisy reached into the pocket of her muumuu, pulling out a heavy key ring. She unlocked the door, then hit the lights and waved us through.

"You know what to do, Jack," she said, then she shuffled off with a phlegmy cough.

I fell into step behind the kid and parroted, "*You know what to do, Jack?* How is it you've come to know all these shady people?"

"Maisy isn't shady," Jack said, motioning to the large warehouse that stretched before us. "She's one of the good guys."

Abram let out a long, low whistle, his dark eyes roaming the shelves. "Weapons."

I followed his gaze and jolted as I realized the closest metal shelves contained stacks of guns. Stacks and *stacks* of automatic weapons. Farther beyond, there were swords and knives, and farther than that, I swear I saw an honest-to-God mace.

"Jesus, it's like a national armory up in here," I breathed, taking a few steps deeper into the room. I traced my fingers over an automatic gun of some kind, complete with scope. "Why are you carrying a sword when you could carry a gun?"

"Guns are easy to find," Jack replied. "Ammo is not. The militia confiscated most of it during the takeover."

Abram hefted a giant gun in his arms and peered through the scope towards the far end of the warehouse. "You could make your own."

"Wasn't there a movie where they melted down toy

soldiers to make bullets?" I mused, picking up a handgun. I couldn't quite recall what movie it was, though I felt like it was on the tip of my tongue. "Do you guys remember?"

Abram and Jack looked at me blankly, both of them cradling guns like little boys with toys. I realized neither would be *any* help in jogging my pop culture memory. Abram wouldn't know the difference between Jonah Hill and the Jonas Brothers, and Jack was too young to recall any movies that came out before the turn of the century.

"Probably you want to go for a knife." Jack pointed down the appropriate aisle, a smile threatening to break out over his face. He thought I was a crazy person.

"Somebody hot was in it," I said, mostly to myself, and headed for the daggers.

Maisy had been building this collection for quite some time. The daggers took up an entire ten-foot section of the warehouse. From rusty, aged buccaneering knives inset with varnished rubies to clinically sharp hunting knives with camo handles, her collection included something for everyone.

I wasn't much of a knife-or-gun kind of girl. I mean, when your entire body—and blood—could be considered a lethal weapon, guns tended to be a backup, not the main event.

Still, I did my due diligence, lifting knives from the shelves to test their weight and the way they felt in my palm. Many of them were too big around for my weirdly small hands, and I dismissed those without even picking them up. Until, finally, I found a small silver dagger with a plain black handle and a shiny blade that tingled in my palm as if it were meant to be there.

The knife beside my chosen one was covered in flecks of old blood. I grimaced and thought, *Jesus, couldn't Maisy have cleaned the bits of the last guy off?*

Jesus. The Passion of the Christ.

I charged out of the aisle and raised my dagger in the air. "Oh my God! I figured it out!"

Something clanged nearby, followed by the thud of heavy footsteps slapping against the floor. Abram and Jack raced from their respective aisles, skidding across the floor toward me. Jack held his broadsword in one hand, and Abram seemed to have found himself a sword, too.

"What is it?" my boyfriend barked, his gaze darting wildly around me as he held the sword at the ready.

"Mel Gibson!" I said excitedly. "*The Patriot!*"

Abram sighed wearily, his shoulders slumping forward and the sword's tip settling on the floor in defeat. He scrubbed a hand over his face, and I thought I heard him mutter something like, "God give me strength," before he walked back into the shelves without comment.

Jack's brow wrinkled. "Mel Gibson? Is that the guy who made all those funny British movies my mom likes?"

I groaned. "No. That's Mel Brooks. And honestly, Lulu, you let your child watch that shit?"

With a grin, Jack added, "'Strange women lying in ponds distributing swords is no basis for a system of government.'"

"Better than supernatural, power-hungry men who want to bleed teenagers dry as a foundation for their dystopian regime," I replied, my thoughts going immediately to Darcus. I'd been so caught up in everything that had happened today, that I'd let the evil bastard slip from my mind.

I can't make that mistake again, I told myself, going back to the knife aisle to hunt down a proper sheath and holster. *Not now, not tomorrow, not ever.*

I'd faced a lot of threats since coming into my powers, but this would be my most dangerous quest yet.

It was well and good to enjoy stealing moments with Abram, or to laugh over stupid movies with my best friend's son. But at the end of the day, Darcus was the main reason I'd been brought here.

And there was a fifty percent chance I wouldn't make it out of this timeline alive.

CHAPTER 5

WE MADE a couple more stops on the way home, though thankfully they were errands for Lulu and not more shady run-ins with individuals doing illegal things. By the time we walked through the door back at the apartment with blades, bags of groceries, and our newly acquired fake identities, it was already dinner time.

The house smelled like bacon and cooking meat. As Jack closed and locked the door, I lugged my canvas bags to the kitchen, where Lulu stood over an open fire and a skillet of sizzling bacon. She greeted me with a pleased grin as she took a couple bags off my hands.

"We don't get to have a shopping spree very often," Lulu told me, setting them on the counter and digging inside the first bag. "Jack had a good week at work. Which means we eat well this week."

I cast a glance at the boy in question as he leaned over a saucepan and eyed the concoction inside, carefully avoiding looking at his mother. After our adventures today, I wasn't *entirely* sure Jack had a proper job. If anything, Jack had picked up some freelance work that likely involved his broadsword and nefarious situations.

Not that I'd say a damn thing to Lulu about it. I'd worry about her son for her. Let her think he worked at a factory or some shit if it helped her sleep at night.

"What's for dinner?" I asked, reaching into another bag to help unpack.

"Burgers and fries. If that's okay? All homemade."

"Like I'm going to turn down a homemade meal. I have curves to feed." I slapped my ass, then leaned over to pop a kiss on her cheek. "Can I help?"

After we put away the groceries, Abram and Jack disappeared into the living room to discuss manly things, and Lulu set me to work slicing potatoes. We reminisced about life before the apocalypse, and it was so hard to wrap my head around the fact that, for me, that was only a few days ago. For Lulu, it had been nearly two decades. A couple times, I thought she would break down from the emotions of it all. Luckily, my "make Lulu laugh" brain still worked.

While I fried the potatoes in the skillet, Lulu mixed up the hamburger patties and fried them. The kitchen stayed over-warm because of the gas stove, but I was too busy enjoying myself to care.

We sat down for dinner around sundown to an achingly familial atmosphere, as if we were simply a family sitting down after a hard day's work to decompress together. Jack had splurged on two bottles of wine, and we popped them both to settle in to eat.

After I enjoyed my first decadent bite of juicy, fire-roasted burger, I turned to Jack and asked, "So what's our next move? We're chipped. We're armed. Next stop—battle?"

"Next stop: allies," Jack corrected, then took a bite of his burger that was bigger than his head. He tried to continue speaking through the mouthful, but sounded like a bad PA system, so I looked to Lulu for clarification.

"Your friends, Briar and Ramsey?" she said, picking up a

fry and dipping it in her homemade sauce. "They've been busy in the last few years."

It was a testament to how much I couldn't comprehend the time travel thing that I hadn't even thought to ask after their well-being. If Lulu's life was ripped apart and turned upside down, the same probably happened to all my friends. "How are they?"

"Surprisingly good, all things considered," she replied. "They have a daughter, Rosie, she's… Oh, I guess she's about fourteen now? They're still living on Grimoult, but the entire island is locked down. Nobody can get in or out thanks to Ramsey's magical barriers."

I dragged three fries through the sauce and shoved them in my mouth, chewing and swallowing before I asked, "So what can they do to help us with allies while locked away in their palace?"

Jack was the one to respond. "They've been spending the last five years building an army. They're basically running a safe haven for supplicants now. Thousands of people safe from Darcus on Grimoult."

"A few good conduits, too," Lulu added. "Not every conduit seeks to overthrow the world with Darcus. Briar and Ramsey welcome them with open arms. The more ammunition we have against Darcus, the better."

"But Grimoult is a plane ride away," I pointed out. "Are you telling me there's still commercial airlines in this dystopia?"

"Definitely not. Passenger planes were shut down within years of Darcus's takeover, and only cargo ships fly by air now." Lulu reached for the wine bottle and topped off her glass. "Ramsey is kind of a miracle worker, in case you didn't know."

As she topped off my glass, I nodded and thought about the entire year we'd spent side-by-side as he taught me how to hone and harness my powers. He'd been my best friend and confidante for so long. Of course, for me that had only just happened. For him, that would have been fifteen years ago.

God, this shit was so confusing.

"So we take…a boat?" I asked, grimacing. "I'm pretty sure I get seasick, and it won't be pretty for any of us if that happens."

Jack guffawed. "No. We take the portal."

"A portal?" Abram asked, finally speaking up now that his burgers and fries had mysteriously vanished. I assumed it took a lot of calories to power all that man-meat, so whenever he focused on his meals with gusto, I just let him do his thing. "Like the portal we traveled through time?"

"Not quite," Jack replied. "This is more 'traveling through space' than traveling through time. We'll leave in the morning. We'll have to walk a while to get to the portal."

Ugh. I guess I should have been happy that I'd brought shoes that were made for walking.

"Are you coming with us?" I asked Lulu.

She shook her head sadly. "I think it's best if I stay here and wait for… Well, you know. In case Alice comes home."

I reached across the space separating us and put my hand over hers. "We'll find her, Lu. We'll bring her home."

Lulu squeezed my hand and offered me a slow, sad smile. "I know you will, Char."

But neither one of us sounded like we had much hope in the process.

AFTER FINISHING off both bottles of wine over three fast-paced rounds of Go Fish, the four of us retired for the evening, mainly so that the traveling party could get a decent amount of shut-eye before we had to leave early tomorrow morning. Jack warned us the trip probably wouldn't be easy, but I couldn't even pretend I'd considered otherwise given the state of the world.

When we'd arrived last night, Lulu had given us her bedroom and opted to sleep in Alice's for the time being so that Abram and I would have a larger bed to share. She had opened the window at some point today, allowing a brisk, refreshing breeze to power through the small, square room. The sun hadn't yet dipped over the horizon, which meant I would have a little longer with Abram in his human form before he had to leave me.

It wasn't a terrible space: The paint peeled in a few places, and the carpet was stained, but Lulu's blankets were brightly colored and clean, and she kept pictures in frames and flowers in vases on every surface. But the room definitely spoke volumes of the life she'd been forced to live. I hated that I hadn't been there for her through it all.

As the door closed behind us, I watched Abram walk into the room and head for the nightstand, carefully unraveling the watch band on his wrist. Even though my brain was sleepy after the day we'd had, other parts of my body weren't so much.

My breath caught in my throat as Abram hooked his thumbs in the hem of his t-shirt and tugged it over his head. Flames from the three oil lanterns situated around the room reflected off the plains and valleys of his muscular torso, throwing the chiseled beauty of him into sharp relief.

I walked toward him like a moth to a flame, his body a magnetic pull I couldn't deny. His shoulders stiffened as I traced my fingers up his back.

I wanted him. I wanted *my* Abram, the broody, sexy partner who'd been the main character in every one of my wildest dreams since the day he pushed me away because his beast had become too strong. I still knew very little about the full year we spent apart, except for that most of the time, Abram himself hadn't been in the driver's seat.

My hand cast shadows that flickered over his skin. I traced the muscles in his lower back, then slid a thumb up the curve of his spine. I twirled my fingers in the divots beneath his shoulder blades, watching the way goose bumps played across his skin.

He didn't move. He hardly breathed, and honestly, neither did I. For so long, I'd been denied the satin of his skin and the scent of his body. Even upon his return to me, things just hadn't felt…right. As if I'd lost a hundred pounds only to find my favorite shoes no longer fit my feet. But I didn't think that was something that would last forever. He was my Abram, top to toe, I had no doubt.

I just had to rekindle the connection. Dig deep inside and coax him back to me.

Stepping closer, I slid my hands around to his front and pressed my cheek to his warm back. The tension in his body loosened as I embraced him, and he sank back against me—just a bit—as I played my fingers over his chest.

I wanted to memorize every square inch of him. What if something happened in this timeline, and I lost him again? My only option was to treasure every last moment I could get alone with him, and to map his heart, body, and soul with the touch of my fingers.

Emboldened by the way he leaned into me, I moved my hands up to his thick pectoral muscles, where I brushed my thumbs over his nipples. He growled, a small, delighted sound, and his nipples pebbled beneath my fingers. I couldn't stop the grin that stretched over my face—with Abram, I was never the one in charge. In the bedroom, he dominated me the way his beast dominated the night, so this was an interesting turn of events.

I swirled my fingers around his nipples and pressed a gentle kiss directly on his spine, earning a hum of pleasure from deep within his chest. Then I slid my hands down, moving over his delectable washboard abs, then lower, my fingers dipping beneath the waistband of his jeans. I relished the sharp intake of breath from him as my hand disappeared into his boxer shorts and wrapped around his thick, already hard cock.

Of course, I might have been *too* bold with the teasing. Moved too quickly to the main event—AKA the amazing fucking erection in his pants. Because in the next moment, he'd whirled on me, his eyes heavy-lidded as he lifted me off the floor and threw me onto the bed, covering my body with his.

I'd lost the upper hand. Too bad. It had been fun while it lasted.

But the moment his lips crashed to mine, I didn't care anymore. This was *my* Abram. I could tell by the achingly slow attention he paid to my lips as he kissed me. His tongue traced my lips and dipped into my mouth, and he slid my shirt up over my chest, flicking the front-closure on my bra open like a pro. My breasts spilled into his hands as his lips trailed over the edge of my jaw, heat rising between us.

His mouth closed over one of my nipples, and I arched into him, my breaths coming in shallow pants. He was moving too slow. There were still too many barriers between our bodies. I was desperate to feel his skin on mine, to feel the thick, velvet slide of him between my legs, filling me. Claiming me.

But suddenly, he jolted away, staring down at me wide-eyed like he didn't recognize me.

"Abram?" I said softly, reaching for him.

He climbed off me, leaving me cold and exposed on top of the bedclothes as he sat on the edge of the mattress. His head fell forward into his hands, and he stayed there unmoving, his breathing shallow and abnormal.

"Abram?" I tugged my shirt down as I sat up, feeling awkward at my nakedness. Had he just…rejected me? Sliding to the edge of the bed beside him, I sank against his side in the dip he'd made on the old mattress, and put my hand on his knee. "What's going on?"

"Nothing." He brushed my hand away from his knee and stood, moving off toward the window with his erection still straining at the front of his pants.

Hmm. He clearly still wanted me—that much was obvious. The bigger question was, what was holding him back?

"Is it something to do with the year we spent apart?" I asked him, staying firmly where I sat, even though I really wanted to go to him. The heat and motion of his body had been imprinted on mine, and I thought I'd go crazy if we didn't finish what we'd started. "If you were...with other people. It's okay. I know you weren't yourself."

He glanced over his shoulder at me, stricken. "No. I wasn't with anybody else."

I let out a breath I hadn't held on purpose. "Oh, thank God. To be honest, the thought was making me a little nuts."

"I wasn't myself," Abram said, repeating my words back to me. He turned his back to me again, leaning on the window frame as he looked out over the alleyway. "You were supposed to stay away."

Irritation lanced through me. I narrowed my eyes at his back and considered throwing something heavy at his gorgeous head. "Need I remind you that *you* came to *me* first."

Abram shoved away from the window and whirled on me again, only this time, it wasn't desire in his eyes, but anger. "You were supposed to stay away. Let me take care of you by protecting you from me. You shouldn't have put yourself in danger to bring me back."

I rolled my eyes. "Abram, I hate to break it to you, but I don't need you to put myself in danger. Danger finds me any damn time it pleases."

Standing up, I walked toward him as I tugged my shirt off over my head. Then I let my bra slide off my arms to the floor. His eyes drifted to my chest, and I recognized the way they glazed over with desire.

Whatever was going on inside his conflicted mind, it had nothing to do with not wanting me, and everything to do with Abram himself.

I stepped into his personal space, my bare breasts pressing against his bare skin and his hard length jutting into my belly. "This isn't about us, and you know it. You need to forgive yourself for whatever happened while we were apart. I've already forgiven you. If you can't let whatever it is go, neither of us are going to have a chance in hell of surviving this thing. We're a team, Abram. In the bedroom and outside it."

The firelight did magical things to his face. We stood still for several long minutes, pressed against one another, our eyes locked, his breath mingling with mine. I would wait this out as long as it took for him to beat down whatever monster he was fighting against within himself.

You would think a man who lived half his life as a beast would be better at beating back his demons.

I tiptoed and gently bit his bottom lip, sucking it into my mouth. His cock throbbed against my pelvic bone, sending another rush of hot desire through my core. Pulling away, I said, "I have every intention of spending the rest of my life with you, whether you like it or not. Might as well get used to it."

Then I kissed him. Long and slow, more torturous to me than even the feel of his body so close yet so far away. His hands drifted over my bare back as if I were precious goods, easily broken, when I wanted him to manhandle me onto the bed and fuck me breathless.

Instead, he broke the kiss, swept across the room for his shirt, and disappeared out the bedroom door. A cold blast of air from the open window surrounded me, turning my skin as cold on the outside as I suddenly felt on the inside.

CHAPTER 6

BY ELEVEN THE NEXT MORNING, it became clear Abram wasn't coming back to the apartment of his own accord.

I'd gone to bed alone and frustrated the night before, expecting to wake up next to him as usual. He often spent the night roaming while under the influence of the beast, and probably caught some beastly Zs curled up under a tree like a cat. But generally, when the beast released him at dawn, he'd come climb into bed with me for a few more hours rest and some make-up cuddles.

Or at least, that's how it had been before we separated.

So I figured as soon as my eyes opened, he'd roll over, take my hand, and apologize for being an absolute crazy person. I'd even planned out the way I would gently accept his apology, tell him I loved him, and then ride him until we both couldn't remember our names.

Except that's not how it worked. I woke up to weak sunshine pouring through the still-open window, and Abram's side of the bed cold and untouched.

All through breakfast, and while choking down two cups of instant coffee, I listened intently for the sound of the door opening, for his footsteps in the hallway. Lulu and Jack did the same, all three of us on edge, munching toast and shooting concerned glances at the door like at some point we would see him walk in. Every door slam and yelling voice in the recesses of the apartment building made our heads pop up from our breakfast plates like valley girls sighting Hollywood's biggest hunk on the city street.

Finally, Jack slammed his mug to the table and said, "We should go look for him."

"Look *where?*" Lulu admonished. "There's a lot of city out there. A lot of places he could be."

I couldn't disagree with her. In my timeline, New York City had been a place you went when you wanted to get famous—*as well as* a place you went when you wanted to disappear.

"Wherever he is, something's wrong," I said, rubbing at the knot in my chest. My anxiety over his absence had manifested as a tightening ball of worry near my heart. I'd already done the whole life-without-Abram thing. For a full fucking year. I wasn't intent on doing it again. "It's not like him to disappear like this."

No need to add "before we broke up" and muddy the waters here.

"If we don't go walk around the city looking for him, what do we do?" Jack griped. "We can't just sit here. The dude's in trouble. Obviously."

Hearing someone else put to words the exact thing I couldn't stop repeating in my head was like taking a bucket of ice water to the face. I gasped through the shockingly cold revelation, and then wracked my brain for our next step.

A while back, my friend Satina and I had done a magical scrying to locate someone we needed to find. It wasn't an exact science, and unfortunately, Satina's strong conduit powers had really driven the show back then.

Remembering her now added to the growing ache in my chest. She'd been a staple in my life—one of the people I could truly call a friend, and unfortunately, she was dead now. For good this time, and resting in peace, I hoped.

But during my year training under Ramsey, we'd done some small scrying exercises. Nothing massive like trying to track down a person in heavily populated New York City, but stuff like finding a missing remote or tracking a passing car as far as I could from my current location. Things meant to build my stamina so that I could ultimately lead up to the big stuff.

Well, here I was. Needing the big stuff, and without Ramsey here to direct me.

"I can scry," I said out loud, even as my head protested there was no damn way I was strong enough to find Abram on my own.

"Magic?" Jack asked.

I nodded. "Magical tracking. I can use something of his to get a bead on him, and then using magic, trace his last steps." Last night, he'd unhooked his watch and set it on the nightstand, where I was pretty certain he'd left it when he grabbed his shirt and hauled ass out of there. "I think I *might* be able to do it. With some help. Lu, do you have a small mirror? Something I can lay on the table?"

"I do!" she said brightly, eager to help. She jumped up and headed toward the back of the apartment, presumably to get the mirror in question.

"Jack, get me a candle," I said, shoving my chair away from the table to stand. "And a knife. A clean one. Meet me at the coffee table in five."

I found Abram's watch exactly where he'd left it, and by the time I returned to the living room, Jack had settled a lit black pillar candle on the low wooden coffee table beside a shiny hand-held mirror that looked like something out of a fairy tale.

Lulu and Jack posted up on the couch, but I kneeled on the floor in front of the mirror and sat Abram's watch on top of it.

"You aren't going to break it, are you?" Lulu asked fretfully. "It was my grandmother's."

"No, I promise I won't hurt it," I assured her, then took a deep breath and let it out to a count of three. I repeated the deep centering breaths three times, until I felt like I had control of my senses.

A thread of doubt filled me as I touched the sharp tip of the knife to my finger and drew a bead of bright red blood. When we'd first arrived here, I'd tried to sense magic using my own powers and had come up short.

I recalled Abram telling me it wasn't my powers that were wrong, but this place. What if *he* was wrong? What if something went fundamentally sideways during the time travel, and I no longer had the powers I needed to defeat Darcus once and for all? I'd had even worse luck in the past, so the idea wasn't out of the realm of possibility.

I made sure none of my blood had been left behind on the blade before I set it aside. Getting even a miniscule drop of my blood on the floor would have been akin to sending out a Bat-Signal that said, "Supplicant blood found here!" Every conduit within a ten mile radius would converge on Lulu's apartment to snatch me for themselves.

Wiping the blood from my finger onto my palm willy-nilly, just to keep it from dripping, I took one more breath and promised myself, *You can do this.*

Then I held my palm out over the mirror and Abram's wrist watch, then closed my eyes.

My power flared warm and golden within me. Heat bloomed up my arm from my palm, the exposed blood strengthening the conduit powers within me. I didn't *need* to cut myself to do magic, but it didn't hurt to strengthen it. Especially when I was flying blind without Satina to guide my hand.

Suddenly, the magic tipped me forward. And I fell...right past Abram's watch and...*into* the mirror?

What. The. Fuck.

Once I passed through the looking glass, the city opened up around me as if I were a drone flying overhead. I hung in the air above Lulu's apartment building, trying to make sense of what I could see far below. A trail of red light, tinged gold, waved upon the air, heading away from the building.

Abram.

I sank lower, gaining speed as I followed the undulating ribbon of energy. It moved down the street before it made a ninety-degree curve onto a smaller side road. I followed it eagerly, knowing somehow that Abram would be waiting for me at the end.

I'd done it—I'd been able to harness a scrying on my own. Just...in a very different way than ever before.

The ribbon stretched *forever*. To the outskirts of Harlem, past Upper Manhattan, all the way along Central Park and into Midtown. But before I could get my hopes way high and do a victory dance that I'd located my errant boyfriend, the ribbon ended. Just...vanished. No energy, red, gold, or otherwise.

I took a good look around me. Everything was shadowy and vague, but I could make out a low glass building that had a strange dodecahedron emblem emblazoned on the door. And across from the building sat a homeless man, dozing beneath a tattered awning.

I surfaced from the mirror with a gasp, my body jolting as if I'd just awakened from a falling dream. Lulu and Jack both reached out to grab my shoulders before I keeled over sideways and knocked my head on the table.

"What did you see?" Jack demanded.

Considering the question hadn't been, *Where did you go?*, I assumed that meant I hadn't *actually* fallen through the mirror.

"I could see his trail. Where he walked after he left," I added to clarify. "But I lost it near a glass building." I explained what I'd seen, with the company's dodecahedron label and the sleeping homeless man. "Maybe that guy saw something? If we can find the building, we can find the man."

"That sounds like the Chatham Industries building," Lulu said, exchanging glances with Jack. "Over near St. Patrick's. It's one of the only all-glass buildings still standing in Manhattan."

Jack nodded grimly. "I think you're right. Our best bet is to head over and see if we can catch that man."

St. Patrick's Cathedral was a staple in Midtown Manhattan, situated near Rockefeller Center. The two-towered, neo-Gothic church had been built in 1879, and four generations of Catholic worshippers had come from far and wide to visit its hallowed halls and pray to God.

Me, I liked it because it was pretty. Like a sharp, fancy cake carved of monument stone and dropped smack dab in the middle of modern Fifth Avenue, where the city's most expensive stores hocked their wares. I wasn't going to pretend there was ever a point at which I visited St. Patrick's that I hadn't also blown hundreds of dollars on high-end fashion.

We passed the cathedral on our way to Chatham Industries, and I was horrified to find the place had just as much damage, and nature overtaking it, as most other buildings in this area. On this side of the apocalypse, people hadn't been able to protect what amounted to a national damn treasure of NYC, and I think that, more than anything, told me nothing would ever be the same again.

Leaving the church behind, Jack led me down a small side street that I immediately recognized from my scrying vision. My heart launched into a song and dance as I realized Abram had been down this road—though I had no idea what the fuck for. Why did he walk so far from Lulu's apartment to begin with? In a dystopian wasteland crawling with militia?

Chatham Industries was in a lot better shape than St. Patrick's. The entire facade was glass, with not a broken window in sight, though the building was dark and lacked obvious inhabitants. Opposite the clean, shiny storefront, a line of stone buildings across the street were marred by gaping, dark holes for windows and piles of trash on the sidewalks.

I opened my mouth to question Jack about the Chatham building—Did they do pharmaceuticals? Accounting? Was it a front for a strip club? Not that anything about dodecahedrons screamed "titty bar," but you never know.

Before I could ask, I noticed movement across the street. A pile of what I'd thought to be trash was shifting, and a moment later, a scraggly head of greasy black hair appeared from beneath.

The homeless man.

"There he is!" I hissed, clutching Jack's arm and pointing with my other hand.

We hurried across the street as the man reached for a nearby bottle, uncapping it before he turned it up over his head. Even from halfway across the street, I recognized the black and gold symbol on the side of the liter. Montezuma Tequila. The man was drinking shit tequila straight from the bottle.

He was going to regret that later.

Jack angled himself in front of me as we came to a stop before the old man. Up close, he looked as worn out as a destroyed bus seat: skin leathery and lined, a strange jaundiced yellow from too much alcohol and rough living, and eyes so bloodshot they looked red in their own right.

It took him a moment to realize we'd stopped in front of him. He lowered the bottle, liquid sloshing around inside, and squinted at us. "Whadya want?"

"Uh, sorry to bother you," I said, peeking around Jack's shoulder and aiming for my most polite tone. "We're looking for information on a missing individual. We have it under good authority that he passed through here last night, maybe sometime around midnight?"

The man cocked a thick, bushy eyebrow. "Whaddya payin'?"

I exchanged glances with Jack, who took the reins. "We aren't paying anything, buddy. Did you see a big guy pass through here late last night? Big, muscular, dark hair."

Homeless Man fell back against the stones and sneered at us. "Kid, you just described half the men in NYC. Can't help you."

Nothing wrong with being down on your luck and being homeless, but this guy was being an asshole, and with my boyfriend missing, I wasn't having it.

I shoved Jack aside and planted my Chucks on the sidewalk in front of him, hands on my hips as I stared down at this sad excuse for a man. "Listen, bud. I don't care what the alcohol content in your pickled body is. I know you saw something happen last night. Something strange. I demand you tell me what you saw."

"Fuck off, lady. You got no right demanding shit." Homeless Man swayed to the left, both hands and bottle hitting the ground as he hauled himself to his feet. Thank God the bottle was plastic and not glass, because it would have shattered beneath his palm. Not that the loss of bottom shelf tequila would have made any angels cry.

Before he could take a single step, I shot a hand out and grabbed his arm. "Hey—"

The man reacted with astonishing quickness. He swung the Montezuma bottle around, aiming right for my head.

CHAPTER 7

I DUCKED the flying Montezuma bottle, narrowly avoiding a close encounter with shitty tequila. Behind me, Jack let out an angry yell, and the next thing I knew, his fist was flying past my head.

Wind displaced all the tiny hairs around my face, and an extremely satisfying—and surely painful—*crunch* broke through my horror as Jack punched the man in the face.

The old guy collapsed to the ground like a ballgown tossed from a window. Luckily, he fell backwards onto his pile of newspaper, giving him a little bit of a softer landing than if he'd hit the sidewalk bare.

Once he hit the ground, he rolled down the hill of papers, sprawled out onto the dirty sidewalk, and lay still. His bottle of Montezuma tumbled away from his fingers and into the gutter.

Whirling on Jack, I screeched, "What'd you do that for?"

Jack shook out his hand, his face pained. "He tried to smash you over the head with a bottle!"

"I ducked!" I groaned, then stomped away from the kid toward the homeless man. "What if you've killed him?"

"I didn't kill him," Jack said irritably, his voice coming closer as he followed me over to the man.

I stared down at the poor soul. The guy had clearly had a rough life, maybe even before the world ended fifteen years ago. He was dirty on every part of his visible skin, and his balding hair was dreadlocked from not being cared for. Though he was short and skinny, he had a potbelly that looked less like "beer o'clock" and more like his insides were eating themselves with starvation.

"Somebody should have told the man alcohol doesn't cover the six basic food groups," I said out loud as Jack posted up next to me, clenching and unclenching his fist. I pointed at his hand. "Serves you right."

"I'm not sorry for defending you."

"You'll have to learn like every other man in my life that I don't *need* your defending," I snapped. "You should be sorry for knocking out the only man who knows anything about Abram's disappearance. Also, I'm telling your mother."

Jack rolled his eyes but didn't comment.

And yeah, I know it was a low blow. But for fuck's sake, I couldn't ask questions of an unconscious man. Jack effectively neutered our only lead. As long as the guy was locked inside his own head, he couldn't give me answers.

A sudden thought occurred to me. I straightened with a maniacal laugh, and then turned to Jack and cupped his face in my hands. "You brilliant boy!"

With his cheeks smooshed between my palms and his face screwed up in utter confusion, he looked so much like the little boy I'd once dragged out of a creek.

"Uh. What?" he said.

I let him go and knelt beside the homeless man, shoving up the sleeves on my sweatshirt. Navy blue—not a great color to go with my winter complexion. "He's unconscious!"

Jack knelt beside me, looking at me like I'd lost my mind. "Yes. That's why you were yelling at me."

"Yes, well, that still stands. Don't punch the people we need to help us," I said sternly, and then placed my hands on either side of the homeless man's head.

"What are you doing?"

"He's unconscious," I repeated, "so I can read his memories."

Jack rocked back on his heels and eyed me warily. "You couldn't read his memories if he was conscious?"

I huffed. "Don't question the logic of my magic. I've been questioning it for years, and there aren't any answers to be found. But there are memories in this guy's head. So hush."

Closing my eyes, I dove into the man's alcohol-saturated mind.

I got in easier than I had the last time I'd tried this, last year when Ramsey had me practicing on the neighbors while they slept. Bad move, by the way. You don't actually want to know what your neighbors have been up to while you weren't looking. That's not information that helps you sleep at night with only a thin, shared wall between you.

But once I was in, making sense of the man's memories proved to be a bit harder. He'd clearly been on a bender for days, so his memories were vaguely watercolored and disjointed, while missing vast swaths of time.

On top of his alcoholism, something else felt weird, too— as if I were trying to read his memories through a veil that separated me from his mind. I could blame it on his drunkenness, but something niggling inside me said it wasn't the man.

It was me. My powers. Something stood in my way, and it originated with me.

Well, I don't exactly have a back up plan, I told myself, sifting through his memories as if they were colored slides on a projector. *Gotta make this work.*

I headed backward in his mind. First, I came across the moment Jack and I arrived—and the entirely disgusting thoughts the homeless man had had over my "lucious hips." Before that, he'd been sleeping, and before he passed out, he'd watched employees come and go from the Chatham Industries building. I kept paging backward, trying my damndest to not listen in on his disgusting thoughts and to just look for Abram.

Finally, I hit paydirt. A single street light illuminated the road ahead of the homeless man as he lounged on his throne of dirty newspapers and opened his fresh bottle of Montezuma. He looked up at the thin sliver of sky between the buildings, and I got the impression he missed seeing stars. Then his attention caught on the steady march of militiamen boots headed his way.

The homeless man burrowed deep into his newspaper cave, inching a sheet aside so he could watch outside his protective barrier. He remembered the last time he'd been picked up by the militia—they'd thrown him in a jail cell, then he'd spent six months in a laboratory being tested on like an animal. It was a miracle he'd been released.

But the militiamen weren't the first people he saw passing beneath the streetlight.

Abram slunk from the shadows, looking big and dangerous in the growing twilight. Homeless Guy thought Abram looked a bit feral and insane, and that wasn't too far off the truth. I could tell by the sweat beading on Abram's strong forehead, by the slight curl of his thick lips and the tension in his muscles, that he was close to shifting.

Homeless Guy gave a fleeting thought to yelling at the strange man and telling him to take cover. Every three days, the militia covered this street on their patrols, and even though his mind was in a fog borne of bad gin and even worse tequila, he was pretty sure this was a third night.

But he kept his mouth shut because the big dude scared him.

Dismayed, I watched as the militia came into view beneath the streetlight and yelled at Abram to halt. My boyfriend had an exchange with the men that looked pretty damn heated, though I couldn't hear a word of it through the veil blocking me. Then there was a tussle, a gunshot, and then Abram slumped to the ground.

I knew my boyfriend was made of stronger stuff, and a bullet wound was hardly enough to take him down. So when one of the shoulders stepped up and plucked a dart from his neck, I groaned out loud.

They'd tranquilized him.

Sons of bitches.

I surfaced from the old drunk's memories and took a deep breath to chase away the lingering cobwebs. The guy was still out like a light, so I swept to my feet and got his tequila bottle, sliding it under his arm so it would be there for him when he woke up.

I joined Jack at the edge of the curb facing Chatham Industries. "He was taken by militia. Right here on this street."

Jack grunted. "I worried that was the case."

"Where do they take prisoners?"

Jack squinted at the building across the street. "Word on the street is the militia operates out of district headquarters. Like the city is broken down into districts, and each district has its own patrolling militia. My guess is he'd be taken back to district headquarters."

"Word on the street," I repeated, getting a sinking feeling from that short sentence. "So...you don't know where the district headquarters are?"

"No one does. They're kept secret on purpose. I guess because they think if civilians knew where to find them, we'd use that information to take them out." He laughed. "They're probably right."

"We'll need to find a patrol group and follow them back to base," I said. "They can't patrol all day and night without going to lunch. Or going to shift change. They're people.

They need breaks." I narrowed my gaze on Jack. "They *are* people, right? Not robots?"

"Far as I know, they're flesh and blood," Jack assured me. "Following a platoon is probably the best course of action."

"Great. Let's get back onto the main street. The militia only patrols this street every three nights, so we won't find them here." I step off the curb and into the cracked street, on a straight line back toward Fifth Avenue.

"How do you know that?" Jack asked, loping to catch up with my determined pace. "About the patrolling?"

"The homeless man's memories. He tracks the militia to stay out of trouble, I guess."

Jack looked impressed. "Huh. I never thought about using the homeless as a form of intel. All the times I've almost been caught—"

He cut off abruptly, and I cast him a withering glance.

"You don't work at a factory, do you, Jack Carroll?" I accused.

He shrugged, giving me a lopsided grin. "I plead the fifth."

"I somehow don't think there are constitutional protections in this timeline. Spill it, kid."

His smile fell away, and he took a deep breath, his blue eyes sparkling in the morning light as we rounded the corner onto Fifth Avenue. "Trust me, Char. It's safer if you don't know."

"Lulu's going to murder you," I pointed out, but I dropped the subject anyway. Jack may have been my best friend's kid, but he was also an adult capable of making his own decisions—even if they were stupid ones.

For it being the middle of the morning, there was a decent crowd of people walking the streets. Of course, fifteen years ago they would have been buying from Gucci, Dolce & Gabbana, or, for the lighter wallets, H&M. Now they were simply passing by the shuttered and crumbling stores on their way to whatever destination.

We stopped at a food truck, where Jack treated me to a couple street tacos and a lukewarm canned Coke. Armed with our lunch, we carried our food to a nearby stone staircase that ended in a boarded up door covered in graffiti, and sat to eat and wait.

After I devoured my first taco, I balled up the tinfoil and reached for the second as I asked, "Is your surreptitious 'job' the reason you think Alice didn't run off to Wonderland?"

He'd just shoved a large bite of taco into his mouth, and I waited patiently for him to clear it out. "Yes and no. I have it under good authority that my sister, and a lot of other teens, didn't make it to Wonderland."

"Are you in contact with Wonderland?" I asked, biting into my second taco with a burst of cilantro lime over my tastebuds.

"Not directly. My superiors are."

"That's why you haven't told Lu—your mom?" I guessed. "Because you don't want her to know you're wrapped up in something way over your head."

"I'm not wrapped up in something way over my head," Jack said wryly. "I'm simply doing my part to take down Darcus."

We ate in silence for a few more moments. Not only was I happy to know that there were food trucks capable of surviving the apocalypse, but these tacos were to die for. I finished off mine, then sipped at my Coke, wishing for ice cubes.

"Your dad would be proud, you know," I said. "You're a kinda soldier, too. He lived and breathed the military and fought for the greater good."

Jack crushed his foil and tossed it at the paper basket at his feet. Pain flashed in his eyes and he avoided my gaze, but he nodded. "Yeah. I've thought about the comparison before, too."

I slipped my arm around his shoulders and tugged him in for a hug. "If your dad were still here, he'd be fighting along with you."

The stamp of marching feet tore through our conversation.

I released Jack and stiffened, sweeping the street with my gaze. The militia came into sight in the distance, moving at a regulated pace toward us. Their legs moved in tandem, their arms swinging, but their voices raised over the thudding as they laughed and cut up like they were out on the town and not looking for civilians to arrest.

"We'll wait for them to pass," Jack said under his breath. "Then follow my lead."

Nodding, I planted my feet on the step beneath me and leaned forward on my elbows in an attempt to look like I belonged there.

Luckily, it was the middle of the day, and people were allowed to be out and about. Neither myself nor Jack earned even a side-eye as the party passed—even with Jack wearing his broadsword. I didn't know if they just weren't very observant, or if even in Darcus's America, the right to bear arms still stood.

After the militiamen passed, Jack watched them intently until they'd gotten a few blocks ahead, then he motioned me to follow him.

We fell into step at a distance, keeping as close to the buildings as possible. Neither of us spoke to ensure we weren't noticed, even though the chances of that were slim considering the way the group of men operated. They never looked back, only ahead, and they kept their attention mainly on each other.

Bros, man. They transcend any time or place.

We followed for nearly an hour, walking up and down the

same streets multiple times as the militia completed their patrol. Until finally, they veered off the normal path. Unfortunately, that meant veering off populated streets and onto empty streets that would definitely give our location away.

"Can I glamour us?" I hissed under my breath to Jack. "Are they human? Or conduit?"

"Human. But there will be conduits in charge, so it won't be safe once we get there."

"Noted." I pulled on my magic, conjuring up a simple glamour to protect us from prying eyes.

This particular spell took less energy, and as a result, I hoped would be less obvious to anyone who might be sensitive to magic. Rather than physically blocking us or changing our appearance, this glamour made it so that anyone who happened to look our way would feel a strong urge to glance away. Their gazes would just move off us without noticing we were there.

Thanks to Ramsey, I was really good at glamours.

The militia men took us deep into an alley, where they halted outside a blank wall with a single metal door. A soldier up front tugged his badge forward, and a distinct electronic beep flashed down the alley before the door opened.

The group began to file inside the large, several-stories-high stone building. Looking in from the outside, nobody would have ever guessed the place operated as what amounted to a police precinct.

As we stopped just around the corner and watched them enter, I closed my eyes and opened my senses. Like I'd done the day we arrived, I searched the building for any sign that someone magical was inside. And there were—five brilliant spots of energy. Four of them foreign, likely the conduit bosses as Jack had suggested, and the fourth I recognized immediately as Abram.

"He's in there," I whispered, glaring at the door as it

slammed shut behind the last of the militiamen. "The question now, is how are we going to get in and get him?"

Jack leaned against the wall and eyed the building from top to bottom, like an operative taking stock of the situation. If he suggested we scale the building like some kind of scene out of *Mission: Impossible*, I was going to lose my shit.

Instead, before he could suggest any course of action at all, voices approached behind us. Two more soldiers were walking down the alley, both carrying duffel bags as if they were coming on duty for the afternoon. They were deep in conversation—one man, one woman.

Jack and I exchanged glances. His sword slid smoothly along its scabbard as he tugged it free.

"No magic," he mouthed so the soldiers wouldn't hear.

No magic. Great. As if I were any good at actual hand to hand combat. "What are we doing?"

He didn't answer. Just leapt at the approaching soldiers, my glamour sliding off him and leaving me no choice but to follow.

CHAPTER 8

JACK HAD BEEN CARRYING the broadsword since he stepped through the portal and yanked me and Abram across fifteen years into the future, but I'd never actually seen him *use* it. Until this moment, I'd treated it like a safety blanket—it made Jack feel better to carry a big sharp sword in a world that had turned dangerous.

He knew how to use it, alright. And quite frankly, he was terrifying even when he wasn't aiming for certain death.

Jack whipped the sword around as if it weighed nothing at all, and the blade flashed in the ambient light as he brought it down on the two passing soldiers. Before I even managed to get my dagger out of the sheath at my hip, he'd used the handle of his sword to knock out both soldiers. He was so quick, neither of them had a chance to react to his sudden presence before they'd been concussed into dream worlds.

Then he snagged the guy's arm and dragged him into the alley, out of sight of the militia's department building.

"Get the girl!" he hissed at me from under cover, motioning to her prone form.

I was still standing on the sidewalk with my dagger

dangling uselessly before me. Both me and the unconscious soldier woman were fully visible; should any more militia appear, I'd probably be shot on sight. Yet there I was, letting grass grow beneath my feet. *Some help I am*, I thought, and shoved the dagger back into its sheath.

Leaping into action, I hauled the woman soldier into the alley beside her partner where Jack was already tugging off the dude's pants.

"What are you doing?" I asked, eyeballing the poor guy's Homer Simpson boxer shorts. The fabric had *not* aged well, though at this rate, it wouldn't have surprised me to find out *The Simpsons* was still running with new episodes every Sunday night. And they'd added making fun of conduits to the narrative.

"Put on her clothes," Jack said, motioning to the unconscious woman. "We're going to pose as them to get inside the building."

I gaped at him. "Are you out of your mind? What happens when we get in there and they figure us out? We'll be offering ourselves up on a silver platter."

Jack unbuckled his broadsword and set it on the ground, then tugged off his shirt. "Got a better plan?"

Jack was *ripped*. His long, lean torso held at least an eight-pack, maybe twelve, maybe twenty, I didn't stop to count. I whirled around with a squeak of indignation and fought the urge to jam my fingers into my eyeballs.

Logically, I knew that he was twenty years old, and not the little boy I used to babysit to give Lulu a break from the mom thing. Even still, I felt completely disgusted by my momentary, silent thought of "Oh, *my*." I conjured up an image of Abram naked to bleach my brain with, thankful I had such an exquisite man bod to turn to in these trying times.

"Put a shirt on, you heathen!" I griped over my shoulder, bending down to reach for the buckle on the woman soldier's pants. "I'm super sorry," I told her under my breath, working the belt from its loop. "This is *so* non-consensual, and I swear to God, I wouldn't be doing this if the entire world wasn't at stake."

"Char—you're stealing her clothes, not her dignity," Jack said, amusement lacing his tone. "Plus, she's the bad guy."

Once we'd traded our clothes for theirs, including their militia badges and their guns, we dumped our own things behind a dumpster where we could come back for them later. Then we fell into step beside each other and headed for the innocuous door.

"I want it known that I think this is a stupid plan," I whispered. "We're both going to die."

Jack grinned and tugged his badge on the lanyard to scan it on the keypad beside the door. "Speak for yourself."

The door opened on a surprisingly bright lobby, illuminated by humming fluorescent fixtures high overhead. The floors were brushed concrete and the walls yellowing plaster, but the place was clean. Busy, too, which added a new level of stress to my worries.

Jack took the lead, thank God, and we headed to the right, following a wave of soldiers through a side door. Nobody paid us any attention, and an inkling of hope rose within me. Maybe there were so many militia in and out of this building that unfamiliar faces were just par for the course. That would make our job easier, and keep the militia from shooting off my beautiful face, but we were still left with the conundrum of finding the holding cells.

As far as I could tell so far, the walls didn't have any helpful *Jail Cells—Third Floor* signs to guide us. That would be too easy, of course.

Jack peeled away from the crowd, and we took a staircase to the second floor. Jack peeked out the door into the second floor hallway, then hauled back and took the stairs once more. I don't know what he saw when he peeked out the door a second time, but it seemed to work for him, because we left the stairwell behind.

Traffic had quelled significantly in this area of the building. We mainly passed offices with closed doors labeled by ranking officers' names. I didn't know if that meant we had more room to maneuver, being currently unseen, or if the first person to catch us would know we didn't belong in this area.

Didn't take me long to find out, either.

A handsome older man with coiffed silver hair and a perfectly pressed uniform stepped out of one of the offices, closing the door behind him. His gaze zeroed in on us. He stepped into the middle of the hallway and crossed his arms. "Lost?"

"No, sir," Jack replied, coming to a halt before the officer.

Jesus H., we're going to die, I thought, terror unfurling inside me. *I'm too fucking pretty to die.*

The man eyed us suspiciously. "Name and rank?"

Jack straightened and tossed back his shoulders. "Darius Winslow. Private First Class."

He said it with such authority, even *I* believed him. When the man turned his beady gaze on me, fear struck me dumb. There was no way I could mimic Jack's acting.

"Laura Robinson," I said, using the fake name Alan had given me on my microchip. Since I didn't exactly know military ranks, I copied Jack. "Private First Class."

The man's gaze slid down to my uniform shirt. "Demoting yourself, *Sergeant*?"

Fuck. I hadn't paid attention to the soldier's shirt, but clearly something about the embroidered patches gave away rank. We were screwed.

In the blink of an eye, Jack whipped his gun up and jammed the barrel in the soldier's chest. "Where are the holding cells?"

The man looked down at the gun jutting into his uniform

shirt as if he couldn't quite believe the nerve. It was so perfectly pressed, he had pleats in the sleeves, so I couldn't very well blame him. "Go ahead and shoot me, kid. I'm not going to help you with whatever suicide mission Wonderland has sent you on."

I was shocked to hear the soldier bring up Wonderland. Did they often have teenagers infiltrating their precincts? Also, I knew I looked good, but I didn't look like an eighteen year old. Even flawless skin from a lifetime of good moisturizers can't stop the flow of aging. I should know, being an out-of-work model booted because I was no longer young enough to appeal to the masses.

Instead of rising to the bait, Jack took a single step backwards and jerked the gun up, swirling the heavier grip end until it smashed into the officer's face. The move was quick and brutal, and took me a few feet further into my theory that Jack was either working for Wonderland or running around New York City like a goddamned vigilante.

Lulu would be *so* pissed.

The officer crumpled to the floor, his eyes fluttering closed and staying that way.

"Come on," Jack said urgently, tugging on my arm, and we took off down the hallway.

We reached the next stairwell before the shouts began. As I followed Jack through, I heard a gunshot, and then felt the obvious displacement of air in front of my face before a bullet embedded in the doorframe.

"Holy shit," I breathed, launching through the door and letting it slam behind me.

"We're out of time," Jack said. "We need a plan."

"We needed a plan twenty minutes ago!" I snapped, then whipped around to stare down the door. It was metal, with one of those push-bar handles that opened the door outward onto the floor. I placed both my palms on the bar and called up my magic, wrapping a tendril of searing hot energy around the mechanism. Then I stepped back as the thing began to melt, effectively locking the door closed.

"I said no magic!" Jack roared. "What the hell, Char?"

"I just bought us some time. We've already been seen; might as well take advantage of it." I closed my eyes and searched the building with my magical radar, looking for Abram's familiar presence.

Outside in the hallway, voices raised and footsteps ran closer as the militia gave chase. I ignored the noise, and the terror that maybe my magic hadn't melted the door after all, and shoved my senses out further. I knew Abram was in this building. I just needed to know *where*.

Finally, I got a bead on him.

"Top floor!" I said, then hauled ass up the stairs.

Jack wasn't super happy with the way I'd hulked out on magic, but the kid was smart enough to keep his grumbling to a minimum as we spiraled up the staircase. Smart, because I was *not* in the best shape of my life, and these stairs might damn near have killed me.

At the top floor, I shoved through the door and into the holding area. The lobby held a few folding metal chairs and a horrific pea-green carpet that had seen better decades. Behind the circular desk, two uniformed officers leapt to their feet, spurred by our sudden explosive entrance.

Before Jack could raise his borrowed gun, I sent a wave of magic arching through the room and dropped them with a sleeping spell.

"Neat trick," Jack said, letting his gun fall.

"This is what happens when Char's allowed to use magic," I told him, then turned my back on him and raced for the side door.

The soldier woman's badge granted us access to the holding cells. The interior hall was dim and quiet with not a militiaman in sight, though the faces beyond the bars proved the room wasn't empty. I found Abram at the end of the hall, sitting on his metal bed with one leg cocked up and his head resting on the stone wall as if he were bored.

"You stupid son of a bitch!" I roared at him, slamming both my palms against the iron bars. Magic sizzled along them, disintegrating them to pieces as he watched me enigmatically from his position. "You couldn't have had a temper tantrum on the roof of Lulu's building? You had to go prancing off through the city as if you were *begging* to get arrested?"

Abram dropped his feet to the floor and glared at me. "You're overreacting."

"I had to take a woman's clothes off to get into this building to save you!" I screeched, fury dampening any feelings I had inside about keeping my voice down so we could remain unseen.

He grinned, a hard glint in his eye. "You had to take a woman's clothes off? How delightful."

"You're a pain in my ass," I snarled, throwing him the gun off my back. "And you owe me some serious wallowing."

"Char!" Jack yelled. "We've got company!"

I motioned for Abram to follow me, and we joined Jack down in the main aisle as a group of militiamen poured through the security door.

"That's the only way out," Jack said, leveling his gun on the crowd. "Can you shut them down?"

"Ha!" I said, widening my stance. "Can I shut them down? Of course I can, grasshopper."

Then I closed my eyes and reached for the magic.

A solid sheet of power blasted from my center, knocking down the entire group in a single blow. They weren't all completely out of it, but they were down for the count—for the moment. So Jack, Abram, and I took off, darting around fallen soldiers until we reached the door and left the jail cells behind.

As we passed back through the lobby, I felt something hot

dripping beneath my nostrils. I touched my upper lip and drew my hand away, recoiling as I realized I'd gotten a nose bleed. It happened sometimes when I used too much power at once, but there was *no* way I'd used enough to justify my body giving up the ghost.

What was going on with my magic?

The door to the stairwell burst open before we reached out, and three large, muscular men barreled into the room with their guns raised. I sent another blast of magic their way, tossing them off their feet and into the wall in the same moment the blood started flowing a bit more freely from my nose. Gathering a handful of uniform shirt, I shoved it beneath my nose, and made a beeline for the staircase.

I could hear the thud of approaching boots from below and skidded to a stop at the top of the stairs. Knocking out that officer had obviously put the entire building into motion, and if we went downstairs, we'd run into a dozen men who would just as soon put a bullet in each of us than let us safely pass.

So I took the stairs up.

"Char!" Jack shouted. "What the hell are you doing?"

"Desperate times!" I yelled back, curving around the landing and taking the last ten steps to the roof exit. By the time I'd opened the door to brilliant morning sunlight, Jack and Abram were at my heels.

I raced towards the edge of the roof, hoping that one of the nearby buildings was close enough to justify a rush and a leap. Unfortunately, there wasn't a chance in hell Jack or I could leap over these alleys without plummeting ten stories to our deaths.

I'd never wished I could fly before. First time for everything.

"What do we do now?" Jack asked, his gaze darting around the roof for inspiration.

I held up my hands. "I don't know. Pray?"

The stairwell doors burst open, and a crowd spilled onto the rooftop. A bullet whizzed past my face, and I ducked behind exposed ductwork, my skin sparking with magic and fear. Jack and Abram both leapt behind walls and air conditioning machines to protect themselves.

We were ten stories up, and our only exit was inundated with militiamen ready to kill us on sight. It wasn't a fair fight when a dozen men carried semi-automatic weapons against three people, one of whom had no weapon at all except magic.

Abram straightened, whipping around to level his gun on the crowd. He got off three shots before they returned fire and he had to duck back behind the wall.

How do we get out of here? I asked myself, curling into a ball behind the ductwork. I didn't have an easy answer. All I could come up with was "Fight."

So I leapt to my feet and launched a full out magical assault.

For several moments, the air was filled with magic and gunfire. I tossed up barriers, catching their bullets in mid-air, and then flung more magic at them until they began to collapse. But it became obvious within moments that this level of magic wouldn't be something I could keep up.

I was bum-rushed by a militiaman who reached for both my hands as if taking hold of me would stop my onslaught of magic. I tried to send another wave of power into him to knock him out, but it didn't work—probably because I'd started tapping out on my powers three onslaughts ago. So I kicked him, sending my Chuck between his legs for a little bit of football.

He grunted, but leapt for me, his hands grappling with my neck. We struggled against one another, my magic sparking uselessly on my fingertips and blood pouring from my nose. I hit a low brick wall, and then used the momentum to shove him into a nearby A/C tunnel.

The guy was made of rubber. He leapt at me again, his momentum sending me flying backwards.

Except, I hadn't realized how far across the roof we'd danced.

Suddenly, my body was floating mid-air, nothing behind me but the ten-story drop to the sidewalk below. And I fell.

CHAPTER 9

I'D NEVER BEEN the type of girl to wish she could fly. Walk down a runway? Check. Wear two-thousand dollar heels? Double check. Fly? Nah, man. That shit's for the birds. Literally.

Luckily, I didn't panic when the militiaman tossed me over the edge of the roof. Well, to be fair, I panicked for about point-two seconds, letting out half a quick screech as my body plummeted toward the concrete below. But then I remembered I was half-conduit, half-supplicant, and all badass, and screaming like a little bitch wasn't conducive to that amazing combination of qualities.

Pulling on my magic, I tried to think fast for a plan. I wasn't entirely certain I could stop a total free fall with my body in panic mode, and my body being the thing needing saving. But if I considered the physics of it all, I was falling, so I needed an equal and opposite force to buoy me. What if I used an outward blast? That was how rockets worked, right? Epic fuck-tons of downward blasting fire power, and the craft could just shoot straight to the stars.

I had a split second to conduct the magic and get it right before I became a Char pancake outside the secret militia headquarters. I managed to rotate my body until I was face-down, which was probably a bad idea considering the concrete was rising at an alarming rate and now I could, in fact, *see* just how alarming a rate it was. Shoving my hands out before me, I channeled a big burst of energy and sent a ball of power careening ahead of me.

It worked…sort of.

The blast hit the concrete with a devastating blow. Shards of broken asphalt pistoned out, and the ground buckled in a meteoric-like crater. I jolted painfully as my downward momentum met the backlash of the energy, but then I slowed. Not enough of a slow down, however. I was no physicist, but I was pretty sure my rate of speed still hovered in "dead on impact" territory.

So I bundled another blast of energy and let it rip, this one stronger. The momentum of the blast shooting outward halted me to a total standstill in mid-air about ten feet above the ground. All the bones in my body protested the sudden stop, no different than if I'd been in the driver's seat during a head-on collision. As the energy faded, I fell again, but hit the ground with a jarring, painful roll instead of a full-on terminal crush.

The alley pivoted madly around me as I rode out the rest of the motion in a barrel roll that made it hard for me to figure out which way was up. I came to a smashing stop against the brick wall opposite the militia building, and despite the fact my head still whirled and my bones felt like they'd been thoroughly mauled, I used the bricks to haul myself up.

As soon as I got my feet under me, I cupped my hands around my mouth and screamed up at the roof. "Abram! Jack! *Jump!*"

I didn't wait for a response. The sooner I could get a safety net in place, the better. I lifted my hands toward the rooftop and sent out a billowing sheet of magic. It hung in the air, lines of energy criss-crossed like a hammock.

Man, my first apartment in New York, I'd had a woven hammock on my tiny balcony. Those were *much* easier days, laying in that gently swinging cradle, a mimosa in one hand and *The Real Housewives* circa 2010 playing on my iPad in the other.

I crashed back to local time as the first of my two companions launched over the edge of the roof.

Jack appeared, his long legs pedaling the air as he pitched towards the asphalt. Damn, whoever would have thought the boy I lost as a toddler while babysitting would grow up to trust me enough to jump off a roof?

I strengthened my net of power, praying I was strong enough to catch him and bring him gently to the ground. He hit the magical hammock on his back, and the impact reverberated in my core. Ignoring the painful tug, I quickly wrapped the energy net around him, encasing him from head to toe. Then let him float toward the ground.

I cackled at my own cleverness. That was *super easy*. The only thing I wished was that Ramsey could be here to see it, so I could shove my prowess in his face and say, *See! I can work under pressure!*

Abram crested over the edge of the roof and spread out like a skydiver on a leisurely—and much safer—jump to the earth. Unfortunately, though, Abram wasn't wearing a parachute.

I had a brief moment of panic where Jack hadn't quite made it safely to the ground yet, and Abram was swiftly catching up to him, and me with no net there to catch the man I loved. Logically, I knew the beast was likely to survive a ten-story fall with little more than some scratches and bruises. But irrationally, all I saw was my raison d'etre heading for terminal velocity.

I leveled my left hand on Jack, keeping a small amount of concentration on his fall and then used my right hand to jettison a new net of power toward Abram. It wrapped around him like a spider web, and I gritted my teeth against the magical weight of having both their lives in my hands. Literally.

But within moments, they were both on their feet, shaking off the last vestiges of my powers.

I sprinted away from the militia headquarters, not even bothering to check if Abram and Jack were behind me. Either them bitches followed my mad dash for freedom, or they got left behind. Now wasn't the time for second guessing or being the Big Hero. But all I needed was the sound of their boots heavy on the asphalt to let me know we were well on our way to getting the fuck out of this mess.

As we passed the alley where we'd taken down the two soldiers earlier, Jack darted behind the dumpster and snatched up our things, but I kept running. The only thing we had working for us right now was the ability to put distance between ourselves and the militiamen.

Otherwise, we'd end up back inside that building, a three-for-one deal. Only this time, we'd be sharing a cell. Or dead.

We ran for what seemed like an eternity. I used magic to boost our speed and gave Jack the lead, since he'd grown up on these post-apocalyptic streets and knew best where to hide.

By the time he skidded to a stop inside an old, abandoned warehouse, my lungs were barely functioning and my legs had turned to jelly. I collapsed against a chipped stone column, resting my hot, sweaty forehead on the cool surface as I tried to measure my breathing before I passed out.

"Where are we?" Abram asked brusquely. He barely sounded winded, and I hated him for it.

"About three blocks from the apartment," Jack said breathlessly, bending over to rest his hands on his knees. His face had turned fire engine red, and sweat dotted his blond hairline. At least he was human and subject to overexertion like me. Plus, he was much more in shape than my lumpy ass, and I'd *still* managed to keep up with him. "This is an old printing factory."

Abram turned in place, taking stock of our surroundings and likely straining with his beastly senses to make sure we weren't followed. I glared at him, clutching a sharp pain in my side and struggling to catch my breath. He was too busy looking for external threats to realize the biggest one stood six feet away and ready to blow—as soon as she could breathe again.

When I finally regained full control of my senses, I launched to Abram's side on my wobbly legs and shoved him with all my might. "You are *such* an asshole!"

To my chagrin, he hardly budged under my blow. My rockin' curves couldn't even put a dent in that mountain of muscle. Even though it was basic physics, it still pissed me off even more than I already was.

"Why'd you run off into the fucking apocalyptic sunset?" I snapped, jabbing my finger in his chest. My voice was still high and breathy from our sprint to safety. "That was a seriously stupid thing to do."

"I needed some air," he said shortly, crossing his muscular arms over his chest.

"We're in danger just by *being* here in this timeline, you jackass. Then you had to go run away in a temper tantrum like a jerk and get taken by the enemy!" I dropped my fists to my sides, still clenched, because I was worried I might actually punch him. And that would *hurt*. Me, not him. When I spoke again, my voice came out small and scared. "What if we hadn't been able to find you?"

"I would have found a way out."

The confidence in his voice sent a fresh rush of fury through me. "Oh yes. Sure. You appeared to be doing such a *great* job at that in your magically enchanted cell."

"Guys!" Jack hissed, angling his body between us. His

baby blues were locked on the door we'd come in, and a muscle ticked in his jaw. "Shut up and hide."

The three of us broke, darting into the shadows at the edge of the warehouse. I headed for a massive machine that stood six feet tall and at least as long. It was a little rusted and falling apart, but the large rollers spaced evenly across gave the underside some cover. I fell to my knees and wedged my hips beneath one of the rollers, army-crawling into the darkness with God knew how many cockroaches and spiders.

Not even the slants of sunlight fighting through the dirty windows high overhead could reach the shadows beneath the roller machine. I didn't have a fucking clue what this thing used to do back in its hey-day, but I definitely felt confident in it as a hiding place. Hopefully, Jack and Abram had found cover, too.

The door screeched in protest, and the shuffle of footsteps on the dusty warehouse floor shifted through the room. My heart did a crash-and-burn, and I went as still as possible, hardly even breathing.

"Are you sure they're in here?" a man asked.

"Civilian said they ran this way. It's as good a lead as any," a second voice replied. "Harvey, take the left. Stan, the right. I'll go forward."

So Harvey would be making his way in my direction. Lovely.

I couldn't peer over the metal edge of the contraption to get a view of any of the militiamen, but I could hear them. They moved slowly and deliberately through the room, moving furniture, opening old trash cans, and generally just mucking up the old factory as they looked for me and my companions.

Were there only three of them? Harvey, Stan, and Mister *I'll go forward.* I closed my eyes, casting my senses out into the room with a small dash of my magic. I found Jack close by, his body twisted into a pretzel inside some kind of protective container. I noted three moving bodies, which confirmed we were evenly matched. And then just to make sure he was okay, I cast my senses further, looking for Abram.

I found the son of a bitch on the ceiling. *How even?*

There was a *slight* possibility we could get out of this unseen. Clearly, we all had decent hiding places. If we could just hang tight, the militiamen would get bored and decide we weren't in this room, and move on to the next. At least, that's the lie I told myself.

In reality, I heard the metal clang of something being opened, and Stan yelled, "Hey!" followed by the tell-tale *snick* of Jack's blade unsheathing.

Dammit. Guess we wouldn't be sitting this fight out.

I wiggled out from under the machine, my boobs smashed into the floor as I did the worm. A gunshot cracked through the warehouse, sending me into panic mode. My hips got caught under one of the rollers, and I had to do a strange shimmy-shake to extricate myself. By the time I got my legs free and rolled over to get up, Harvey was standing over me with his gun trained on me.

"Hey, sweetheart." The older man grinned, exposing three missing teeth. "Aren't you a looker?"

Then a wild blur of motion rammed into the militiaman. Harvey grunted and pitched sideways, smacking the concrete as his gun slid across the floor.

Abram offered me a hand. "He hit on you. So I have to hit him now. Okay?"

I stood and brushed off the seat of my jeans, giving Abram a little growl. "You do you, bad boy."

While my boyfriend leapt on poor Harvey to defend my questionable honor, I looked across the factory to find Jack yanking his sword out of another militia man's chest. The third was already in a crumpled, blood heap on the floor next to an old mailbox—presumably where Jack had curled inside to hide.

"Well," I said, planting my hands on my hips as Jack and Abram joined me by the roller machine. "I like when I don't have to lift a finger. But I'm *starving*. Can we get out of here before more assholes show up?"

~

AFTER A LATE LUNCH of bologna sandwiches and instant coffee that tore a time-space continuum in my gut, I had an extremely tearful goodbye with Lulu. The guys gave us space, either because they were kind and compassionate men or because the blubbering sounds we were making were more terrifying than the roar of a chainsaw next to a Versace gown.

Either way, I promised that both her son and I would return to her in one piece. Probably a really dumb promise to make when I couldn't back it up with experience or science or even an astrological horoscope, but I did it anyway.

Then Abram, Jack, and I set out on the first leg of our journey.

Nobody waited outside the apartment for us as we skipped down the cracked front steps and Jack led us north. For whatever reason, only those three militia guys had followed us to the warehouse through whatever redneck investigation they'd been running. So we'd been able to return to the apartment and prepare for departure without harassment.

Regardless, we walked quickly and silently so that we wouldn't draw any undue attention to ourselves. Jack kept us to side streets, alleys, and shadows as we headed north. We were in the home stretch, and getting caught now would have been like blowing a heel in the first five minutes of Coachella.

We weren't on foot for long before the kid pointed at a parking garage and pressed a finger to his lip to remind us to stay quiet. The garage looked a little worse for the wear, with ivy growing up the outside and several chunks of concrete missing, exposing the inner rebar. The closest entrance-slash-exit had caved in on itself, so clearly no cars were coming in and out of this piece of junk.

But Jack ducked through a slit in the chain-link fencing surrounding the garage, and then leapt over a low concrete wall to the interior. Abram and I exchanged glances that said, *Alright, this kid is nuts, why are we following him?* But I just sighed and wedged my butt through the fence to join him on our next great suicide mission.

Kid's been fence hopping since he was a toddler, so there was that.

The inside of the garage was even more silent than the world outside, and the concrete hadn't fared much better. Full grown trees jutted up the center courtyard, and weeds stretched out among various cracks and holes. More than once, we had to re-route to avoid a massive sinkhole. Our footsteps echoed off the low ceilings, and somewhere nearby, water dripped incessantly. Even the air seemed colder in here, rushing in off the water and lowering the temp enough to make me raise the hood on my sweatshirt.

Jack led us up a nearby staircase, where the steps seemed like they might crumble beneath our feet. They held steady anyway as we circled several times up the narrow stairwell and then exited on the top floor.

There were cars up here. I blinked into the cloudy daylight, estimating at least thirty vehicles spread across the open roof. Jack reached into his shirt and pulled out the necklace that held his house keys, then tugged the cord over his neck. A moment later, an alarm chirped two rows over

"You have a *car?*" I asked, surprised.

"Mom's old car. She pays my pal Benny monthly to store it here."

"Your pal Benny, huh? What nefarious rebellious thing is he up to?" I made sure to let a note of teasing into my words so he would know I was just messing with him. "Why haven't we seen any cars until now?"

"We aren't allowed to use cars within city limits, since we could mow down the militia in a single go. But Darcus hasn't cut us off completely from being able to leave the city. There just isn't much gasoline to come by." He lifted the bag he'd been carrying by hand and unzipped it, revealing an old plastic gasoline can. "I got us enough for a trip to New Haven."

I gasped. "New Haven? But you said it was gone."

"It is. Mostly," Jack added, cringing. He cut through a line of cars, making a beeline for a little Honda CR-V with its lights on. "But it's also one of the most powerful vortexes of supernatural energy in the area. Ramsey had to harness that power to build his portal to Grimoult. So that's where we're headed."

Conversation ceased as Jack carried his gasoline canister to the gas tank to fill 'er up. I had to admit a pang of nervousness about going to my childhood home. I'd hardly had a chance to come to grips with the idea that New Haven as I knew it had been razed by Darcus in his rise to power. Now, I would have to see the damage for myself, which made it all too real.

Before I had to decide what door to open, Abram folded himself into the back seat of the CR-V. I didn't recognize the car—Lulu had been driving something nicer the last time I stayed at her house. I circled around and climbed into the passenger seat, fastening my seatbelt with my heart pitter-pattering a bit faster at the road that lay ahead.

A moment later, Jack slid behind the wheel and cranked the engine.

"I can't believe Ramsey and Briar have completely taken over Grimoult," I said, baffled at the thought. "It's a tourist destination!"

"*Was* a tourist destination," Jack amended, shifting the car into reverse. "It hasn't been that for about ten years now."

"Is any tourist destination still around?" I asked. "Bora Bora? Turks and Caicos? The Maldives?"

Jack laughed. "I don't know. You'd have to ask someone who has the means to find out. I'm not carrying an airplane in my pocket."

As he pulled out of the parking spot, I said, "Not be *that girl*, but how are we going to get out of the garage? The entrance was completely covered over and there are more holes in the floors than my Grandma Nancy's homespun lace."

Jack raised an eyebrow at me as if I'd asked a silly question. "The secret entrance."

"Oh. The secret entrance. Duh," I said sarcastically, then slouched down in my seat for the ride.

And in fact, there was a secret entrance below ground, with a ramp that spilled us out onto the main road. Jack turned north and headed for the edge of the island, where we would have to take a bridge to the mainland.

I watched the overgrown husks of buildings creep by, catching a glimpse here and there of a couple walking or a child playing on sparse grass. But even up here, away from the epicenter of midtown, the once beautiful hustle of NYC had faded into memory.

I was having a mental meal at my favorite trattoria when we slowed to a stop. Jerked from my daydream of chicken parmigiana and fifty dollar cabernet, I sat up to look out the windshield and see what was holding us up.

We were at a standstill behind a line of vehicles waiting at the edge of the bridge. In the original New York, waiting to exit the island was a fact of life.

But here—there was a militia checkpoint.

"Jack, why are there militiamen on the bridge?" I hissed, my heart pumping.

"They do this sometimes," he said absently. "Like a quality control check. No big deal, they'll just scan us and send us on our way."

"Except Abram was just in jail!" I reminded him.

"They scanned me multiple times during booking," Abram added helpfully, as if a reminder of his costly temper tantrum was good right now.

Jack's eyes turned toward me, luminous blues as big as saucers. "Well, shit."

CHAPTER 10

JACK and I stared at each other for half a moment as the reality of our situation sank in.

"*Well shit* is not helpful!" I finally snapped, my mind whirling. I propped an elbow on the door and laid my head in my hand to control the dizzying feel of the world collapsing around me. "This would be just our luck. Seriously. First, Mr. Man-Tantrum back there, now this."

Abram shifted forward, his upper body closing in between us over the center console. "It was not a 'man tantrum.'"

"Honey, I love you," I told him, cupping his gorgeous face between my hands, "but you're the king of man tantrums. Now get back there before someone sees you."

Abram growled, his face settling into an annoyed glare as he disappeared back into the backseat. I'd probably pay for that later, but whatever damage had turned him into this shadow of his former self wasn't helpful for our situation. I didn't know how to fix him, but I swore to myself I'd figure it out eventually. At the moment, however, we had more pressing issues. Like not getting caught because of his man tantrum and subsequent jailing.

The black sedan ahead of us eased forward as the line

shifted, and I gritted my teeth. "We need a plan. Can militiamen sense magic?"

"Definitely not," Jack said without hesitation. "They're almost always human. And conduits never staff these blockades."

"Makes sense. Conduits wouldn't dare demean themselves into being government lackeys." I rolled my eyes, then whipped around in my seat to meet Abram's dark gaze. "I can turn you into a dog. They don't chip dogs do they?" I directed the latter at Jack.

"Not that I know of."

"You're not turning me into a dog," Abram growled. "As if I'm some animal—"

"You are at least *part* animal," I cut him off coolly. "But you can't be the beast unless you want them to kill us with those big guns. So stop being a diva and give me permission to make you a dog."

"Just make me invisible!" he roared as the car inched forward once more.

Jack shook his head. "See that black arch ahead? It's a thermal scanner. They're going to know there are three of us in this car before we reach the bridge checkpoint. It's a failsafe to make sure no one leaves the island unaccounted for."

I turned in my seat again and glared at Abram. "Hear that? You've got two seconds to give me permission before I do it anyway. I'd rather not do it against your will, but I will to save your life. And mine. And Jack's, because Lulu would kill me, which would also save mine times two, so the odds are really stacked against you here."

A muscle ticked in Abram's jaw. "I want it to be known that I protest this situation."

"Protest it later after we survive it," I told him, then called on my magic to do my bidding.

With as little fanfare as possible, I wrapped my power around Abram and coaxed his form to morph into a big, fluffy black dog. In my adult life, I'd never had a pet, so I didn't have a well of lost loves to pull from. But after my dad disappeared and was never heard from again, my mom decided to get a "guard" dog. Fluffy had been a big bear of an animal and on sight, she was frightening as hell, but in reality, she was the biggest baby. She was the most useless guard dog, but a steadfast cuddler.

The spell clicked into place, and Abram's body shimmered and changed. His long legs shortened, his arms tucked into his barrel chest, and his torso folded in on itself. His head was the last to morph, which was oddly terrifying, before his nose elongated like a B-movie werewolf and dark fur sprouted all over his skin.

Then, it was no longer Abram sitting in the backseat.

"Oh my God! You look just like Fluffy!" I lunged between the seats to bury my hands in the soft, slightly curled hair around his floppy ears.

Abram growled, baring his sharp, white canine teeth at me as he backed away from my touch. Petulant jerk.

"Is that anyway to treat your master?" I cooed at him, getting entirely too much enjoyment out of the situation. I reached for him again and earned a soft nip at my fingertips, but if I wasn't mistaken, there was a hint of amusement coming from my doggy boyfriend, too.

At least he wasn't *completely* furious with me. Or maybe he was amused by thoughts of how he would make me pay for it later...though I'd never minded his ideas of payback before.

We finished our creeping momentum toward the bridge in strained silence. I clutched at the seatbelt crossing my sweatshirt as if it could anchor me to the car. Too quickly, we watched the car ahead of us drive away up the ramp and onto the bridge, and then...it was our turn.

Jack eased between the roughshod orange traffic cones and followed the instructions on the sign ahead to cut the engine, then put the keys in the cupholder.

Fight or flight turned my body to a livewire. I didn't like having the car off. At least with the engine running, Jack could have floored it to get us out of there if the situation turned dangerous. I focused on taking deep breaths, forcing the panic back where it came from.

Two men in green fatigues were waiting in the middle of the road, clutching their machine guns with placid faces. In the seconds after the engine shut down, they split around the front of the car, one heading for Jack's window and the other for mine.

My heart fluttered so quickly I thought it would stop altogether before the militiaman even made it to me. Fortunately, I didn't have a heart attack, nor did I stop breathing, so I rolled down my window as he approached.

"Morning, ma'am," he said, tipping his black New York Yankees hat in my direction. I somehow didn't think the Yankees were playing ball anymore, and considering the distressed look of the ballcap, the damn thing might as well have been considered a relic at this point. But the guy was older than me, maybe late thirties, early forties, and had likely been a fan long before the world ended.

I offered him a wan smile. "Officer."

From outside Jack's window, the other man spoke up. He was younger—hardly older than Jack—and looked a lot more jumpy with his finger hovering near the trigger on his weapon. "Where're you folks headed?"

"Connecticut, upstate," Jack said with a charming smile. "We received word that one of my elderly aunts needs help. She's been living in her house alone for fifteen years now, and she's ailing. We're headed to pick her up and bring her back to live with us here in the city under Darcus's protection."

"Good plan," the militiaman said approvingly. "You are aware that every new resident to the city will have to be registered upon entry?"

"Yes, sir. I'll ensure we have her birth certificate and prior government ID on hand before we reach the checkpoint."

Jack had clearly done his homework and knew how this kind of thing went. Probably that came with the territory in his secret life as a rebel.

My attention had remained firmly on Jack and his verbal sparring partner, so it took me a few moments to realize that the man outside my window had trained his shrewd gaze on the backseat.

On Doggy Abram.

My heartbeat seized, and my magic rolled over beneath my skin, ready to fight. Could he sense that there was something a little too human about the dog? Did he have some kind of weird magic sense that told him something was off? Every muscle in my body tensed, and I tuned out Jack and the other soldier, who were still chatting amicably.

As if he could feel my gaze on him, the militiaman looked away from Doggy Abram to me. For a brief moment, his craggy face looked suspicious, but then he broke out into a smile. "Newfoundland?"

Relief washed over me, and I laughed. I'd been so close to screaming, however, that the laugh came out a tad too high-pitched and damn near hysterical. "How'd you know?"

"I love dogs!" the militiaman said. The tone of his voice and the way his smile turned his face years younger made him look like less of a threat. "Is he friendly? Can I pet him?"

"He's very friendly," I said, giving Abram a pointed look. I snaked an arm behind my seat and hit the button to roll down the automatic window.

Abram growled under his breath as the glass rolled down.

"Well, hello, handsome man," the militiaman cooed, reaching in to ruffle Abram's ears. "Who's a sweet boy? You're a very sweet boy."

I bit back a grin as I watched over the seatrest. Okay, yes, it was *highly* dehumanizing for me to let an enemy soldier love all over Doggy Abram. But we were only in this mess because Abram got stuck in his own head, ran away instead of talking about his feelings, and got himself locked up. If he'd just talked to me last night, we could have worked through his issues like adults. Instead, he screwed up all our plans and landed himself a starring role as Fluffy.

So as far as I was concerned, this was his just desserts.

~

ONCE ON THE highways beyond the city, my heart rate found a level closer to living woman. I undid the spell on Abram, albeit begrudgingly, and the three of us lapsed into silence as the landscape whipped past.

This wasn't the world I knew. Obviously, I'd already come to understand that inside the city, but out here, the idea that everything had changed really sank in.

A few gas stations still operated here and there, but for the most part, everything we passed looked like cannon fodder. Nature had begun its creeping descent to take over abandoned houses, long-dead businesses, and roads now less traveled. Very few cars joined us on the road, and even fewer could be seen navigating any of the side streets off the exit ramps.

It really felt like we were all alone in the world.

When old, chipped street signs began to announce upcoming New Haven exits, I sat up straighter and watched my surroundings for any hint of familiarity. I'd driven this highway a hundred times during the early days of my mother's sickness, coming back from working in the city to check in on her, to make sure she had food and comfort.

But...even this didn't look familiar.

Jack seemed to know exactly where he was going, though. Considering they'd moved to the city when he was just a kid, I had a feeling his familiarity with the outside world had a lot to do with his super secret rebellion job.

Every time I remembered that he'd placed himself in a dangerous position, I had to bite my tongue and shove away an almost motherly panic that something might happen to him. Because seriously, it wasn't like what we were currently on the road to do was any safer than whatever he got up to on a daily basis.

We took the first New Haven exit. I knew from past experience that this was the outskirts of the city, a leap and a jump from my mother's old neighborhood in the downtown area, and even farther from Lulu's suburban home which sat on the other side of town.

Or used to.

Jack navigated down a broken road, watching the pavement with unblinking eyes so he wouldn't run over debris or chunks of asphalt. The road buckled and waved beneath us —nature had done its job a little too thoroughly here. We passed a dead McDonald's, a strip mall with all its windows blasted out, and then turned into an old Wal-Mart parking lot.

The parking lot was empty, and the giant warehouse store had been bombed to pieces. It was missing half its roof and an entire chunk of one corner, and the bank of glass doors had been destroyed so that a craggy maw opened onto darkness.

"Going shopping?" I asked Jack as the car bounced over the cracked parking lot.

He scoffed. "Nothing left in there but wildlife. Most everything was looted after the blast."

I shivered, trying not to think of how many people I'd once known in this town. How many might have died.

"We're going to park out back," Jack went on. "Then take a path through the woods. Ramsey's portal is a couple hours on foot."

Behind the Wal-Mart, Jack pulled behind a giant dumpster that had been knocked on its side, half-hiding the car from view. I shoved my door open and stepped out into a chilly, gray afternoon, broken glass crumbling beneath my boots as I slammed the door and went to get my bag from the trunk.

None of us spoke. I couldn't speak for Jack or Abram, but the eerie silence cut through me. There should have been cars whooshing past on the road. Voices calling from the front of the building. Heavy machinery cranking and whirring nearby as new buildings were constructed. This may not have been the heart of New Haven, but it wasn't a rural area, either.

Yet it was deathly silent.

"Don't leave the path," Jack said as he shouldered his backpack and then reached over his head to shut the trunk door. "Not for anything."

Chills froze me to the ground. "Why?"

Jack's gaze flicked to me, then back to the forest stretching dark and foreboding ahead of us. "When Darcus blasted the veil between this world and the supernatural world, things came through that shouldn't have. Ramsey's magic protects the trail, but not the woods. And that's where *things* like to hide."

I clutched my canteen against my chest so tightly my fingertips began to grow numb. After Jack got his pack settled, he motioned for us to follow him to a narrow, slightly overgrown dirt path that arched off the parking lot and into the pitch black trees.

Abram stepped up beside me and put his arm around me. He squeezed me against his side and pressed a kiss to my temple—seemingly forgiving me for the whole dog thing in the face of my fear.

"We'll be fine," he assured me, and then gave me a gentle push ahead of him. "I've got your back."

I nodded and swallowed back the pounding of my heart as I followed Jack into the forest—and hoped the *things* wouldn't find us.

CHAPTER 11

I'D DONE my fair share of stomping through the woods as a teen. Mostly, those trips involved a lot of rough-and-tumble guys, my giggly girlfriends wearing peak "notice me" fashion, and a case of the cheapest beer Roger Moore's older brother would buy us. The days were long and the nights were longer, and I'd kissed most of those boys by high school graduation. Including Roger's older brother.

But this trip into the woods was so far removed from those days of underaged drinking and dreaming of a life outside New Haven, that I couldn't firmly grasp the idea we were still *in* the city where I grew up.

The moment we passed into the thick, dark wall of woods, we lost all ambient light. Not even a hint of red, evening sunshine pierced through the heavy canopy overhead. Suddenly, we were in a tomb-like dark, even the path invisible under our feet. The atmosphere felt heavy and oppressive, weighing on me like twenty-thousand leagues of ocean over my head.

Jack's arm brushed against mine, and I heard him unzip his bag. The darkness was so absolute, I couldn't see his form beside me, even though we were close enough to touch. A moment later, a round beam of light clicked into existence, eerily illuminating the gloom. Then he passed a second flashlight to me, and a third to Abram. At least he'd come prepared.

"Have you been here before?" I asked him as I switched on my flashlight, adding more light to our little circle.

"Once," he replied. "A couple years ago. Ramsey brought me out here before he and Briar went through to live on the island permanently. So I'd know how to reach them if I ever needed them."

I thought of my old friend in his tweed coat, patches on his elbows as he led a younger version of Jack onto this path. My friends thought I'd disappeared, along with Abram, but even in our absence, they'd kept in touch with one another. Protected one another. A tingle of warmth suffused me. Sometimes the families you make along the way are the ones that last.

Armed with light, we set out, leaves and twigs crunching beneath our boots. The path had overgrown a bit, with weeds and wildflowers growing up in the middle of the dirt path and branches hanging in head range, particularly dangerous for Abram, who's noggin lived north of the clouds. Despite that, however, there was still a clear delineation of the path versus the rest of the dark forest, which eased some of my worries. Though...I wouldn't have put it past myself to veer off the path by total accident and get eaten by some otherworldly beast.

The way was too narrow for any of us to walk side by side, as much as I wished I could cling to Abram's strong, sturdy arm. I followed in Jack's wake, while Abram hovered close behind me, a Char sandwich moving farther and farther into the hell woods.

I was okay, holding it together with my flashlight and a prayer, when I caught a flash of movement in my periphery.

I came to an abrupt halt and jerked my flashlight toward

the woods. Abram had no warning and bounced off my back, then gripped my shoulders to keep me from punting off into the trees. But not before my flashlight leapt from my numb fingers and hit the path, skittering into the trees.

The scuffle alerted Jack that he'd lost his ducklings, and he circled back to join us. "What's wrong?"

I stared into the deep abyss of the forest, my heartbeat fluttery and weak. "I saw something."

Jack glanced at the woods. "You're going to see a lot of things out there. Your best bet is to keep your eyes straight ahead and stay on the path. We're safe on the path. Ramsey made sure of it."

"What if Ramsey's protections have failed?" I asked, my voice coming out low and a little more fearful than I wanted it to.

"Are you a conduit or not?" Jack asked impatiently. "You have an entire world of magic at your fingertips."

"Monsters are scary, okay?" I shot back with a withering glare. People seemed to have this misconception that magic fixed everything, but that was far from the truth. Especially for a girl who'd hardly cracked five percent of what was possible with her powers. Maybe if my father had stuck around for my teen years, I might have been a little more capable.

Instead, I was just a scared little girl.

Jack opened his mouth to retort, but then he glanced at my empty hands. "Where's your flashlight?"

I pointed at the trees. "It fell."

"You dropped it," he clarified.

"I wouldn't have dropped it if Abram hadn't bumped into me!"

"You stopped so fast, it's a miracle *you* aren't lost to the trees," Abram snarled.

I pursed my lips, taking a deep breath before I asked, "Could we not pick on Char right now? She's fragile and wearing supermarket denim."

Jack rolled his eyes, and Abram tried to cover a smirk. But they both dropped the subject.

As Jack whirled on his heel to get us back in motion, I thought about breaking the tension by coming up with something motherly to screech at him, like "Don't walk away from me when I'm talking to you!" But I was too on edge, even for humor. Abram nudged my lower back, and I set off after the kid, thinking a good smack in the back of Jack's golden head still wasn't off the table.

I tried desperately to ignore the constant rustling. The streaks of gray and white beyond the barrier of trees. The low growls of things much bigger than us. These woods were alive with all manner of ghosts, ghoulies, and monsters, and the worst part was just how close the trees were. If I even stumbled and threw an arm out to catch myself, my hand would disappear into the darkness. Prime catchings for a quick cryptid. One grasp, and I'd be jerked into the woods quicker than Naomi Campbell fell off her blue, nine-inch mock crocodile heels at the '93 Paris Fashion Week.

So I kept my arms coiled tightly against my torso. The beam of my flashlight bounced wildly ahead of me, and mostly on Jack's back which did little to help light our way. But I liked my arms still attached to my body.

Off to my right, a massive thump in the undergrowth sent terror skating through me, and I shrieked, then whipped around to grab Abram's flashlight. I jerked it out of his hand and shone it on the area where the noise had originated, attempting to swallow back the heartbeat in my throat. It wasn't even that I wanted to see the monster—it just seemed better to have my sights set on a real, visible threat instead of an invisible one.

But the flashlight couldn't pierce through the pitch black.

Abram placed an arm around my shoulders and tugged me into his chest. I leaned in, letting his warmth suffuse the chill I couldn't shake. His lips pressed against my forehead, and his fingers squeezed my shoulder. "You are safe with me."

"I thought you were mad at me," I griped, glancing up at him. Jack had stopped farther up the path, his light beaming onto the ground as he gave us some privacy.

In the soft glow of his flashlight, Abram's elegant eyebrow arched up. "You let the soldier *pet* me."

"You liked it," I teased. "I saw the way your eyes closed and you leaned into his ear scratches."

"Absolutely not," Abram said, "And I'll make you pay for it later. But I am not mad at you. I am…mad at myself."

"Do you want to talk about it?"

"Not here." He glanced around us, his dark gaze searching the woods. I couldn't help but wonder if he could see things I couldn't with his heightened beast senses. "I'd like to keep moving. If you please?"

Honestly, his admission that he wasn't mad at me went a long way in soothing my nerves. I damn near glowed like a Swarovski crystal necklace on Beyonce's rockin' collarbone.

I tiptoed and kissed him soundly. Perhaps a little too soundly, with my boobs pressed against his chest and a bit of a hip gyration that earned me a low growl of approval and a slap on my ass that I felt in my panties. In my defense, Jack couldn't see us, and it had been entirely too damn long since I'd taken my boyfriend to bed.

But, unfortunately, this nightmarish hellhole was *not* a bed, and I had to end the kiss. Eventually.

I was still tongue-deep and raging with desire when something poked me. Not the good kind of Abram poke, which I was thoroughly enjoying the feel of against my pelvis, but a sharp, rough jab in my neck from behind.

I screeched and leapt away from the touch. Abram snarled, throwing himself bodily in front of me, while Jack's footsteps pounded on the path as he raced back toward us.

How could one walk through the woods have been so wrought with chaos?

I peered over Abram's shoulder and shoved the flashlight I'd stolen into his hand, looking for the source of the poke. God forbid it had just been a low hanging branch, and I'd come out looking like a hysterical princess.

No. This wasn't a natural low hanging branch. A humanoid shape just beyond the tree line chuckled, waving the spindly branch in his hand around in front of Abram. It was taller than Abram, with glowing red eyes and a body formed of gray smoke.

"Your lust smells delicious," the creature hissed. "Won't you come into the forest so I can lap it up?"

"Ew," I breathed, clinging to Abram's shirt. The back of my neck prickled, and I just knew that the other side of the forest was watching this behind me. A hundred monsters, waiting for one of us to fall off the path and become a four-course meal. Nowhere was safe.

"Keep walking," Jack said sharply, tugging me ahead of Abram. "He can poke you with a stick, but he can't get to you on the path. Also," he added, glaring at Abram, and then me, "keep it in your pants."

We fell back into formation, moving quicker than we were before. After having my delightful moment with Abram rudely interrupted by a monster who wanted to "lap up" my desire, I had no desire left but to get the *fuck* out of these woods.

THE REST of the walk took another thirty minutes of doing my damnedest to ignore my surroundings. Ramsey hadn't held back on making sure the portal to Grimoult was isolated and protected. As much as I hated him for putting me through this, I also understood why he'd done it.

Finally, I saw the opening in the trees ahead of Jack.

Purple twilight spilled beyond the barrier, growing larger as we trotted toward the end of the path. Blessed relief rushed through me, and I picked up the pace, holding my breath until we passed beyond the trees and into a wide, open clearing.

High overhead, stars were beginning to wink to life as the sun made its descent to the horizon. The air here smelled fresh and clean, like snow on mountains, and the oppressiveness of the forest had vanished beneath the sky. Though the woods still surrounded the clearing on all sides, a thick, dense fog undulated around the perimeter, as if to hide the nightmare from view for anyone lucky enough to have found their way.

I took a deep breath of that crisp, cool air and then folded dramatically onto the soft grass. Cool blades, slightly wet from the fog, tickled my cheeks, and I rolled over to stare lovingly at the stars. "Oh, thank God. No monsters here. The stars are beautiful, like a shimmery, pearlescent foundation on the face of the earth."

Abram stopped beside me and gazed down at me, amusement clear on his face.

Jack ignored my theatrics and headed toward the center of the clearing, where a single thick-trunked tree grew straight up into the sky. He circled around, disappearing on the opposite side so we couldn't see him. A second later, the disruption of magic vibrated on the air, and then Jack groaned.

"The way is shut down for the night," Jack said, glancing at the purple sky as he came back around the tree to join us. He hovered over my head, addressing Abram. "We're too late to make it through tonight. The magic will reactivate at dawn."

I cringed. "This is my fault, isn't it?"

"The woods are hard to deal with. Nobody blames you for the delays," Jack replied. "We'll just have to make camp and wait for sunrise."

I motioned to the forest. "We have to sleep surrounded by *that*?"

"The fog will shield us. That's what Ramsey put it there for," Jack assured me, dropping his pack to the ground. He nodded to a nearby circle of stones, filled in with dirt and gravel—a fire pit. "Think you can get us a fire going with your magic?"

"Sure." I rolled to my knees and stood, brushing dirt and grass off my butt as I walked to the fire circle. Once I got a fire whipped up, the light and heat chased away some of the fear I felt over being surrounded by the forest.

We settled around the fire, and Jack popped the top on three cans of pre-made beef stew. He set them within the fire to cook, using a metal kebab stick to stir them so that they heated evenly. Surprisingly, the stew turned out to be *not* awful, if a little salty, and it did chase away the final niggle of terror chilling my bones.

"What are you going to do about the beast tonight?" I asked Abram. I could tell he was holding back the transformation as much as he could, but eventually, he wouldn't be able to stop the beast from coming out. The night was his domain. "You can't exactly go into the woods."

"Why not? It might be good sport." He tipped up the last of his stew, and then tossed the can onto the ground.

"There are like a thousand of them with a thousand different ways to kill you, and only one of you. I'd rather you come back to me in the morning."

A gentle smile spread across his handsome face, and he pulled me close, tucking me against his side. "I'll sleep here. In beast form."

I wanted to talk to Abram and dig into the reasons behind his attitude problem of late. Even I knew that dredging up old pain and illogical worries while isolated in a clearing with Jack wasn't a great idea, but I hated this big thing hovering between us and keeping us from being who we were before our year apart.

But he let out a weighted sigh, and reluctantly released me. He couldn't fight the beast off any longer, anyway.

Jack and I began to clean up our things from dinner to give Abram some semblance of privacy. He stalked off towards the edge of the clearing, the fog swirling around his hulking form like a curtain. I shoved our three empty cans into a plastic bag and deposited it into my backpack, trying not to listen to the snaps and snarls taking place within the fog.

Then a moment later, Abram returned.

His beast had always reminded me of a wolf, though much larger and walking upright on his back paws, like a human, though he could run like a wolf if he needed to. Coarse, black fur covered his body, and he had a long snout with fang-like teeth that could do some serious damage in a fight. His already large, muscular torso became bigger, and his powerful hind legs made him incredibly fast.

He was terrifying, but also kind of beautiful. Maybe that was because I loved him.

Jack and I unfurled our bedrolls and got under the threadbare blankets we'd brought. I had no pillow on which to lay my head, so I had to make do with my backpack. Abram curled up on the other side of the fire, his dark, beastly gaze trained on the roaring flames. I was extremely thankful he'd stayed tonight, especially after the mindless panic I'd been through the night before when he disappeared. So I fell asleep watching his form waver beyond the firelight.

Something awoke me much later.

The flames had died down to glowing embers, and the clearing had grown cold without its heat. Sunrise touched the sky with hints of rose and amber, and the fog still formed a barrier between us and the woods.

I shivered beneath my thin blanket as consciousness crept

back in with icy fingers. It took me several moments to realize what had awakened me.

Beeping.

Every muscle in my body protested as I sat up too quickly and looked around, trying to place the source of the sound.

Beep. Pause. *Beep.* Pause. *Beep.*

My gaze landed on Abram beside me. At some point while I'd slept, he'd moved around the fire to join me. He was in human form, the beast having gone back to hibernate now that the sun was rising, but he was still curled up on the ground instead of his own bedroll, dressed in a change of clothes he'd packed.

And in the wrist where Alan embedded his tracker, a red light flashed under his skin in time with the beeping sound.

Beep. Flash. Pause.

"What the..." I reached out and shook him awake. "Abram! Your wrist!"

As his eyes blinked sleepily open, a masculine scream emanated from the woods. Followed by another. Then another. Until we were surrounded by terrified cries and panicked gunfire.

Jack leapt to his feet, unsheathing his broadsword, just as a handful of militiamen barreled into the clearing.

CHAPTER 12

Surprise rendered me useless for about two-point-five seconds. I sat on my uncomfortable bedroll with every root and stick beneath me digging into my ass while half a dozen men in fatigues rolled into the clearing brandishing automatic weapons. I couldn't even lift a finger through my haze of shock.

How the *fuck* had they found us? We were in the middle of nowhere! New Haven didn't *exist* anymore beyond being a crater in the ground with a few big box stores and laundromats rotting on the outskirts. Even accounting for the fact Jack's car could be easily found in the Wal-Mart parking lot if someone were looking, the soldiers would have had to *find* it to begin with—and we were almost two hours away from the city. In an abandoned dead zone.

But...there was the beeping. The flashing red light inside Abram's wrist.

Mother fucker. They'd tracked us. That was the only explanation.

Beside me, Abram launched to his feet and raced across the clearing, heading for the mass of militiamen. I expected him to reach for the sword he'd picked out back at Maisy's pawn shop. The sheath was propped up against his backpack near the dying fire, easily accessible and ready to be wielded. But he lunged right past it.

Instead, he morphed into the beast.

My skin raced cold and rooted me even more to my seat. Beastly Abram barreled into the soldiers—who looked as surprised by this turn of events as I felt—and I just continued to sit on my happy ass, reveling at the fact my boyfriend had just gone beast in the daytime. On command.

Abram's curse had always been to turn at night. He lived a half life as an immortal human, and the other half as the beast. But I'd never seen him just transition whenever he felt like it or whenever the situation warranted it. It was a nifty trick, and one that would likely save our lives.

But...I understood now that the Abram who had come back to me wasn't the Abram I knew before. Even his beast had changed. I needed to be a little more patient and sensitive with him, clearly, since he was going through some shit.

Balk later, I told myself. *Get up and blast these guys now.*

Jack's sword clanged nearby. I swiveled toward the too-close sound and panicked as I realized the kid was parrying sword-to-gun with a militiaman, and they were both headed my way. They were also both unaware of my body in their path.

I kicked at the covers, only to find they had managed to tangle around my legs in a kind of irreversible sailor's knot. The soldier side-stepped closer, still trying to get his gun up beneath Jack's blows to shoot him, and I kicked even more frantically. What the hell had I done in my sleep? It was like trying to get out of wet Spanx.

Before I could unentangle my legs and get out of the way, the soldier backed right into me. He tripped over me and went down hard, his gun flying out of his hand and bouncing across the grass.

Jack raised his sword to make a killing blow, but I

panicked. I had no idea what Jack did for the rebellion, and frankly, I didn't want to live with that knowledge because it might make me blubber. Adult or not, he was still little toddler Jack in my head. So the fewer people he murdered in cold blood, the better for my conscience. Totally selfish, I know.

I threw both my hands up, deflecting Jack's blow with a blast of white magic, while casting a sleeping curse on the soldier with my other hand. The militiaman conked out immediately, adding his snores to the rest of the chaos erupting around us.

Jack glared at me for intervening, but at my sheepish grin, he stalked away to help Beast Abram with the rest of the soldiers.

I rolled to my hands and knees. The woods were redolent with the echo of gunfire—presumably from the dumbasses who had left the path and found themselves up against creatures a lot worse than a ragtag band of rebels. Air displaced near my face and my hair whipped forward, then a split second later, a great clod of dirt burst up from the ground.

Holy shit, I almost just got shot.

I leapt to my feet and reached for my magic, all of my limbs tingling with fear. Abram was in the middle of a crowd of soldiers as their guns barked. Lucky for my boyfriend, his beast skin was tough and nearly indestructible.

Jack, on the other hand, was not graced with bulletproof hide. As magic gathered in my fingertips, a militiaman lifted his gun and aimed for Jack.

Oh hell no. I promised my bestie I'd bring her boy home safe.

I let loose with a volley of fireballs that made my hands look like a flamethrower. Orbs of fire seared through the group, skirting around Abram and Jack, but sending all the soldiers stumbling away with their hands thrown up to protect their faces.

Both Abram and Jack took advantage of the distraction to leap in with killing blows, while I switched from fire power to more sleeping curses. Even though these men had come here to either kill us or take us into custody, they were only doing what their superiors ordered. I couldn't in good conscience just let my two companions murder them all. Not when there was another option.

I blasted two men back-to-back, sending them to snoozeland, but before I could aim for the next, a fist came out of nowhere. The blow hit me on the side of my face, and I went down like a sack of bad, off-the-rack Liz Claiborne tops. As I slammed into the ground, Abram snarled, and then hot blood spattered my body.

Ugh. Blood was a bitch to get out of cotton.

My head still rang from the punch, but I managed to get back to my feet and knock out a few more soldiers until the clearing fell quiet. All the scuffling and shrieking in the woods had petered out, too, and I doubted that was because those soldiers had gotten away.

A few feet away, Beast Abram hovered menacingly over a fallen militiaman who was cowering on the grass, whining like a puppy. I hurried over to them as Abram morphed back into his human form.

Jack joined us and pointed his broadsword at the man's neck. Abram put a boot to the man's chest, shoving him firmly into the ground, and I cringed at the distinct crunch of bones cracking.

"How exactly did you find us?" Abram asked, a dangerous edge to his voice.

"Don't bother lying," I added. "I'm pretty sure I've already figured it out."

A trickle of blood traced its way down the man's face as his blue-eyed gaze darted between the three of us. He gulped. "Your chip," he rasped, addressing Abram. "When you were locked up, they turned it into a tracker. Standard procedure."

"Is it standard procedure to chase an escaped prisoner across state lines?" I asked.

"It is when his escape killed four people," the soldier barked.

"Touché. No need to yell." I lobbed one more sleeping spell and put him to sleep before Jack could get angry enough to skewer his neck.

"Dammit," Abram snarled, his voice low and gravelly as if he were still in beast form. He reached for Jack's sword. "I have to cut the chip out. We can't allow them to follow us to Grimoult."

"Not necessary," Jack said, pulling his sword from Abram's grasp. "Not having a chip is a death sentence in this world. If the militia sense you don't have a chip, they shoot first, ask questions never. Once we get to the island, we'll be out of range for their technology. Ramsey can get you a replacement."

Suddenly, a brilliant flash of magic illuminated the clearing from the central tree. I tossed up an arm to shield my eyes and thought, *What fresh hell…*

In the aftermath of the glow, black dots danced around in my vision, and I felt the tell-tale sensation of magic rippling through the clearing. Then Ramsey Duldridge himself appeared from the other side of the tree.

Tall and thin with striking, aristocratic features, Ramsey had dark hair combed over and wore a lame cardigan sweater over pleated pants with wire-framed glasses perched on his nose. Not for the first time, I wondered how on earth Briar had fallen for such a professor type. During the years we'd been each other's competition in the industry, her tastes had run more toward sexy jocks and my ex-boyfriends.

Regardless, Ramsey had been my closest friend for the past year of my life, which for him was a decade-and-a-half ago, but seeing his friendly, familiar face was exactly what I needed.

He looked around, his mouth dropping open ever-so-slightly at the bodies strewn about the clearing.

"Most of them are alive," I called out, just to clarify.

His gaze whipped over to me, and his mouth opened even more. "Oh my... Char!"

I grinned. "Hey, old friend."

Ramsey loped across the clearing and snatched me up in a big bear hug. "You're not dead!"

"Well, it was touch and go for a while," I joked as he released me back onto my feet. "These militiamen like their guns."

Ramsey cupped my face in his hands and turned me left, then right. "You're going to have a bruiser."

"You should see the other guy," I quipped. "He's asleep. That's all. I'm as lame as your corduroys."

Ramsey laughed. "Still the same old Char." He released me and turned to greet the others. "Jack Carroll. You've grown a foot."

Jack offered Ramsey his hand. "Good to see you, man."

"You remembered the code," Ramsey said approvingly as they grasped hands. "I got your message the moment I awoke." He turned to Abram, shaking his head in disbelief. "I'm so glad to see you both alive and well. Fifteen years, we've thought you were... Well. Miracles do happen, huh?" Then Ramsey took another good look around the clearing, letting out a long, low whistle as he surveyed the damage. "Looks like you guys had some fun here."

"Is *fun* the word we're using?" I asked with a grimace. "How about we get out of here before my sleeping curses wear off? I somehow don't think they're going to wake up any less angry."

Ramsey nodded. "Indeed, that seems safest. Follow me!"

He led us back to the tree, with a brief stop at our small campsite so we could grab our things. As I rolled my bed pallet back up, I noted there was a swirling portal superimposed on the tree. It looked a lot like the portal Jack had used to get us to this timeline.

"Are we going back in time again?" I asked as I lugged my backpack over to the tree, where Ramsey waited.

Ramsey's eyebrows lifted towards his hairline, and he looked at Jack, impressed. "I'm going to need to hear *all* about that. But no—this is a portal through space. It shortens the distance between two places like an accordion. One step, and we leave New Haven for Grimoult."

"Well, what are we waiting for?" I asked, shouldering my bag. "The beaches await!"

GRIMOULT TURNED out to be the only place that looked anything like it had fifteen years ago.

When Abram and I vacationed there in the previous timeline, the small, tropical island boasted clean, white beaches, quaint strip malls, well-maintained beach houses, and its own cursed monarchy. We'd shaken things up a bit, broken the curse, saved a bunch of lives, restored the palace, locked away the mad king, and given the whole damn island to my arch-nemesis Briar Templeton.

On the other side of the apocalypse, all the stores and restaurants still existed, even if the strip malls were being used for things other than tourist dollars nowadays. The beaches stretched below the cliffs like ribbons of white satin, even now dotted with sunbathers. Seeing Grimoult like this helped me deal with the way everything else had changed. One constant in a world of chaos helped.

And another constant was Briar herself.

Briar's vivid red hair was pulled up into a ponytail as she sashayed down the front steps of her castle home and made a beeline toward me.

"It's about time you fucking showed up," Briar hissed,

poking me in the chest with a glint in her cat-like green eyes. But then her glare fell away, replaced by an even, white smile I knew she'd paid several thousand to have, and she tugged me into a hug. "God, Char! We thought you were *dead!*"

"Nope, we were just kidnapped," I said into her ponytail. "Jack stole us right out from under you and Ramsey the night after we saved the genie."

Briar stepped back, her elegantly red-lined lips falling open. "So you've been in the future for the past fifteen years?"

"Well, no. That night was just a few evenings ago for us." I shrugged helplessly. "Time travel, man. It's a weird thing."

She reached out and squeezed my arms, her gaze roaming over me as if she were seeing me for the first time. "Regardless, I'm glad you're here now. Come in out of the heat! I'll have Angelica whip us some snacks and drinks."

Even during the apocalypse, ex-cover girl Briar Templeton kept staff. I couldn't even be surprised.

We passed into the castle, which was cooler and dimmer than the bright, beachy world outside. The place had been a lot more dreary and rundown the last time I saw it, but now I could see touches of Briar in every aspect of the interior decorating. She'd always had expensive taste, and it appeared she hadn't lost her desire for beautiful things at exorbitant prices. Sculptures and original artworks lined the halls, and expensive tapestries helped tame the drafts inside the giant stone castle. I peeked into rooms as we passed them, noticing that none of the original furniture even still existed. Briar's credit card had been busy.

We paused outside a pair of polished wooden double doors, and Briar kissed her husband on the cheek. "Go on in, sweetheart. I'll inform Angelica that we have guests."

She reached out and took my hand, squeezing my fingers with a fond smile, then tapped away in her high heels.

What a queen. I hated her as much as I loved her.

The dining room overlooked the backside of the castle,

where a dramatic cliff swept down to the beach. Abram and I had dined in this room multiple times before, accompanied by a raunchy, misogynistic king with a BDSM complex. Of course, our time here had also led to some of the hottest sex I ever had in my life, so I could hardly complain.

I peered out the window at the ocean, where the waves rocked and rolled against the shore. On Ramsey and Briar's little slice of paradise, you couldn't even tell the rest of the world had come to a halt.

"Are Huntsman and Stacey here?" I slid into a seat at the table and smiled up at a petite brunette who appeared from nowhere and set an ice cold glass of lemonade before me. "Lulu didn't really know them, so I figured she wouldn't have an update."

Ramsey's face fell. "Oh. Um, well, nobody has seen Huntsman since your disappearance. He hardly ran in our circles, though, so his running off wasn't all that strange."

I inclined my head. "You're right. But Stacey? How's our resident psychic witch?"

Ramsey glanced down at his own glass without answering, and a pit yawned open in my stomach. I narrowed my gaze. "What happened?"

He cleared his throat, still avoiding catching my eye. "Stacey lived with us here on the island until about six months ago. She accepted a mission into the city..." He trailed off and heaved a sigh.

"Ramsey, spit it out," I snapped. "What happened to Stacey?"

Finally, he lifted his gaze to meet mine. "We have reason to believe she was taken...by Darcus."

CHAPTER 13

Nausea rolls in my stomach. I think of Stacey, with her boy-short haircut, dyed pale pink, and the matching lipstick that made her look like a cupcake. She was a short and petite pixie, like Tinkerbell, and she was a chain-smoking, trash-talking oracle. The last of her line, in fact.

There's no way she had a chance in hell of surviving Darcus.

Oracles weren't made for war. Their only superpower was talking in circles about your future until you wanted to throttle them.

While I was lost in my thoughts and reeling from the news, Briar returned and slid into the chair beside her husband. She took one look at my face, then slapped Ramsey on the shoulder. "You told her."

"She asked!" he replied, waving his hands uselessly in the air.

The little bit of normalcy in their relationship wasn't enough to make me feel better about Stacey. Everything in this timeline had gone topsy turvy. My friends and family—which is what I considered Alice—were in danger.

"How?" I asked quietly. "How did he get his hands on Stacey?"

"We aren't sure," Ramsey said, a note of defeat in his tone. "She went with a group of rebels into the city six months ago. They were tasked with surveillance on Darcus's compound so that we could pump up our dossier on the place. We never heard from any of them again."

"So you're just guessing Darcus took them," I clarified, relieved.

Ramsey reached for the lemonade on the table in front of him, but pulled his hand away before he picked it up, as if he didn't know what to do with himself. "No, unfortunately not. Stacey sent us a message before their communications stopped. All it said was *Darcus*."

The backflips in my abdomen came back and kicked the bass up a notch. "Oh. I guess that's pretty damning. But no one ever went after them? To see if you could save them?"

"We don't exactly have a huge army," Briar spoke up snippily. "Every team that goes on a mission knows they're on their own if something goes wrong. We can't put everyone in danger when there are so few of us."

"But the island looked full! I saw a hundred people lounging on the beach when we arrived!"

Ramsey smiled sadly. "All the citizens of Grimoult are still here, Char. We didn't kick them off the island when we decided to provide a safe haven for supplicants."

Some of my earlier excitement about what they'd been doing here oozed away. I'd let myself believe we were walking into a ready-made army, and all I'd need to do was figure out how to lead the charge. Instead, Ramsey and Briar had gathered a bunch of scared kids, and we were no closer to defeating Darcus than when I stepped blind through the time portal.

Beside me, Abram slid his big arm around my shoulders, and I leaned into him, drawing strength from his presence. In the year we'd been apart, I'd missed this—how he always seemed to know when I needed comfort.

"So what's the big plan, then?" I asked after a few moments of silence dragged on and made my skin crawl. "All the supplicants just hide away in a tropical paradise while Darcus destroys the world?"

Briar bared her teeth at me in an expression highly reminiscent of the day I took the Gap commercial out from under her. "No, *Char*. We have a plan. A long term plan."

"I don't think we're looking at a 'long term' in which to stop Darcus before he turns this world into The Hunger Games," I pointed out.

Ramsey placed a hand on Briar's shoulder as if to say *Down, girl*. She immediately melted back against her seat and crossed her arms over her voluptuous chest. He would have been a handy man to have around when the two of us were constantly vying for runways.

He sat forward and leaned on his elbows, catching my eye. "We could build an army of supplicants thousands strong, and still, we wouldn't have enough to beat Darcus and his army of conduits."

"Then what's the purpose of all this?" I fluttered a hand in the air, indicating the whole of Grimoult. I glanced at Jack, who was sitting in silence on my other side. "Jack said you were preparing an army. If that's not what you're doing…then what *are* you doing?"

"The way I see it," Ramsey starts, "is the only way we'll have a fighting chance against Darcus is to bridge the gap between conduits and supplicants so that both sides are fighting for the same rights."

"You're talking convincing an entire race of beings that Darcus, their leader who is offering them the world on a silver platter, is evil. Ramsey, that's not possible. Convincing people to sway their beliefs is a pipe dream."

"Maybe in the world of yesteryear," he said coolly, adopting that professorly tone I'd come to know and loathe. The man could be sweet and kind, but when he felt like he knew more than you, he turned into a mansplainer. "But this world is different. Even conduits feel the oppression. Darcus may be pretending the conduits are free to use their power and live their lives, but only on his terms. Many have already come to recognize his dishonesty."

"Okay. So ignoring the idea that getting conduits to switch sides is *crazy*," I said, "how on earth do you plan to get supplicants to agree to this? Every supplicant I've ever seen provide blood for a conduit was doing it under duress. Either begrudgingly because they needed to save the world or being bribed into it for something they needed in return."

"I'm not sure, but I have a feeling we can make it happen," Ramsey said firmly. "Especially now that we have you to guide us."

Right. No pressure at all.

～

WE SPENT much of the day getting a tour of the island's supplicant neighborhoods. Despite Ramsey's *'throw glue at the wall and hope it holds'* method, they had built something pretty impressive here on Grimoult.

There were five neighborhoods of modular homes that each housed several supplicants. Each neighborhood had been provided with a training area, both an indoor arena and outdoor fields, in which to work with the island's few resident conduits on their magic.

And despite my misgivings, there were conduits on the island. Ramsey hadn't been pulling my leg. Quite a few of them, who'd seen right through Darcus's plot from the beginning. Abram and I spent some time talking to all of them, both supplicants and conduits, and getting a feel for the climate. Most of them wanted a chance to take down Darcus —they were just waiting for the missing link.

God help me, but that missing link was me.

The sun was already sinking over the sapphire ocean when Abram and I walked into our room at the castle. I'd specifically chosen this room—the one we'd stayed in when it had been King Archibald in charge. Briar had done a bit of redecorating and given the room more of a feminine, designer-esque touch, but the bed was still the same hulking four-post monstrosity Abram had bent me over and whipped me on before fucking me senseless.

I slid my fingers over the fresh white duvet, a pulse between my legs as I imagined sliding between those soft, expensive blankets with a naked Abram. After everything that had gone down since the moment we walked into this apocalyptic wasteland, I was *done* waiting to touch him again. So I whipped around with my best, most seductive face, and sat on the edge of the bed. Straightening my back to put my boobs on display, I opened my legs and bit my lip.

And probably looked ridiculous. I wasn't used to being in off-the-rack jeans and a hooded sweatshirt, but I had to work with what I had.

"Do you remember what happened the last time we were in this room?" I asked him, keeping my voice low and husky.

Abram's eyes darkened. The effect was so immediate, it sent a thrill racing through my body. But he remained rooted just inside the door, his gaze raking over me like he could see through my clothes. "I do."

Okay. His interest was a good sign, but the fact he was still holding back made me think I needed to pull out heavier artillery. I tugged my sweatshirt off over my head, taking my time as I exposed my bare skin beneath. I was wearing a borrowed bra from Lulu, and bless her but it wasn't exactly a sexy La Perla of satin and lace. So I reached behind my back and released the clasp, then let it slide to the floor.

Abram's lips parted and he stalked several steps forward. I could see the long, delectable length of him pressing against the front of his jeans.

Progress.

I turned around, giving him my back as I unbuttoned the jeans. Hooking my fingers in both jeans and underwear, I slowly peeled them down my body, bending over until my bare ass was in the air. Then I stepped out of the pile and crawled onto the bed, keeping my back to him and my legs open. Cool air from the open window brushed against my already throbbing pussy, but I wanted it to be him touching me.

"Do you remember the way you punished me?" I asked over my shoulder. The floor creaked under his feet, and I shivered. I could feel his gaze on me.

He drew up behind me, and his presence seemed to suck all the air from the room. "I remember you liked it."

I rotated my hips and spread my legs wider on the mattress. "Do you want to do it again?"

A low growl rumbled in his throat, and Abram's hand smacked into my ass, then his fingers squeezed. "You push me."

I moaned as the smack made my body tremble. I felt it deep inside me, and I wanted him to do it again. Sliding back on the soft blanket, I hitched my ass higher in the air and lowered my upper body toward the mattress. "You aren't going to push yourself, so someone has to."

I wanted *my* Abram. Our reunion sex hadn't felt right—it hadn't been enough. Then we'd immediately been whisked away to save the world again. All I wanted was to feel this man's body on mine, to taste his love on my lips.

He just had to take it.

Abram's breathing had grown shallower. He gripped both of my ass cheeks and spread me wide, and I could feel the burn of his gaze on my folds. One hand drifted over until his thumb slid between my legs and dipped into my wet core.

"*Abram,*" I moaned his name and backed up against his thumb, pressing it deeper into me.

He readjusted, and his index finger slipped in. With his other hand, he slapped my ass again. Then he crawled on the bed with me, his body arching over mine as he slipped another finger inside.

"You are the most exquisite creature," Abram murmured, his voice reverberating through my chest. His fingers worked between my legs, building a delicious heaviness inside me. "How do you do this? Make me feel like all will be fine?"

"Because everything *will* be fine," I said breathlessly, rocking against his hand. "This is us, Abram. The real us."

But suddenly, he stilled. Every muscle in his body grew tense, and another low growl rippled through him. His weight disappeared from my back, and the absence of his hand left me shivering just beyond the edge of my orgasm.

"Abram?" I turned around on my knees.

His nose had begun elongating. The beast—it was coming out. He gave me sad, puppy dog eyes that reminded me of Doggy Abram, then he raced from the room.

Of course. Just when we were about to make a breakthrough.

I took my time in the lavish jacuzzi tub, shaving all my bits and parts while using up way more of Briar's expensive soap than necessary. Then I wrapped myself in a fluffy robe and sat on the edge of the bed to comb out my hair.

At least this time, Abram hadn't been running away from me and the idea of being intimate again. He'd been ready to open up to our past, to revisit what we had before we lost everything. Even better, I knew he would be safe out on the island tonight as the beast, and I would be safely cuddled up in bed, waiting for him to return. We would be okay. One day.

I froze, the brush stilling in my length of wet hair, as movement caught my eye on the floor. My first thought was *Mouse! Rat! Vermin!* And I leapt to my feet on the mattress, holding the brush out like a weapon, as if I'd get close enough to a mouse to beat it with the damn thing.

But it wasn't a rat. It was a *cat*.

He had vivid orange fur striped through with darker orange tabby stripes. He had a smooshed nose and wide face, and his tail was the longest I'd ever seen.

"Oh my goodness," I said as my heart rate pulsed back to normal. I sat back down and patted the covers beside me. "Look at you! Where did you come from?"

The cat looked at my hand patting the blankets, flicked his tail twice, and then launched up to join me. He sat on his haunches, wrapping that long tail around his front legs and began to purr as I scratched his ears.

"You came out of nowhere," I told him, rotating my fingers under his chin. His purring grew louder and he closed his eyes, leaning into my touch. He had silky soft fur that begged to be petted. "I didn't take Briar for a cat person."

"She's not," the cat said.

I screamed and rocketed away from the little cat, falling off the other side of the bed and onto the hard floor. I took half the blankets with me, tumbling into a tangled up pile on the Oriental rug.

The little cat didn't seem too surprised as he padded over the remnants of the blankets and peered over the edge of the mattress at me. "Are you alright?"

"Y-you can talk!" I pointed at him, as if there were some other talking animal in the room.

The cat sat down in that same regal pose. "Indeed I can," he agreed. Seeing a cat's mouth move like a person's was incredibly alarming, and the voice was craggy and deep like the ocean. "I'm an ancient god. I could dance for you, too, if you wish."

"Please, no," I said meekly. "The talking is enough."

"As you wish."

I disentangled myself from the bedclothes and stood,

putting a little more distance between me and the cat. I realized I was still holding the brush, and quickly placed it on the dresser behind me. "Did you, like, possess a cat? Or are you a shapeshifter?"

He laughed—a deep sound for such a tiny thing. "I can take whatever form I wish."

"So a *god* took the form of a *cat*, and walked through time and space into my bedroom."

He blinked. "Yes. Though it does sound quite mad when you put it that way."

"Okay. I'm processing." I crossed to the lion-footed armchair in the corner behind the bed and sat heavily, rubbing a growing knot of tension between my eyebrows. *When I thought things couldn't get any weirder...* "Why are you here?"

"I am sympathetic to the plight here on Grimoult," the cat said simply. "I've come to give you some information that might help you make your way."

Swiping my hands back through my wet hair, I pulled the whole mass off my neck and then motioned for him to go on because I didn't trust myself to speak.

"Wonderland is a rebellion group being run by an old friend," the cat said. "They will be allies to you, and I've sent word to them regarding your arrival here."

"Um, thanks?" I said, wondering if he meant an old friend of *his* or an old friend of *mine*.

"You're most welcome. Unfortunately, there is a downside. Darcus is operating a small subterfuge to undermine Wonderland. He's issuing propaganda and siphoning off kids who are seeking the real Wonderland."

Shocked, I let my hair fall back to my shoulders and said, "Jack was right. Kids are being kidnapped, but not by Wonderland. But Lulu's right, too. Alice *did* go to join the rebellion. She just got hoodwinked by Darcus."

"That seems to be the long and the short of it," the cat

said wryly. "If a little confusing, put into your own terms. May I continue?"

As if the god cat was being *any* less confusing. I held up both hands in apology. "By all means."

"Ramsey has the right idea," the cat went on. "You must find a way to bring the supplicants and conduits together so they're fighting for a common goal. This is the only way you will defeat Darcus."

"That is an impossible task," I pointed out.

"Perhaps you should believe in impossible tasks?"

"Ugh!" I threw my hands up in the air and stood to pace the floor. The wood creaked and groaned beneath my bare feet. "Can't you give me *any* advice?"

"The gods do not interfere in mortal affairs."

I paused in my pacing and narrowed my eyes at him. "Yet you're here now."

"With information," he said shortly. "Jack Carroll is hiding things from you. It is long past time that you have a chat with the boy."

"About the rebellion stuff he's doing in the city?"

"No. About who he is and how he managed to pull you and the beast Abram from the past to join this fight."

I stopped pacing again and faced the cat, my hands dangling at my sides as I considered what he'd said. Jack had definitely been withholding, but it wasn't as if I'd asked questions. I'd made it a point to stay out of his rebellion stuff so that I wouldn't be suspect with Lulu. But was there more than just his work in the city? "How *did* he find me and bring me here?"

"Only blood can find blood," the cat intoned.

I made a face. "That's helpful."

"I can give you one piece of advice to take with you into tomorrow," he offered, as if he were giving me a pair of two thousand dollar heels, and not more cryptic *information*. "Seek the real Wonderland, where your allies are waiting for you."

"And how do I find the real Wonderland?"

The cat shrugged. "Perhaps you'll do impossible things in the morning."

"If you talked in bigger circles, you'd talk us right off the cliff out back."

The cat leapt daintily off the bed, his paws silent as he strolled. His tail swished behind him as he walked toward the door, and I rounded the edge of the bed to watch him go.

He paused in the middle of the floor, where the glow of the moon slanted through the open window and illuminated his fluffy little head. "Heed this, Charisse Bellamy—the battle will be dangerous, and there's a very real chance you might not survive."

Then he vanished, disappearing slowly like ashes on the wind until nothing was left but moonlight.

CHAPTER 14

Brilliant Grimoult sunshine spilled through the open window on a breeze heavy with salt and sea. I stretched and rolled over beneath sheets that felt like clouds on my skin to find Abram asleep beside me.

For about ten seconds, I gave myself this little bit of peace —to watch him breathe, the sunlight turning him into a golden god, while the room smelled like the islands. In another lifetime, we would have been here on vacation, eating until we couldn't move, buying tropical beverages with little umbrellas from street vendors, and turning into lobsters on the beach.

And making love. Lots and lots of making love.

Then I got up, quietly threw some clothes on, and went to interrogate Jack. As much as I wanted to stay right where I was, that wouldn't get me any closer to answers, or any closer to defeating Darcus and making the world okay again.

I found Jack sitting on a bench in the palace gardens overlooking the ocean. He was sharpening his broadsword with a blade tool, and even though his hands were moving confidently through the motions, his eyes were on the horizon.

Instead of launching into a tirade about how a talking god

cat told me Jack was keeping secrets I needed to know, I perched on the bench beside him and casually said, "Hey."

He glanced at me, his boyish face enigmatic. "Hey."

"You okay, bub?"

Jack shrugged. "Did you know when Mom was a kid, her family went on a vacation to the beach every summer?"

"Yeah, I did know. I've been on a few of those vacations with her."

He nodded, looking down at his sword and sliding the sharpener purposefully with a metallic *snick*. "She used to tell me stories. She always planned to do the same for me and Alice, but then…"

"The world ended."

"Yeah." *Sniiiick.* "So I guess it just kinda sucks to be here. Like Mom would love it, you know?"

"Why didn't you guys just move here?" Now that I really thought about it, I knew Ramsey well enough to know he would have offered for them to come the moment Grimoult became a safe place.

"I think she always hoped more of our family would show up. She doesn't know what happened to any of her cousins."

I nodded, looking back out over the ocean. Lulu had always been a family kind of girl. If she had any feeling that her cousins might still be out there somewhere, I could see her making the decision to stay and be there to help when they arrived.

"Have any cousins ever showed up?" I asked.

"One. He lives in our building. Liam."

I grimaced. I'd had a few rounds in the sheets with Liam when we were teens, then I apparently "broke his heart." This according to Lulu, of course, who never let me live it down.

But basically, I was just wasting time talking about anything but what I came here for. I couldn't keep putting off the reason I'd sought him out, even if I hated to pry into his life. He was just a kid. One look at his face was enough to remind me of that.

"Jack, something happened last night."

His lips quirked up into a half-smile. "Char, I adore you, and Abram seems like a nice man, but what you do in the bedroom..."

"Ew! Oh my God, you perv." I punched him in the arm, but his ridiculous amount of muscle just hurt my fist. "No. A cat showed up in my room. A talking cat."

At that, Jack laid his sword in his lap, the sharpener stilling in his hand. He raised a pale eyebrow. "Cats don't talk. Not even in the apocalypse."

"This one did," I said stubbornly. "And he told me that you're keeping secrets I should know. Something about how you were able to time travel to get me. Only blood can find blood. Or something."

Jack's blue eyes slid away from mine, and he stared down at his sword. It gleamed in the sunshine, so brightly it burned my eyes, but he didn't seem to notice. "I guess I should tell you. You have a right to know."

The subdued note in his voice made me want to instantly remove my question from the conversation. "Shit, Jack. What did you do?"

He took a breath and set his sword and sharpener aside, then turned to fully face me. For a brief moment, he was a toddler again, turning to face me on Lulu's massive couch as he raised his small, chubby hands. *Patty cake, Aunt Char?*

This Jack, twenty-year-old Jack, raised a hand and shoved it through his mass of blond hair. His dad's hair. I kept forgetting he'd lost his dad before he ever had a chance to know him. At least I had my dad for a decade of my life before he shouldered a gun and walked into the woods, never to return.

Jack spoke. "I'm a conduit."

I clutched the edge of the bench because I felt I'd sway

right off if I didn't latch on. A breeze filtered past me, coming in off the ocean, and I closed my eyes and breathed deep. "Why didn't you tell me?"

"Nobody knows. Not even Mom."

Opening my eyes again, I said, "What about your…the rebels you work with?"

He nodded. "They know. But nobody else."

"You should have told me," I said sternly. "Being a conduit isn't a bad thing. But what about… So you're a beast like Abram?"

"No, actually, I'm not." He blew out a breath. "The rebellion did a…procedure. It's a separation of the magic and the beast. It was risky, so that's another thing I'd like to keep from Mom."

"Risky, but it worked?" I clarified.

He nodded.

"Wow." I slouched over and let my elbows rest on my knees. "Things just got real weird, real fast. What about Darcus's conduit army? Are they de-beasting?"

Jack shook his head. "No, this was a procedure created by someone in the rebellion. The same someone who helped me time travel to you."

Only blood can find blood. "Who?"

Jack reached out and took one of my hands in both of his, then met my gaze. "Your dad."

Chills raced across my skin, though I wasn't sure if they came from the cool breeze or Jack's words. "My dad's dead."

"No. He's not. He's here—well, he was," Jack added, releasing my hand as his eyebrows knitted together. "We were in constant contact during my procedure, and while we were concocting the time portal. But I haven't been able to locate him since we returned."

My heart thumped painfully in my chest as I sifted through this new, and alarming, information. "But he never came home. He just…left. I never saw him again."

Jack shrugged helplessly. "I don't know his story. Only that he told me he was your dad, and he wanted my help getting you here."

"*He* was the one who brought me back? I thought that was you and Lulu!"

Before Jack could elaborate, we were interrupted by Ramsey coming down the path. He waved, a big grin on his face. He looked dapper in a sweater vest, Oxford shirt, and pleated khakis, with his wire-framed glasses perched on his nose and his brown comb-over windblown.

"Breakfast is ready in the dining hall," he told us, motioning back toward the castle.

Honestly, I opened my mouth to say, *Oh, good. I could eat a Gucci bag.* But what came out was, "I want to go to Wonderland."

Jack and Ramsey both looked at me like I'd lost my damn mind. To be fair, I wasn't entirely sure I hadn't. Between New Haven being blown up, talking cats in my bedroom, and now a resurrected father, my sanity had become a tenuous thing.

"Nobody knows how to get to Wonderland," Jack told me.

"Well, actually, I might know someone," Ramsey said as he shoved his glasses farther up the bridge of his nose. "But it's dangerous to get to where he lives."

I rolled my eyes. "As if everything in this godforsaken world isn't dangerous? Who's the guy?"

"I don't actually know *who* he is, only that they call him mad. He apparently hatched a plan against Darcus, and worked with Wonderland to put his plot into motion, which means he knows who they are and where they are. But when he was caught, Darcus cursed him to his current predicament."

"What's his current predicament?" I asked, my skin tingling at the thought of what Darcus could have done to this poor rebel.

Ramsey held out his hands. "I don't know. All I know is it's driven him insane."

"So we're going to seek help from an insane person," I said. "Good. Great. I love how our plans get stranger and stranger. What's next? Flying elephants? A turtle fashion pageant?"

As Jack and I got to our feet, I continued listing weirder and weirder things on the walk to the palace, until both my companions were laughing so hard their sides hurt. I shelved our conversation about my dad for a later date. Seeking out a crazy man who'd been cursed by Darcus didn't feel like any kind of a normal—or safe—plan, but it was the only plan we had.

I just hoped we didn't die along the way.

WE LEFT the castle after breakfast—me, Jack, Abram, and Ramsey, holding overnight bags stuffed with clean clothes, a few non-perishable items, and weapons.

Lots of weapons.

On the steps of the palace, Briar kissed her husband like she would never see him again, and it didn't make me feel any better about our chances.

Ramsey led the way, and I wasn't too entirely sure where he was leading, but he seemed to be confident about his choices. I was, too, until it became clear we were walking out onto a dock toward a little motorboat.

I skipped ahead a few steps, leaving Abram behind with Jack, to tug at Ramsey's sleeve. I'd told him in no uncertain terms he couldn't traipse about saving the world in a sweater vest, so he'd changed into jeans and a t-shirt. I hardly would have recognized him if not for the glasses. "We're going on a *boat?*"

He hummed his agreement and stopped on the gently

waving dock to face me. "Wonderland doesn't exist in this realm. It exists in a half-world—a place between this world and the next."

"There's a *next* world?"

Ramsey looked at me over his glasses. "Char, do keep up."

I fought the urge to shove him right off the dock into the warm Mediteranean waters. "I haven't been on a boat since Kanye's yacht party, and I got seasick and threw up over the side in front of Leo."

"I don't know what that is or who those people are, but I'm sure you'll be fine." He tossed his bag over the side of the boat, then crawled in after it.

Once we were all settled in our seats—and I'd buckled myself into a lifevest—I clutched the handrails at my side and Ramsey set us into motion.

As expected, my seasickness reared its ugly head about ten minutes into the ride. Abram must have noticed how green I looked, because he gently pushed me over the railing and began rubbing my back in soothing circles. Of course my boyfriend would be so perfect that the constant up and down of the boat wouldn't affect him.

I closed my eyes and let the spray fly off the water into my face. Surprisingly, it helped. The cold mist gave me something else to focus on, and it cooled the heat rising in my cheeks. I stayed hunched over the railing the whole ride, and I didn't even throw up.

I'd be a yacht club member yet.

Ramsey cut the engine, and I sat up abruptly, thinking we'd made it to our destination. But the boat drifted completely out at sea, not a landmass in sight. I didn't trust myself to speak, because there was still a chance vomit would emerge, so I just looked at him in confusion.

"The portal is just ahead," he told me. "We can't go through with the engine running. It messes with the magic."

For a few moments, Ramsey hit the motor, then shut it off

multiple times, urging the boat forward at a slow, halting pace. I had to bend back over the edge of the boat and squeeze my eyes shut, so I didn't even see when we finally drifted through this supposed portal.

But I felt the magic wash over me.

Instantly, my seasickness disappeared. The portal passed over me like a cold waterfall, soothing all my aches and pains, calming my stomach, and even easing some of my worries. I sat up, glancing around for at least a glimpse of this healing portal, but instead, I saw an island looming right ahead.

The island jutted out of the water, long, wide, and mountainous, covered in dark forest and a vaguely threatening mist. A line of white beach gleamed beneath the sun, but the trees didn't seem to absorb any of the light at all. It was like the forest back at the New Haven Wal-Mart.

"The half-world," Ramsey explained. "Wonderland exists somewhere in this realm. And so does the man who can help us find it."

"Do hell-monsters exist in those woods?" I asked with a shudder.

"I honestly do not know," Ramsey said, his voice way too cheerful.

Great.

We parked the boat at a dilapidated wooden dock that hardly looked sturdy enough to support a dog, much less Abram's bulk and my curves at once. I braced myself as I shouldered my pack and stepped out of the boat, but chilled out when the dock didn't immediately crumble beneath me.

"Do we have a map?" I asked Ramsey as he joined me and Abram on the boards. Jack was strapping into his broadsword, his expression hard as he gazed at the dark woods.

"Well, no," Ramsey said with a grimace.

Jack stepped over the edge of the boat. "We're walking into *that* without knowing where the hell we're going?"

"Or what's in there," I added, rolling my eyes. "This is a suicide mission. We might as well go back to Grimoult. At least it's safe there."

Ramsey grimaced. "Char, need I remind you that you are the one who wanted to go to Wonderland. This is the way we get there."

I huffed and tugged the straps tighter on my backpack as I took off towards the shore. The longer I stood on this dock, the more I felt like I'd fall into the sea and be dragged away by the kraken. "This is not my fault."

"I do have a plan," Ramsey said from behind me. "Abram, this man is being held in an area of this island known for its grapevines. Do you think you could scent out the grapes and lead the way through the forest?"

I scoffed, about to say there was no way he could do something like that, when Abram said calmly, "Of course. I smell the grapes from here."

Apparently, I was wrong. And ew.

Abram took point, leading us toward a small, overgrown path in the trees. The beach radiated heat from the sand that I could feel through my boots, and I wished I could rip my shoes off and dance around with the sand between my toes. Instead, I followed Abram into the shadow of the trees, where the temperature dropped several degrees all at once.

And then we were inside.

Unlike the hell forest back at Wal-Mart, at least these woods seemed slightly more normal. Sunlight did pierce through the canopy, though it was dim and murky, as if we were walking underwater. Normal forest sounds surrounded us —the chittering of insects, birds singing and flitting through the trees. Those things went a long way toward convincing me strange humanoid beasts weren't going to try to eat me here.

We walked for a time before we had to leave the path. Every few feet, Abram would stick his nose in the air and sniff, and each time we remained on the path—what little path there was. But eventually, the time came when he sniffed the air and led us into the undergrowth.

I glanced back at the path, feeling as if we'd left the only thing protecting us. I knew it was a leftover feeling from Ramsey's magically protected path at Wal-Mart, but I couldn't shake the sense of foreboding.

The forest grew darker the farther we walked. Abram continued his sniffing and turning, while I studied the trees around us, hoping to see nothing bigger than a bird so I wouldn't run screaming.

My first clue that something wasn't right came when a tree branch slapped me in the back of the head. If the branch had been anywhere near us as we passed, it would have gotten Abram and Ramsey first, considering they were both taller than me. But it slapped against my head, and behind me, Jack unsheathed his sword with a surprised yelp.

I grabbed the back of my head, more surprised than hurt, and the three of us turned to look at Jack. He was staring up at the branches overhead, his eyes as wide as saucers. "It reached down and hit you, Char. On its own."

"The *tree*?" I balked.

Abram moved closer to me, pressing me behind his back as his dark gaze roamed the forest. "We are not alone."

The shadows had deepened around us. The only sunlight shafted down intermittently, forming spotlights on the pitch black forest floor. I realized then the birds had stopped singing, and the bugs had ceased chirping.

Movement flashed in my periphery. As one, our group jerked around to look that way, and I caught a glimpse of something pale passing just beyond one of the spotlights. Another flash, this time from the other side and too quick to be the same creature. Abram's claws lengthened and twisted, his beast reacting to the threat.

Then a tree branch snaked around my torso with preternatural speed and lifted me off the ground.

CHAPTER 15

I FLEW THROUGH THE AIR, leaving my stomach somewhere down on the ground with the guys. The strange, spotlighted forest pinioned around me as I rose, and adrenaline raced through my veins, making my heart thud painfully against my ribcage.

A tree had *picked me up*. Like it was a living, breathing monster.

The tree's branch gripped me beneath my arms and around my boobs, one titty in, one titty out in a *very* uncomfortable position. Luckily for me, being pissed about the uncomfortable grip on my breasts was enough to shove me past fear and panic and right into *Okay, what next?* territory. How best to pry my luscious curves from the tree's grasp?

"Char!" Abram roared from below my feet.

I glanced down to see him leaping beneath me, his hands swiping at my shoes. He was just far enough away that he couldn't reach me.

His voice spurred me on. I struggled against the branch, trying to dig my fingers in between my sweatshirt and the bark. The branch wasn't *that* thick, so if I could get my hands around it, maybe I could break it and allow for room to maneuver. But it dug so firmly into my body that I only succeeded in ripping off a few fingernails. It had me in a death grip.

I considered slipping out of my backpack and sweatshirt. Abram was *just* out of reach of my feet, and the tree hadn't yanked me any higher—yet. I had a spare shirt in Abram's backpack, since I was carrying food in mine, mostly. Not because I was a fat ass or anything, but because non-perishables were pretty light, all things considered, and I had the upper body strength of a lipstick tube.

But what would we do if the tree didn't let the food go? We'd be left in this weird, alternate realm without anything to eat.

Another branch began to snake around my legs, and I felt the distinct sensation of lifting. The beast was dragging me even farther into the canopy. If I let it do that, I'd get too high for a safe dismount.

Losing the backpack and shirt seemed like a better choice than two broken legs. That decided it for me. I ripped my arms from the backpack, finagled my poor, smooshed tits down beneath the branch, and then slid out of my sweatshirt, leaving me in only my jeans and tank top as I fell.

Abram caught me with a small *Oof*, and the two of us hit the forest floor, then rolled down a small incline. Ramsey cried out our names, but Jack hissed, "Everyone shut up!"

Abram's arms were warm around me as we came to a halt against a fallen tree. As we lay side by side on the ground, he looked over me, checking me for injuries. I wanted to quip that I thought I'd left my nipple up on the branch, but the silence that fell after Jack's command felt charged.

Something was happening. Something that was more than sentient trees and silent forest.

Abram pulled me to my feet, and we hiked back up the incline to join Jack and Ramsey. Movement in my periphery gave me pause, and I strained to see into the darkness, hoping like fuck it was only birds. Or squirrels.

But it looked bigger than that.

Jack held his broadsword out as he turned a slow circle, surveying the forest around us. Ramsey trembled beside him, holding a smaller knife that hardly looked big enough to skin a possum, much less take down whatever was hunting us.

More movement made me jerk to my right. Whatever beast flitted about out there was playing cat-and-mouse with us. I expected it to vanish, just like it had been doing. Instead, an abnormally tall, thin woman paused beneath one of the spotlights beaming through the canopy. Dull black eyes met mine, and a chill rippled through me.

She was completely naked, nothing but saggy skin and protruding bones. Raggedy black hair hung down her torso in clumps, full of debris from the woods. There was nothing in her eyes—no recognition, no focus, nothing even remotely human. Her skin was so pale, she glowed in the sunlight.

Then she ran, disappearing so fast, she was gone before I could blink.

I gripped Ramsey's arm. "Who is that?"

He shook his head, more times than necessary. "I-I'm not sure."

More movement from the left of our little group sent all four of us whirling around, weapons raising.

Another figure had entered a spotlight. A naked young man, so short and doughy that he was roughly the size and shape of a zero. He also had translucently pale skin, long dark hair filled with twigs and leaves, and those cold, all-black eyes. He vanished as quickly as the woman had.

"What the fu—" But I didn't finish my statement. The branches made a move again, and one wrapped around my face.

Abram swatted the stick-arm away from me and shouted, "Run! Get out of the forest!"

I fell into a sprint, listening to my three companions crash through the undergrowth behind me. We were in the thickest portion of the woods, with plenty of obstacles in our way, and I was *definitely* not an American Ninja Warrior. The first log I had to jump over took me down like it had reached up and grabbed me, and I would have disappeared into the brambly undergrowth if it weren't for Abram's beast-like reflexes. He put me back on my feet with a gentle shove, and I took off again.

Every tree we passed reached for our bodies. Jack's broadsword swung freely all around us, chopping off limbs before they could make contact, while Abram did the same with his half-formed beast claws. But even with the two of them working together, they weren't fast enough to catch every single one. Thin limbs scratched my face and bare arms as I ran, and I felt the warm drip of blood down my skin. A thick branch managed to wrap around my tank top and grind me to a halt, but Jack's sword took it out and we kept moving.

On the edges of my sight, the woman and man raced along with us. They were splashes of white in the darkness, dodging in and out of the sunlight beams with eerie loping motions. Where the four of us made as much noise as possible racing through the woods, those two made none. Just… utter silence. I wasn't sure what was more frightening—them, or the trees trying to steal me away.

I was moving so fast that I lost track of my surroundings. Everything was a blur. Trees whipped by, their branches waving wildly, some of them catching me, yanking my hair, scraping my skin. The strange spotlights blurred around me, and the woods became a strobe effect of light, dark, light, dark, light, dark…

I didn't realize when the ground angled down. Not until the last moment, and it was too late.

I pitched forward with a surprised yelp, but this time, Abram was on my heels and caught off-guard by the change.

Not even his beastly reflexes could save us when gravity took over. He flew forward with me, and then all four of us tumbled over the incline and began to roll.

The forest wobbled around me as I flipped ass-over-teakettle. I hit my head on something hard and stars burst in my vision, and the last few feet turned blurry and disorienting. The ground rose up to meet me with a jarring thud, and I rolled twice more before my momentum came to a halt on blessedly flat ground. Seconds later, Abram, Ramsey, and Jack barreled over me and stopped just beyond my grasp in a tangle of arms and legs.

"*Ow,*" I said, raising a hand to my head where I'd bashed into a rock or something equally as hard and unforgiving. Blood flowed freely from a deep gash in my scalp, and the wooziness in my vision told me I'd hit that rock harder than I thought.

Ramsey shouted, his voice breaking the unnatural silence, and then a commotion rose behind me. All three men began to yell and thrash. Jack's broadsword thunked against something solid.

But I couldn't move. I tried to look around for my friends and figure out what was happening, but the blow had incapacitated me. Somehow the signals were getting crossed from my mind to my limbs. I let my head fall back to the ground, trying to blink away the darkness edging my vision. I felt hard, rough branches entwining my body—roots, I thought absently, coming up from the ground. The trees had used our fall to their advantage.

My discombobulated brain didn't register the danger right away. Not until my ass began to sink into the ground like it was made of quicksand.

My eyes shot open, and I gasped, struggling against the branches. But there were a lot more this time—more than I could count, more than I could swat away. They were stronger, too, which in my addled brain made total sense, since roots were the strongest part of a tree. Long, snake-like branches wrapped me from my neck to my ankles, each of them exerting pressure on me, pulling me into the dirt.

"Abram!" I screeched as my legs vanished into the ground. Soil pressed in heavily on my body, and once my legs were underground, everything else followed a *lot* quicker. Some of the fog in my brain from my blow to the head dissipated, and my wits returned.

His answering call was garbled. All three of my companions were in just as much trouble as I was. And I realized with devastating surreality that no one was coming to save me.

But I had magic. I could save us. If I could just push past the spiderwebs in my head.

I renewed my struggling, lifting my head off the ground to keep it away from the dirt and the branches. As long as my head was above the surface, I could breathe and I could fight. I dug down deep and pulled on my magic, rotating through my options and landing on *Burn the fuckers off.*

I gathered as much power as possible, then with a yell, released it, putting massive amounts of force and intention behind the energy. My plan included slicing through the branches and watching them burn away—a two-fold slice and burn spell. Except something went wrong. Magic arced out from my body and shot through the forest around me...but the branches remained unaffected. Still squeezing. Still tugging me downward.

Son of a bitch! The dirt was to my belly button now, and my heartbeat jackhammered so hard, I was sure the branches could feel it. Were the trees immune to magic?

I resumed my thrashing, shoving my arms and legs against my bindings in an attempt to gain a little bit of leeway between them and my skin. They held tight, not budging, digging into me with supernatural strength.

Warm blood worked its way down my scalp. My blood

pressure was probably through the roof at this point, and so my scalp wound had begun bleeding again. At this rate, I'd bleed out on the forest floor before the trees could yank me underground and suffocate me. I gave a flick of my head to keep the blood from getting into my eye, and droplets launched off me onto the ground.

The minute my blood hit the dirt, it flashed bright gold.

I'd forgotten that this happened, honestly. When my conduit-slash-supplicant blood touched something supernatural, it reacted by glowing with magical light. Bad when a girl just wanted to hide from the supernatural things. Considering this whole forest seemed to be powered by the paranormal, it was no wonder my blood turned into a burning, mini-sun.

I turned my face away from the brilliant light as a horrible *screech* filled the air. The sound seemed to be coming from all around me and reverberated through the branches pinning me down. Several of the branches closest to my head—and thus closest to the spilled blood—recoiled, and my arms popped free. Shocked, I stared at my hands for a brief moment, then rubbed my fingers in the blood spilling down my face and swiped them on the branches around my navel.

The affected branches screeched louder and peeled away, and I let out a yell of triumph. I wasted no time painting my blood on the remaining branches like I was the Pablo Picasso of eviscera, and within moments, I was able to kick free of the dirt and launch to my feet.

"Char! What's going on?" Ramsey said, his voice small and pained. He was closest to me, the branches wrapped tight around his body as he sank into the ground. Beyond him, Jack and Abram were in similar cocoons, though Abram's head was nearly underground.

Panicked at the thought of my boyfriend suffocating in the dirt, I leapt over Ramsey and promised, "I'll be back for you!" Then sprinted to Abram's side.

The blood had begun to slow from my head wound, but I was able to get enough on Abram's branches to get him free. His torso burst up from the dirt and he coughed, rubbing at his chest as he caught his breath. I couldn't imagine the way the ground must have felt pressing in on his lungs. I really didn't want to imagine just how close I'd come to losing him.

Now wasn't the time for some sweet, romantic reunion in which we both declared our undying love, unfortunately. So I left him to disentangle his feet from the last of the branches and moved to Jack's side.

Jack's broadsword was sticking up from the ground beside him. The hilt was still clearly in his grasp under the dirt, but the blade was angled up, jutting half out of the ground and sinking by the minute. Before I could think twice, I grabbed the sword's blade and slid my palm up it to open a new wound, then smeared my blood all over Jack's branches. Blinding, golden light flared, and I tried desperately not to think of all the dirt and bacteria being rubbed into my wounds. There was a definite possibility that before it was all said and done, I'd get gangrene and die.

Whoever said I wasn't an optimist?

As I repeated my motions to free Ramsey, new screaming joined the trees' pained screeches. Angry screaming.

The naked woman and man stood beside one another in the nearest cone of sunlight. The woman held one arm up, her finger pointing dramatically at me and her mouth hanging unnaturally wide as she screamed. The man raked his hands over his face, fat wobbling, his own scream in harmony with hers.

Suddenly, the screaming stopped.

I hauled Ramsey to his feet, and Abram and Jack flanked us, both of them still holding their weapons. The ground beneath us was a wreckage of destroyed branches and roots, all of it still glowing faintly with the light from my blood.

We stared at the unmoving monsters. The whole forest seemed to be holding its breath.

Then they changed. Their faces grew sallower, the hollows deeper and darker. Two sharp rows of teeth elongated in their open mouths, and claws like daggers grew from their fingers.

My skin chilled. I clutched Ramsey's arm, both of us breathing faster.

The monsters charged.

This time, I didn't need someone to tell me to run.

CHAPTER 16

IF WE THOUGHT the two naked demons were simply playing with us before, they weren't now.

The trees had thankfully stopped trying to strip the skin from our bones or drag us into hell, but the monsters pursued us relentlessly as we crashed through the forest. Both demons moved *fast*. Too fast to see them properly.

Too fast for us to outrun.

Ramsey went down behind me with a frightened yell, and I whirled to find the man-demon crouching over him. The monster opened his mouth wide over Ramsey's head, all of his teeth sharp like tiny knives. Panic made my heart fluttery, but my hands and mind seemed to work on their own in the face of someone I cared for being in danger.

I tossed a ball of magic at the man-demon, brighter and more deadly than the magic I'd tried to use against the trees. The magic hit the man's bulbous body and ricocheted right back at me, so that I had to throw myself to the side to avoid being burned by my own magic.

Fucking hell. Did he have some kind of magical force field protecting him? Why was nothing in this forest affected by magic?

Abram appeared and swiped at the monster with his half-formed beast claws. Where my magic had failed, Abram's dagger-like claws opened deep wounds on the demon, and the man screamed. He launched to his feet and sprinted off into the forest.

I wasted no time yanking Ramsey back to his feet, and then we were off again.

"He didn't bleed!" I yelled as I leapt over a small bush and kept running. "Ramsey, *he didn't bleed!*"

"Yes, I saw!" Ramsey called back, and we both simultaneously skirted around a giant rock sticking out of the ground. "I think they're dead!"

I glanced over at him, horrified. "They're *what?*"

I'd miscalculated having the time and safety to look over at him. I rammed into something solid and glowing white, then bounced back onto my ass in the underbrush.

The woman demon. She opened her mouth and hissed at me, then lunged.

That preternatural blur of her body moving way too fast fell over me. Sharp claws pierced my torso, and her mouth opened over my head. But then Abram swiped at her like he'd done with the man.

His claws left deep divots in the skin of her face. Her skin puckered and opened, but inside was just black. No blood. No muscles. No bone.

Pain radiated from where her claws were still sunk into me. I struggled to breathe through the agony. Every move she made, her claws dug deeper, opened wider wounds. I realized a strange numbness was seeping over my body, radiating out from where she'd dug her claws in.

Holy shit. Was I being drugged by something on her hands?

She lifted her head and screamed at Abram, but then leaned in to finish me off.

"Hey, nightmare bitch!" Jack yelled. His voice was way out of place in the dark and the silence, but wholly welcome.

I glanced over to see that he had skewered the man-demon. His broadsword was buried to its hilt in the man's back, and the demon was trying desperately to swipe at Jack, but he was too quick and wily. It would have been comical, if I wasn't about to die.

"Abram, you wanna do the honors?" Jack asked. "I bet your claws could take off his head!"

The woman was distracted, her black eyes riveted on Jack and her companion demon. I took advantage of the distraction, dipped my fingers into the blood she'd drawn on my stomach, then rubbed it on her face.

It had worked on the trees, so it had to work on her, too. Right?

Wrong. She looked more ghastly with my bright red blood swept over her face like a warrior's paint.

She howled at me, then retracted her claws from my stomach and shot over the forest floor to her friend. Abram snatched at the man-demon, yanking him off Jack's broadsword. He dug his own claws into the demon, and began to transition fully to his beast.

"Run!" he growled. "Get out of here! I'll be right behind you."

As Abram kept his claws dug into the confused man-demon, he became a full beast and clashed with the female monster.

I tried to roll over so I could get to my feet, but whatever the demon had injected into me had turned my limbs to half-finished noodles. I was as useless as an intern on a runway in platform stilettos.

Lucky for me, Jack had the instincts of a damn soldier and could tell right away that something was wrong. He loped to my side, sheathing his broadsword on the way, and then put an arm around my waist to haul me to my feet. For such a bean pole, he was packing some serious strength under that sweatshirt.

He pulled my arm around his shoulders, lugged my curvaceous ass against his body, and screamed at Ramsey, "Go!"

Honestly, I did my best to make my legs work. Some part of me knew Jack couldn't carry me through the forest to safety. He didn't have Abram's supernatural strength. But whatever poison had seeped into my system from the demon's claws had re-routed all the sensations in my body and turned me to mud.

I was still clinging to consciousness when Jack carefully laid me on the ground in blinding sunshine. Somewhere close by, the two demons screamed.

"Abram?" I asked, terror working its way back through my paralyzed body.

"He's coming," Ramsey assured me, glancing over at the trees. "Tell me what's wrong."

I waved a hand over my bloody stomach. "She stabbed me with her claws. I felt—numbness. My legs and arms won't work right."

A flurry of emotions crossed his face, too fast for me to keep up.

"Char, listen to me," Ramsey said urgently. "You need to perform a healing on yourself. And this is important—focus on your kidneys."

"Like I know where my kidneys are, you walnut!"

Jack leaned in and jammed his fingers in both my sides. "Here," he grunted, and left his hands in place.

"How do you know where kidneys are?" I shrieked at him, focusing on the only thing that didn't scare the shit out of me right now. "Are you killing people and selling their kidneys on the black market?"

Jack gave me an amused look. "Punching someone in the kidney is a good way to take them down without killing them."

"You need to conjure water and hydrate your kidneys,"

Ramsey went on, worry crinkling the space between his eyebrows. "Flush out the poison."

Abram arrived, mid-transition from his beast, and loomed over the three of us. "I think we're safe. Those two cannot come out of the forest, it seems." Then he really looked at the current tableau—me prostrate on my back, Ramsey hovering worriedly, Jack with his fingers jammed in my sides. "What's going on? Char? Are you all right?"

"Don't tell him, he'll just freak out," I told Ramsey sagely, then I closed my eyes and reached for my power.

Despite my totally-not-working limbs, my magic had no such qualms. It burned to life around me and beneath my skin, and I grounded myself, focusing on the hard dirt beneath my shoulder blades.

The numbness made it so that I couldn't *feel* Jack's fingers digging into my side, but if I concentrated with my magic, I could *sense* where the electrical impulses in his body were firing against mine. My heart felt like ocean waves pounding against the beach, and it thundered in my awareness. I'd never gone this deep inside myself before, and the range of sensations I was getting were overwhelming.

And beneath it all—the demon's poison.

It spread through me like a spiderweb of black smoke. Tendrils curled around my nerves and organs so that it looked like my body was powered by smoke instead of blood. How could just healing my kidneys get rid of *all* of this? There was no way!

I'd failed. I was going to lay here on this ground in some weird, freaky alternate dimension and die.

But Ramsey had never steered me wrong. In the year I'd been apart from Abram, Ramsey had been my staunch partner, my mentor, and my teacher. He'd taught me everything I knew about using my magic, and he'd done it with kindness, affection, and an ever-present smile.

So I focused on Jack's electric fingers, then dove into my organs beneath them.

I found two identical sacks of viscous black poison, and chastised myself for doubting Ramsey. The demon's poison had clearly pooled right here, and then been dispersed through my body using my own renal system against me.

That bitch.

I'd conjured water a few times before when training with Ramsey. It was a fairly easy charm, because water existed around us at all times—droplets in the air, hidden wells and springs beneath our feet, even the clouds overhead in the sky. So drawing on those things to create a pool of water was easy.

Now, drawing on those things to make a pool of water *inside my fucking organs…* Well. I guess I'd done stranger things.

My magic danced around me, searching for the water it needed. It swirled and swirled, drawing in the energy it needed, and then I focused the nexus of the swirl inside the first of my two blackened kidneys.

Water spilled up from inside the swirling ball of energy, filling the organ with fresh, clean liquid. I re-focused my energies on the second kidney, and did the same thing, until I was full to bursting with clean water. I waited with bated breath as it began to circulate through me. With every pump of my organs, the poison began to thin. I had to fill myself up twice more before the water ran clean. While I was at it, I knitted together the largest of my injuries—the few puncture wounds in my stomach, and the gash where I'd hit my head in the forest.

My eyes popped open, and I found all three of my companions leaning over me with identical expressions of dismay.

"I'm going to need you all to back up," I said, "because I need to go pee *yesterday*."

~

AFTER I EMPTIED my overly full bladder of cloud water, we took stock of what we'd lost in our flight through the woods. My backpack full of food was gone—lost somewhere back in the trees, probably dangling twenty feet off the ground. Abram had lost his backpack, too, which meant no replacement shirt for me. At least the weather here was slightly tropical, so I could function in a tank top for the time being. It just meant the entire alternate reality would get a good view of my generous cleavage.

Jack passed out a few sticks of beef jerky—what remained of our food that had been in his bag and we munched as we recalculated.

We'd come out on the other side of the forest, closer to the massively tall mountains that formed the interior of the island. Though the ocean was hidden from view behind the inky forest, I could still smell the salt on the air.

"Can you still scent the grapes?" Ramsey asked Abram.

Abram hadn't left my side since I'd returned from peeing in the grass like a dog. He lowered his beef jerky and tilted his nose up to the air. "Yes."

"Good," Ramsey said with a nod. "We'll continue heading in that direction, as best we can."

"I think we should all be prepared for the next obstacle," Jack said as he shoved his empty wrapper back into his bag. "This island is clearly dangerous. We shouldn't let our guard down."

"Indeed," Abram agreed, handing Jack his own empty wrapper. "Let's get moving. I shudder to think what we'll face when night falls."

Abram took the lead with his beastly nose, and Jack fell back to watch the rear, his hand hovering by his broadsword as if he anticipated trouble. Without a path to guide us, we followed Abram's nose like the crow flies and headed off over the plain toward the mountains.

I settled in beside Ramsey and asked the question that had

been burning me up inside since he told me to flush my kidneys. "How did you know about the poison?"

"Ah, well, I had a hunch what those *beings* were," he said, straightening his glasses on his nose. How he fled through an entire forest, falling all over himself in the process, and still managed to keep those things in place, I'd never understand.

"What were they? Demons?" I offered. "That's how I've been thinking of them."

Ramsey glanced at me and inclined his head. "It's not a bad description, per se. They're Shades, I think. Beings not fully alive, yet not fully dead, either, which explains why no weapon or magic could work on them."

"Abram's beast could hold them off," I pointed out. "He's a weapon."

"He has preternatural strength and quickness to match their own. The forest is their domain, and the trees operate as their soldiers. Once your blood defeated the trees, Abram could step in with his matched strength and give us a chance to escape."

"So are you just making guesses here, or do you know of them through some kind of monster encyclopedia?"

Ramsey flushed. "Ah, no. In fact, I believe they're the subject of a common nursery rhyme from Grimoult." He cleared his throat and recited:

When the forest falls dark and birds stop their song,
Run, my dear, run for something is wrong.
Not dead, not alive, with eyes burning like coal,
The Mother and Child will come for your soul.

A SHIVER PASSED through me as the last of the rhyme faded. Even out here in the hot sunshine, with birds passing overhead and clouds making wispy shapes on the vast blue sky, the nursery rhyme took me right back to that forest.

"The Mother and Child," I said, shuddering. Somehow, their names made them even *more* eerie. "Would have been nice if the original creator had included an addendum on how the hell to beat them."

"I think nursery rhymes are meant to keep us *away* from dangerous things," Ramsey said wryly. "So that we don't need to know how to defeat them in the first place."

We reached a small incline slightly steeper than a hill, and for a while, nobody spoke as we climbed up and over the barrier. On the other side, the hill pitched down even farther into a narrow ravine between two enormous mountains, so getting back down turned into an even suckier way to spend my afternoon.

Eventually though, we found ourselves back on flat ground, and Abram led us down the ravine, promising we were getting closer.

I typically trusted his beastly senses, but I wasn't too sure about this grapes thing. I smelled dry dirt like rust, ocean salt, and…rain?

I glanced at the sky, noting the dark clouds rolling in from over the mountains. Down here was already dimmer than the plain we'd just left, and within moments, the clouds blocked all sunlight from reaching us, turning the ravine to twilight. Rain drops began to patter on the dirt, intermittent at first, then growing in size and quantity until we were caught in the middle of a torrential downpour.

Abram took off at a slow lope, motioning for us to follow him. The rain soaked me through quickly, and my boots turned to wet lead on my feet. We passed beneath an overhang in the mountain and spent a few minutes wringing out our hair and clothes.

"We'll have to wait it out," Abram said gruffly. "I can't smell anything in the rain."

"But the rain itself," I added, sniffing the air appreciatively. "It always just smells like new, to me. A good rain freshens up the world, don't you think?"

Jack raised an eyebrow, and amusement touched Abram's dark eyes, but Ramsey squeezed my shoulder and smiled. "I agree, Char. And we could use a freshening up after the nightmare in the woods, hmm?"

I took a seat against the wall of rock and stretched my legs out before me. Ramsey and Abram sat on either side of me, while Jack positioned himself at the edge of the overhang, just out of reach of the splattering rain.

Abram reached out to touch my wet face. "No more poison?"

"Not as far as I can tell," I assured him, turning my face into his hand so I could kiss his palm.

"Good. I was worried."

"You're always worried," I teased. "We made it, though. We're safe. And when this rainstorm is over, we'll get back on the road and find this madman who can supposedly get us to Wonderland."

I leaned into his side, and he wrapped his big, strong arm around me. I felt like a hundred years had passed since I'd slept last night in Grimoult's palace. My body ached from running through the woods. All the little cuts and scrapes on my arms and face burned from sweat and rainwater. But Abram's arm gave me a sense of comfort that nothing else in the world could, and before long, I fell into a light doze.

Then awoke with a jerk as the ground rumbled beneath my ass.

Abram's arm fell away, and he sat up straighter, his gaze roaming the ravine. The rumble hadn't stopped. It was gaining in intensity, almost roaring like a freight train coming down the tracks.

"What is that?" Ramsey asked, stumbling to his feet.

Stones bounced across the ground by my fingers, and fear prickled along the back of my neck.

Down the ravine, from the direction we'd come, water splashed around the corner. The trickle became a deluge, and the deluge became a wall of flood water heading right for us.

I stumbled back against the wall, everything in me screaming to run, but nobody could outrun a flood.

The water barreled over us and swept us away.

CHAPTER 17

On my best day, I wasn't a very good swimmer. I could walk a runway in six-inch Manolo Blahniks that cost more than my car note, but when it came to swimming, I had a tendency to sink rather than float. Once, at Taylor Swift's annual Fourth of July pool party, Briar told me I only sank because I was full of shit. Since I'd just eaten three hot dogs and tossed back four shots of tequila, she wasn't wrong. Though maybe not in the manner she meant. Taylor, no stranger to being bullied, kicked Briar out, and that was the highlight of my year.

Now, add in the whole *Char sinks* thing with water moving faster and more violent than the Colorado River rapids, and I was pretty certain death had locked its gaze on me.

I rolled over and flipped wildly beneath the surface, getting caught in undercurrents of the rushing flood wall. I couldn't see any of my friends. Hell, I couldn't see anything at all—just dark water all around and the disorienting tumble of my body through the ravine. I'd lost all sense of which way was up and which was down.

And I *really* needed to breathe.

I slammed into rock and all the breath I'd been holding in my lungs expelled. I clawed at the water around me, desperately trying to find the surface. Even a single head pop above water could gain me precious moments. As the river continued to carry me faster and faster, I hit more rocks, slipped through more debris fields, and without a single opening to take a breath, my vision began to blacken.

No, no! I thought, trying to swim, trying to move my arms and orient myself to the surface. But my body had given up. I was battered and losing oxygen.

Death had come.

I thought of Abram somewhere in these waters. Maybe he'd make it through safe and go on to live his life. I hated that we wouldn't be together, but it seemed vitally more important to me that he survive even if I didn't. I couldn't imagine a world without him in it. And Ramsey—he'd promised Briar he'd come home from this trip. Hell, I'd promised Lulu I'd bring Jack home.

Broken promises everywhere.

Just like that, my time was up. My vision went black. My body went limp. And still the water raged on around me.

Something slimy wrapped around both my wrists. With my last vestiges of consciousness, I thought, *EW! Mother fucker, can't I just die in peace?*

Then slimy lips pressed against mine.

My first thought was *Abram! Abram found me!* Which was absolutely asinine, as we were both tumbling through a devil canyon. This mouth most definitely did not belong to my boyfriend.

When the lips opened over mine, I tried to pull away, but I didn't have the energy.

Then a burst of air filled my lungs.

I sucked it in greedily, latching on to the slimy lips as I realized the air was coming from them. The slime around my wrists wasn't seaweed or anything ick in the water—they were hands, holding me firmly in place as the creature gave me oxygen!

I felt the tell-tale tingle of magic racing over my skin, originating from the connection on my wrists. My body grew buoyant, as if I'd been filled full of helium, and I started to rise to the surface with the slimy creature still connected to my lips. At the last moment, the lips disappeared, and the hands gave me one last push so that I broke the surface of the water.

The moment my head breached the surface, I gasped in blessed fresh air over and over until it chased away the black in my vision. Whatever magic the slimy creature had used to make me buoyant kept me above the water—which was a nifty trick I was going to have to learn, considering my history with bodies of water. Up ahead, I could see three little heads floating along the river with the same strange buoyancy, so apparently the slimy things had helped my companions, too.

Abram. Thank God.

Unfortunately, I couldn't even attempt to make it to the side of the canyon and grab for safety. The magic kept me aloft as long as I didn't move. The moment I tried to tread water or do a breaststroke, I teetered over and was nearly ripped back under the currents. So I let my arms and legs hang limply and floated down the river, trying to pretend I was in an inner tube at an amusement park and not another wrong move from death.

The rain stopped abruptly only a few moments after I broke the surface. Overhead, the clouds parted and hot sunshine beamed down on the canyon. The heat felt sticky on my wet face, but the sun reminded me that I hadn't died, and that was the emotion I clung to as the river continued to carry us away.

Now that my life wasn't in immediate danger—as far as I knew—I could appreciate the beauty of the canyon. I figured by now we were *deep* in the island's central mountains, and the sheer height of the two walls on either side of us seemed to corroborate that. The cliffs were dusky red and painted with strips of lighter tan, so that the rock face seemed like an artist's watercolor canvas. With my head above the dark water, I could see that it was a strange royal blue that complemented the red rock in such a way, none of it looked natural to earth.

Though I guess we weren't in Kansas anymore.

Every so often, we passed an opening in the cliff faces, and I'd catch a glimpse of a sandy beach and trees beyond. The sightings helped me remember the world didn't start and end with this canyon. Ideally, we also wouldn't just float along forever, either, and we'd be back on that solid land soon.

It took a couple miles for me to realize the water level was dropping. My first clue came when the cliff walls ahead started to glint like diamonds in the sunlight where the water had splashed against them during the initial deluge. Then the cliffs seemed higher than they did before, and I thought, *Fucking hell, am I* shrinking? Finally, my boots began to scrape ground.

The river was still too fast and furious to stand up in, even with my feet touching mud, so I braced myself and followed the water level all the way down. I hit the floor of the ravine and clutched at the mud as the last of the river funneled past me, turned into a trickle, and then disappeared entirely. The slimy creature's magic faded away as I flipped over onto my back and let the sun warm my chilled skin.

I only lay there a few seconds before a shadow darkened the light on my eyelids. I peeked out of one eye to see Abram looming over me, his hair wet, his clothes clinging to every delicious muscle in his body. He looked primal, like a gruff mountain man who could break trees with his bare hands, and my libido liked it a lot.

"Hey, stud. Come here often?" I teased.

He darted down and grabbed both my biceps, yanking me to my feet. He folded me into his arms and his lips crashed to mine, then we were kissing frantically, like two people who had almost just drowned.

His hands splayed across my back, holding me tightly to

his hard chest. I tiptoed, one arm snaking around his neck and the fingers of the other hand tangling in his hair. Abram's mouth was hot, his tongue dancing against mine so erotically I turned into a living flame in his grasp.

He broke the kiss, his lips trailing down my cheek and neck as he murmured, "I thought I lost you."

"I thought I *was* lost," I replied, tilting my head back to give him better access. One of his hands wrapped around my ass and tugged me against his obvious arousal. "I should almost die more often, if this is the greeting I get."

"Woman, you drive me mad," Abram growled, then moved his lips back to mine.

If we weren't soaking wet, standing in half a foot of muck, and traveling with two other people, Abram might have ripped my clothes off where we stood and had his way with me. Even with all those other things standing in the way, I wanted him to do it. This was the Abram I'd been searching for since he was returned to me.

It just took certain death to get him there.

Finally, he broke the kiss, both his hands moving to cup my face as we pressed our foreheads together. We stood there, breathing hard, drinking in each other's presence for several more minutes before we finally broke apart.

The river had petered out near one of those sandy alcoves. About fifteen feet off the ground, the mountains broke open in a rocky crevice, showing more blue sky beyond, as well as the tops of trees. Jack and Ramsey had apparently already climbed the canyon wall, leaving trails of mud behind that guided us to follow them.

I was about as good at rock climbing as I was at swimming, so getting to the sandy beach was an interesting experience that included a lot of Abram's hands on my ass. I might even have slipped on purpose a few times just to make him touch me. But eventually, I crawled out of the canyon and onto smooth, hot sand, where I flopped onto my back in the sun to catch my breath.

Abram sat beside me, wiping sweat off his brow as he glanced around the small valley.

"Do you smell the grapes?" I asked him breathlessly.

"I do. They're close."

"That's good. I like good news. We need more of that."

Ramsey appeared and held out his canteen. I took it and chugged back lukewarm water, thinking how strange it was to be so thirsty after almost drowning.

"There's a path up the valley," Ramsey told Abram as I drank. "It cuts up part of the mountain and then disappears over the ridge."

Abram accepted the canteen from me, then sniffed the air. He pointed toward the far right. "Over there?"

Ramsey glanced in that direction. "Yes."

"Perfect. That's where we need to go," Abram said, getting to his feet. His blue jeans were covered in sand, and his boots with mud. I couldn't imagine that I looked much better.

Jack strolled up to join us, readjusting his sword's sheath on his back. It looked like neither Jack nor Ramsey had lost their backpacks in the flood, though anything inside was likely waterlogged now.

"Can't we rest for a moment?" I whined, remaining firmly planted on my back. The sand was so warm, I could have closed my eyes and slept for days.

Ramsey smiled down at me indulgently. "We can't stay here forever. Catch your breath, and let's get moving."

As the three men moved off talking about our next move over the ridge, I took a couple deep breaths. My adrenaline had worn off, so now all I wanted to do was take a nap. But I knew Ramsey was right—ever since stepping foot on this island, it had been one deadly obstacle after another, and if we stayed still too long, the next one would find us before we even caught our second wind. Or third wind, whatever.

I was still on my back watching a puffy white cloud in the shape of a bunny float by, when the talking cat appeared. This time, he didn't saunter up like he owned the valley—he popped into existence floating over my chest.

"*Argh!*" I sat up, my heart doing palpitations right out of my rib cage as I scrambled away from him. "What are *you* doing here?"

The cat walked a circle around me—still floating in mid-air. Then he plopped on his haunches and eyed me enigmatically. "You're lucky the frogmen found you worthy. They usually let humans drown in their floods."

"The frogmen?" I thought about the slimy hands on my wrists and the slimy lips touching my mouth. "Ew."

"They usually keep to themselves," the cat said with a tiny feline shrug. "Gentle creatures, really. They call the rains and ride the floods for fun. Anyone who gets caught in the way… well. They aren't overly concerned. This isn't the human realm, after all."

I crossed my legs on the sand and shifted to better face him. "What realm *is* it?"

The cat opened his mouth, but the word that came out was like nothing I'd ever heard before. I blinked at him, trying to make heads or tails of the twelve syllables he'd just spoken. "That's not even English."

An eerie smile spread over his face. "Well, this isn't even human, now is it?"

Somehow, this tiny orange creature had a way of making me feel like a fool.

"You never answered my question. What are you doing here?" I repeated.

"Watching you."

"What am I, some form of entertainment?" I rolled to my knees and stood, then swiped at the three inches of sand embedded in my jeans.

"Perhaps," he mused, standing up and walking around to

join me. The floating cat routine was nearly as alarming as the talking part. "Perhaps I simply have a marked interest in whether or not you complete your mission."

"Where were you when I was about to drown?"

"I said an *interest*, Charisse Bellamy. Gods do not interfere."

"You're a real pain in the ass, you know that?" I told him, then stomped away, heading for the path carved in the valley ahead where my three companions waited.

The cat didn't follow. Not physically, anyway. But I had a feeling he followed our every move as we left the valley and headed deeper into the mountains.

Abram fell back into tracking mode, so I took up my usual spot beside Ramsey while Jack covered our backside with his big ol' sword. Nobody seemed particularly talkative, though, and I could hardly blame anybody for the silence. After battling the trees, the Mother and Child, and the flood, I was running on less-than-fumes, and I couldn't be the only one. The three of us didn't have Abram's beastly strength and virility.

The path led out of the valley through a jagged scar in the mountain, then crested up over a small ridge. From there, it carved up the side of the mountain, curving around and out of sight. It took some fancy footwork to reach that segment of path, and once there, we had to move in a single file line as rocks loosened and fell away from our feet.

But halfway around the mountain, an entirely new world opened ahead of us. A plain stretched far into the distance, much further than I expected on an island this small. More mountains cradled the plain far, far away, nothing but shadows on the horizon all around. It was as if a small landmass had been plopped magically into the middle of the mountains.

Green grass spread as far as the eye could see, bisected by forested areas, wildflower meadows, and patches of fog. I thought I glimpsed a few buildings here and there, but anytime I looked right at them, they vanished. Magic was at work in this place.

Big magic.

We found an incline that wasn't too steep and began our descent to the plain. The sun was high and boiling, and I added a sheen of sweat to my already muddy, sandy, river-water covered body.

Once on flat ground, we passed through a small copse of trees that was blessedly full of sunshine and wildlife. After the hell forest behind Wal-Mart and the sentient forest manipulated by the Mother and Child, I had serious forest-phobia. But we passed through this one quickly with nothing more than a few annoying flies batting about our filthy bodies, and then stepped back into the sunshine.

A small town waited for us on the other side of the trees. Several streets stretched around us, and a few dozen small, squat houses perched along the edges of the roads. Decorative trees and bushes swayed in the wind, and a swingset on a nearby playground creaked ominously.

But…there was nobody in sight.

I exchanged glances with Ramsey. "Where are the people?"

He shook his head, glancing out over the empty town. "I don't know. I mean, I suppose perhaps it wouldn't be 'people' living here."

Abram's fingers wiggled at his sides as the beast braced for action. "There doesn't seem to be *anyone* here. People or not."

"No need to beast out just yet," I told him, gently touching his hand. "Let's keep going. Follow the grapes."

Abram nodded once, then moved off, his nose in the air.

Jack broke away to peer into a few windows, his broadsword clutched in hand. I watched his movements, way too aware that my back was exposed and I no longer had a weapon thanks to the trees who stole my backpack.

"Nothing," Jack said, returning to our group. "Houses are all furnished, but nobody's inside."

"It's a ghost town," Ramsey said with a shiver. "What would make people just up and leave a perfectly good village?"

We turned down a side street, and I stared in astonishment as the houses broke off—replaced by a massive field of grapevines.

I strolled over to the nearest pole and gasped as I saw giant, juicy berries growing on the vine. "Holy shit, Abram. You really could smell the grapes."

He looked at me, affronted. "Did you think I was misleading you?"

"Of course not. Just…whoa!" I plucked a grape off the vine and was about to pop it in my mouth when Ramsey batted it away.

"We don't know that those are safe," he told me exasperatedly. "Please do not ingest anything in this world unless we know it's not poisonous."

"Look." Jack pointed beyond the fields. "A house."

Not just any house, but a massive Victorian painted in a riot of bright colors: coral, sapphire, emerald, yellow. A spire reached into the sky from one corner, and a number of gables arched from various points on the roof. From our vantage point, only the top floor and the roof were fully visible.

"Is that our destination?" I asked Ramsey.

He nodded resolutely. "That's it. Our madman lives there."

We followed the dirt road through the grapevines, the house growing steadily closer. Now surrounded by the orchard, even I could smell the grapes, and the scent was cloying—too close, almost rotten—and I was glad Ramsey had kept me from eating one.

The dirt path opened beyond the grape fields on a sloping yard before the house. I'd expected just another empty yard like all those we'd passed in the village, but instead, we found a large table, flanked by six chairs sitting right in the middle of the lawn.

As we got closer, I could see the table was set for a meal. A lacy white tablecloth draped over it, rippling in the breeze. Fancy China coffee cups and saucers waited at every place setting. The center of the table was weighed down with plates of scones, danishes, croissants, and every manner of pastry I've ever snuck into my mouth between photo shoots.

At the head of the table, a man sat nursing a steaming mug. A teapot rested by his elbow, and a top hat sat atop his dark, curly hair.

My skin ran cold from the roots of my hair down. A rush of heat and the ache of lost affection roared over me.

The madman wasn't just some stranger.

He was my father.

CHAPTER 18

SHOCK FROZE me to the ground as I stared unblinkingly at the man occupying the front yard dining table.

He looked exactly as I remembered him: his dark hair, the exact chocolate brown of my own, was on the long side, shaggy and in desperate need of a cut. A black top hat sat perched on his head, shadowing his face, but I could still see his bright blue eyes beneath the brim, sparkling with good humor as he kept up his conversation with his invisible tea partiers.

My mom always joked how he had cheekbones that could slice bread, and he especially looked that way now, given that he'd lost some weight in the past twenty years. His old, dirty suit jacket hung off his frame like it was made for a much larger man. But even with all that, he hadn't aged a day since the last time I saw him.

My brain tried to process the situation, but it wasn't an easy feat since my father walked out of our home when I was young and never came back. I watched him through the window as he disappeared into the woods behind our house in New Haven.

I found out later, after I met Abram, that he had known

my father—actually, he'd been *friends* with him. Went fishing and all those gross man things that weren't good for my manicure. During some of my earliest conversations with Abram, he'd indicated that he thought my father was dead. Even though I'd always *assumed* the reason Dad never came home was that he met a terrible end somewhere out there, Abram was the first to confirm it.

But now…Jack was telling the truth.

"Son of a bitch," Jack murmured, sheathing his broadsword. "Char, it's…"

"Yeah. I know." My voice came out wrong. Distant.

"No wonder I haven't been able to contact him since you got here," Jack said, shaking his head. "He's been trapped by…this."

Abram's strong hand closed around my shoulder, and I looked up at him in time to see him swallow hard. "It may not be him. We do not know what secrets this place keeps."

"Looks a helluva lot like him." I pulled my shoulder from Abram's grasp, then fell into a jog toward the strangely empty tea party.

"So did the curse!" Abram called after me.

My father didn't acknowledge our presence or the sound of our voices, even though we were plenty close enough for him to hear us and see us. The only way I'd find out if it really *was* my dad, was to march right up to him and figure it out for myself.

Behind me, Ramsey's low voice faded into the wind. "What's going on? Do you all know that man?"

A gentle hill sloped up toward the foreboding house, putting the long table at an awkward angle, all the chairs pitching dangerously to the side as if the merest touch might send them careening downhill.

My legs burned as I climbed up and closed in on the man that could possibly be my father, and Abram's reminder burned hot in my memories. The last time I'd "seen" my dad,

I'd stepped into a magic room with Abram that had been occupied by his curse—the one that made him a beast. The curse had taken my father's form and said awful things to me. Things that haunted me for quite a while afterward, even once I knew it wasn't my real father who'd said them.

Seeing his face now brought back those memories, and my heart ratched up, getting faster the closer I got to him. What if it was a shade of my dad? Something evil and vile like Abram's curse? But it could also be him, and what would I do if he was *made* wrong? I couldn't decide which option seemed easier to deal with.

He was talking out loud, sometimes under his breath while he stared into his fancy mug, and other times, he addressed the empty chairs around him.

"Lawrence, could you please pass the cheese danish?" he said jovially, looking at the chair to his right. "I'm famished."

I slowed and eyed the chair, searching for any evidence that a person or beastie sat there drinking tea with him, but if anything was there, it wasn't in any kind of form I could see.

I drew up next to his chair, my heart hammering in my throat. "Dad?"

He turned to a chair at the other end of the table. "Well, I'm not sure, Marion. Two hundred degrees, perhaps?"

"Dad." I touched his shoulder.

He tensed up, then shivered and offered a jovial laugh. "Somebody just walked over my grave, gents! We need more jam. Do you mind, Neville?"

I hovered next to him a moment longer before Abram gently took my hand and tugged me away from the table to reconvene with Jack and Ramsey. We circled up a few yards from the tea party, though I kept the table, and my dad, in my periphery.

"Something's wrong," I said, glancing back over at him. Dad was pouring from a steaming kettle, but nothing liquid was coming out. "He's, like, insane or something."

"Ramsey, is this our man?" Abram asked. "Is this the man who knows how to find Wonderland?"

Ramsey nodded and shoved his glasses up his nose. "It has to be. The grapevine orchard is a dead giveaway, and they all say the madman is forced to wear a hat. And well, he does seem mad, doesn't he?"

I narrowed my eyes at the top hat. My father laughed, and the hat bobbled precariously, but didn't fall off.

"He wasn't like this when we met a month ago," Jack said vehemently. "He was *normal* when we met for the last time, when he brought me the time traveling supplies."

Ramsey paced away, his gaze on my dad and his face screwed up as he thought. Then he walked back as if he wasn't sure what to do with himself. "Well, rumor does state Darcus punished him when he uncovered his plot. Perhaps this is the punishment? Some kind of magical imprisonment or…"

My dad accepted an imaginary something from an imaginary someone. "Oh, Lawrence, you brought your homemade crumpets today! Lovely. This calls for more butter, wouldn't you say?"

"He doesn't even sound like himself," I said, rubbing my hands up and down my arms to chase away the goosebumps. "Darcus must have done something to his mind."

"Is there something we can do to fix it?" Jack asked. "Fight magic with magic?"

"Maybe." I thought of the homeless man on the street, his liquor bottle in the gutter while I delved into his memories. "I can go inside his mind."

Jack immediately understood what I meant, since he'd been there for the homeless man, and nodded knowingly.

"Your power is to see into a person's memories," Abram said. "How will that help you?"

"It's all the same thing, right? The brain." I motioned to my dad. "I'll just dive in and find the real him. Or maybe I'll find a memory of when Darcus put the spell on him and how it can be broken."

"I don't like it," Abram said with a definite shake of his head. "I don't want you in danger."

"I think I've been in danger a few times since we met," I pointed out, rolling my eyes. This man's sense of White Knight-ery ran *way* too deep for having a magical girlfriend with a destiny to save the world.

"It's rather smart," Ramsey told me. "I'll spot you on this end and pull you back if anything goes wrong."

A rush of affection and relief flooded through me. I had my magical wingman back.

I took the chair to my father's left, my stomach in knots. Ramsey stood beside me, his face belying his fear, and Abram posted up on the other side of my father where he could see me in full. Jack unsheathed his broadsword and began walking the perimeter.

"Ready?" Ramsey asked softly. I had a feeling he could sense my fear and that I was nothing more than a little girl, scared it wouldn't be her father on the other side of this.

I nodded. Then I reached out and laid my hand over Dad's.

My magic rose, tendrils of energy wrapping up my father's arm. Around and around until it reached his shoulder, then his neck, and finally, his head. I could feel his consciousness resting against my coils of power, and I made a tiny shift to shove my magic inside him. My own consciousness wouldn't be far behind.

But it didn't happen as easily as it usually did. His body rejected my magic, pushing back on me. My first thought was that Darcus had laid a safeguard on his punishment— something meant to keep any magical intervention from happening. Except this didn't feel like a magical pushback. More like…my power was struggling to complete the task.

I shoved harder, my skin raging so hot with energy that

sweat broke out along my hairline and dripped toward my eyes. What the *fuck* was going on? I'd just completed this same act on a stranger only a few days before, and now, I couldn't do it?

No, I snarled inwardly. I tightened my grip on my father and put another burst of magic behind the first, sending it out in a furious shockwave. My magic finally barreled into Dad's mind, and so did I.

I opened my eyes on the exact same place I'd closed them, only this scene was slightly different. While my father was alone in real life, he wasn't in his mind, and his companions weren't exactly what I would have expected.

To his right, and directly across from me, sat a giant, humanoid rabbit. His legs and arms were long and spindly, elongated like a person's instead of crooked like a real rabbit's. He had solid, glowing red eyes and two vicious vampire-like fangs extending from his pert snout. Next to the demon bunny was a bulbous gray mouse, bigger around than a beach ball and roughly the size of a child. Like the bunny, he too had red eyes and sharp teeth.

The fourth occupant of the table sat beside me and was a seemingly normal man. He was pale all over—pale skin, pale eyes, pale hair, even his eighties era clothes were pale. The paleness of everything else made the blood on his lips stand out stark, like a bloody Rorschach test.

Then I realized they *all* had blood on their lips.

Even my father.

Before I could investigate further, Dad's other hand lifted away from his tea mug and settled on top of mine, where I still clung to him.

His blue-eyed gaze leveled on me and all the distant crazy was gone. "Char! Is it really you?"

"Yes! But…how did you know?" I eyed him suspiciously, because the man hadn't seen me since I was a kid. I wasn't exactly the gangly limbed child he'd abandoned.

He released me and fumbled inside his pants pocket. He extracted a single small picture—a snapshot of me and Lulu not long after Jack's birth. "Jack gave it to me. I mean...I asked him for it. For something so I could see the woman you became." His voice clogged, and he shoved the picture back into his pocket. "You made it."

"What's going on here?" I asked, glancing furtively at the bunny, mouse, and pale man. They were all three still partaking of their tea party—the bunny nibbling at what looked like a human hand, and the mouse sloshing viscous red liquid into his mug, while the pale man selected a couple of steaming fresh fingers from a platter in the center of the table.

Not a tea party, then. A blood party.

Ew.

"Darcus," my father said darkly. "I'm trapped in here with Lawrence, Neville, and Marion."

I blinked at my father's angular face, then glanced around at the group. "I don't even want to know which name belongs to who." Returning my gaze to my father, I said, "Okay, so what do we do? How do we break the spell?"

He shrugged helplessly. "I don't know. If I knew, I would have already tried. Every day, Lawrence brings a body that looks just like me and then they cut me into tiny pieces and drain my blood into the tea kettle, and they feast. Some days, I'm so hungry, I eat with them."

Nausea flipped inside me, and I fought the intense urge to vomit. *Darcus. What a son of a bitch.*

Suddenly, the rabbit spoke. "Have a crumpet, Bellamy." He held out a bloody finger, his face oddly placid, even for a bunny.

My father nodded with overexaggerated motions and accepted the piece of his own corpse. "Yes, of course, Lawrence. Thank you."

When he nodded, I thought I caught sight of something else bloody beneath the wide brim of his top hat. I hopped out of my seat and stepped close to him, lifting the brim of the hat to verify what I'd seen.

Stitches. Raw, angry skin and coarse black stitches sewing the top hat to his head.

"Oh my God," I murmured.

My dad looked up at me, his eyes wide. "What is it?"

"The hat—" I didn't get a chance to finish my sentence. The rabbit lunged from his chair and rounded the end of the table, his strangely humanoid fist slamming into my face.

I went down hard, landing on my side on the grass. My head bounced off the dirt, and black danced along the edge of my vision. The pain was too real, and I realized with dawning horror that even though I was in my father's mind— this was reality. These monsters weren't here to keep my dad company.

They were here to make sure no one removed the hat from my dad's head. To make sure no one broke Darcus's spell.

Blinking away the wooziness, I rolled onto my hands and knees, where I opened and closed my jaw a few times, trying to chase away the tingling behind the pain.

"Char!" my father cried as he attempted to get out of his chair. But the beach ball mouse clamped a small hand to his shoulder, pinning him in place with inhuman strength.

The pale man slipped from his chair and slowly walked toward me, long, slender fingers extending into knife-like claws. His voice was oddly melodic as he said, "The human is a threat. She must be annihilated."

I swayed as I stumbled to my feet, then widened my stance so I wouldn't fall over. The rabbit, mouse, and pale man converged on me, not moving fast, but moving with purpose.

Planting my hands on my hips, I threw my shoulders back and said, "There's only one problem with that."

The pale man cocked his head and peered at me with those strange white eyes.

"I'm not human," I told him, then unleashed a massive fireball toward the maniacal group.

The magic seared into them, frying skin and singeing fur. Three shrieks of outrage filled the yard, and then they all leapt for me, trailing flames and embers.

The pale man's claws swiped at my stomach, and I dodged the blow, though I went too far left and placed myself right into the rabbit's path. He punched—obviously the brute strength of the group—and I rolled with his blow, taking some of the power out of it.

I rolled twice over the ground, then launched another energy attack, focusing the full force of it on the rabbit. I couldn't fight all three of them at once, but if I could systematically destroy them one by one while taking a few hits, the odds would be better.

The bulbous mouse threw himself on top of me in the wake of my explosion. He was the size and weight of a small boulder, and all the air expelled from my lungs as his teeth sank into my shoulder.

Agony tore through my skin and ran down my arm, and I sent another fireball out, right into the mouse's fat torso. He squealed as the energy tossed him away, and he bounced across the grass, his fur aflame.

I sat up to find both furry creatures on fire, rolling around on the ground screeching as they attempted to put out the flames. While they were otherwise occupied, I could put down the pale man, find a sharp object, and cut the hat off my dad's head.

I shoved off the ground and stood, whirling around as my gaze searched out the pale man.

Only for four sharp claws to sink into my torso.

CHAPTER 19

I STARED down at the pale man's claws in my side, surprised that I didn't immediately feel pain. His knife-like nails had gone so deep, there was *no* way he'd missed all the vital organs. A trace of fear trickled up from within me, but I shoved it away. I couldn't be afraid right now, no matter how much my terror screamed for me to give in.

Grabbing the pale man's wrist, I held his arm in place and stepped away from his claws. They slid from my skin on a rush of heat and agony that stole the breath from me. His other hand raised, and he prepared to bring it down on my head, and an angry snarl twisted his face into something evil.

But before I could come up with a plan or figure out my next move to keep him from decapitating me, I heard a dull *thwack*. The pale man tensed, his entire body going rigid, then his eyes rolled up into his head and he crumpled to the ground.

Dad stood behind him, holding the metal teapot over his head, his eyes as big and round as the moon. Our eyes met, and he dropped the kettle and rushed forward, his hands hovering over the wounds in my side. "Oh, God. Oh no."

I batted his hands away. "Stop. I'm fine."

"No, you're not," he said harshly, grabbing the hem of my tank top to better see the injury. "If you die here, you die in real life."

My fear prickled back into my consciousness. I really didn't want to die. Though I guess most people didn't. I wanted a future with Abram, a wedding, maybe even a family. I wanted my dad there, because I was no longer an orphan and that very thought sent excitement for my future racing through me.

But surprisingly, I wanted even *more* for my father to get out of this alive and free from this horrific spell. *Look at that—Charisse Bellamy, putting someone else ahead of her own life.* It's like I didn't even recognize myself.

I slowly crouched down next to the unconscious pale man. Pain rippled through my torso, and every movement felt like it would be the one to send me into a coma. But there was no way I could leave these things alive in my father's head. So I took hold of one dagger-like claw and kneeled on the base of the pale man's finger. The claw snapped off easily, and I hefted it in my hand, pleased at my makeshift weapon. *Charisse Bellamy—selfless guerrilla warrior.* I was surprising myself left and right.

Then I jammed the faux knife in the pale man's throat and tore across his skin, severing veins and tendons, scraping bone, and damn near taking his head off in my quest to ensure he wouldn't be coming back to life.

Still clutching my now-bloody knife, I got to my feet and swayed dangerously, but stalked to the two burning monsters. My magical flames had done a number on them, and they were both unmoving and, at first glance, not breathing, but I ripped open their necks like I'd done to the pale man. I wasn't satisfied they were dead until their blood slowed to a trickle on the dirt.

Returning to my father's side, I wiped the blade on my pants in a vain attempt to clear away the blood. "Come here and hold still," I told him. "We need to cut the hat off. I think it's the source of the spell."

"The hat?" Dad reached up and tugged at the top hat, then grimaced. "Ow."

With him standing next to me, I remembered just how tall he was. When I was a kid, I'd thought he was larger than life, a giant of a man who had my whole heart in his big hand. After he left, it felt like my heart would never be the same.

And now I have him back. I clutched at that lifeline and fought through the pain in my torso. I could worry about that later—right now, taking care of my father was most important.

He knelt on the grass so I could more easily reach the hat without putting undue pressure on my wounds. The pale man's claw cut through the stitches one at a time, carefully so that I didn't rip any chunks of skin from my dad's head, until I could remove the hat entirely.

The world around us dissolved. Colors merged and flooded, seeping away like water running off into the gutter during a summer rainstorm. I glanced around, stunned by the beauty of it, like a movie scene fading out as another faded in. I watched as Jack, Ramsey, and Abram filtered into view, and the world became whole once more.

I still sat at the long table to my father's left, my hand resting on his in the exact position I'd taken to dive inside his mind. The only differences were his missing top hat and the talking cat sitting by my elbow, an eerie, humanoid smile on his furry face.

"Your wounds!" my father said gruffly, leaning over to check my stomach.

To be honest, I'd forgotten about them. I'd been too focused on defeating the demons in his head and getting that damn spell off him to remember that the pale man had skewered me like a shish kabob. But I lifted my shirt to find smooth skin, unmarred and free of blood. The wounds had been *very* real inside my dad's mind, but they didn't follow me out here. Neither had the angry stitch marks on Dad's hairline —his skin was golden tanned and unblemished.

We exchanged glances, and then we both laughed. It was relieved laughter—a coping mechanism to shake off the heavy weight of what we'd just gone through together. I realized with a pang of emotion that our laughs sounded *so* similar, and I might never have known. My heart ached with the knowledge. It was strange also how my father hadn't aged. When he'd left me, he'd only been in his early thirties, which made us close in age currently. But when I looked at him, I still saw my dad—older, wiser, my protector.

Dad's gaze moved over the table. "Jesus, is that real food?"

Before I could stop him, he snatched a danish off a nearby plate and shoved it in his mouth. He moaned happily and finished it off in two more bites.

The four of us, plus the cat, watched him for any sign of something going wrong. All I could think about was Ramsey batting the grape from my hand before I could eat it and telling me we didn't know if it was safe to eat anything in this realm.

But nothing happened. Dad swiped the back of his hand across his sugary lips, then picked up another pastry. As if only now realizing we were all staring at him like he'd, well, gone mad, he raised an eyebrow and said, "What? I'm famished. You eat your own corpse for a month and see how you feel."

Abram looked at me. "His own corpse?"

I shrugged. "You don't want to know."

The cat's tail swished over the wooden table. "It appears this food is safe. Perhaps you might all fill the aches in your bellies?"

Dad dropped his danish into his empty tea cup, blinking rapidly at the cat. "Did it just…talk?"

I rolled my eyes. "There was a murderous humanoid bunny with fangs in your head, and it's the talking cat that does you in?" I glanced around at my companions. "You guys better sit down. I think we all have a lot of catching up to do."

~

BY THE TIME my friends and I went over the recent events that had led us to this front yard, the sun had begun to fade in the sky overhead. I was tired and achy after everything we'd been through, and all I wanted to do was go to sleep. But I burned with all the questions I wanted to ask my father. *Why did you leave me? Where have you been? How did you end up in Wonderland?*

But I reined myself in and simply said, "Your turn."

Dad blew out a breath and leaned against his high-backed chair, shoving both his hands through his long dark hair. "I don't even know where to begin."

"The beginning is usually a good place to start," I quipped.

"I guess the beginning would be the Oracle," he replied, staring out over the grapevines where the sun sank over the horizon in a brilliant red ball. "She approached me when you were about five years old. Maybe six. She told me you would be an important part of saving the world one day, but that you couldn't do it alone. She had a one-way ticket to the future for me, so that I could make sure you had what you needed when the time came."

"And you believed her?"

"Of course not," he said, laughing. "I thought she was a charlatan looking to swindle me, and I laughed her right out of my office. Before she left, she warned me that you would be a powerful magical being, and soon, creatures would come for you. Told me maybe when that happened, I'd believe her. I ignored her and forgot about that visit for several years. Until a beast tried to break into our house to get to you."

Shocked, I said, "But I don't remember an attack on our house."

He nodded grimly. "You were sleeping. So was your mother. I felt him prowling in the yard, sniffing around your bedroom window. We fought, and he injured me, but I managed to take him out before he could even wake you. But it was then I understood the Oracle had been telling the truth."

"And that's when you left?"

"That's when I left," he agreed. "I went to see the Oracle using the little bit of information she'd left me. When I finally tracked her down, I wasn't given a chance to go back and tell you goodbye. She said we were running out of time, and I needed to go into the future immediately if I wanted to save your life."

"So you left me in the past to save me in the future." I reached out and squeezed his hand. "You manufactured the time travel components for Jack to come back and get us?"

Dad grinned with a hint of modesty. "I did."

"Okay, so what happened next?" I asked, before we got out of order. Not that time had any meaning in this situation, but my poor brain needed to cling to a linear set of events. "When you got here? How did you end up punished by Darcus?"

Dad reached for the kettle and topped off his tea—he'd scrounged some from the house to go with our pastry-laden dinner. "When I arrived in the future, Darcus had not yet begun his takeover. I met with a few other scientists who were also supplicants, and we began working on the technology needed for time travel. The only thing we knew at that point was that Darcus was coming—soon—and we needed to be able to get you to the future.

"But when Darcus showed up, he found us almost immediately," Dad went on, face falling. "I don't know how. It was like he knew, like someone had tipped him off. He enslaved us all and put us to work in his own lab."

"For what purpose?" Abram asked.

"Darcus sees Char as his biggest threat," Dad told him, then looked back at me. "He came to the future to build an army big enough to destroy you when the time came. He figured this way, you'd be older when the two of you finally faced one another again, and at that point, he'd no longer be outmatched by your combined conduit and supplicant powers because he'd have an army on his side. He didn't count on me, though."

I grinned. "What did you do?"

"Darcus had me working on a weapon he intends to use to defeat the gods. I threw myself into the project so that he wouldn't suspect me of treachery, but in my spare moments, I continued working on the magic needed for time travel. And then Jack showed up..."

I glanced at the kid, who'd remained silent and listening up until now. "I thought my dad came to you?"

Dad laughed. "Maybe in a roundabout way, if you want to believe in serendipity. Jack and his rebels stormed the prison and freed us all—an entire unit of supplicant scientists. We had to go underground to steer clear of Darcus, so I tasked Jack with retrieving you. For the magic to work, it had to be done in a certain time frame and done by a conduit using my blood. He was the perfect man for the job. Clearly, since you're here."

"And then Darcus found you," I guessed.

Dad's face darkened, and his gaze slid down to his tea. "He did. I was discovered and punished with the eternal mad tea party inside my head."

"Mad blood party," I corrected with a shiver of disgust.

"I'd like to never speak of those atrocities again," Dad said, blanching. He looked around the table at Abram and Jack, and Ramsey who he'd just met. Then he smiled. "Thank you. All of you. But most importantly..." He reached out to touch my face. "Thank you for being brave enough to leap into my head and save me."

I flushed. "You're my dad. You'd have done the same for me."

We spent a bit more time together as the sun finished cresting over the horizon. But not long after my father finished his tale, five of us headed into the big house to get some shut eye, while Abram prowled into the grapevines with his beast.

The moment my head hit the alarmingly dusty pillow inside the big Victorian, I slept like the dead. It felt like we'd boarded our tiny boat to this realm seven days ago, not less than twelve hours before. Sometime early in the morning, I felt Abram's weight roll in behind me, and his strong arms pulled me into him before I fell back into a peaceful, dreamless sleep.

When we awoke, my father had built us a feast on the outdoor table, and we shared one last meal in the place where he'd been imprisoned. It felt like the last bit of normalcy we might have for a while.

"So how do we reach Wonderland?" I asked as we gathered on the lawn to depart. "And please tell me it doesn't include demons, floods, or psychological torture."

Dad reached into his pocket and brandished a key so small it hardly looked big enough to open a mouse door. "With this."

"Is Wonderland contained in a safe deposit box?" I joked.

Dad held up a finger with a knowing smile, then he leaned over and slid the key through the air just above the ground, as if there were an invisible door. The air waved with magic, shimmering and sparkling as colors rearranged. When the magic faded, it revealed that there was, in fact, a tiny wooden door, though I imagined the key conjured it, and not the other way around. Dad turned the key and opened it.

"Wonderland is just through here," he said.

I exchanged glances with Ramsey. "Dad, that door is four inches tall."

"Well, yes," he said apologetically. "We'll have to use magic to go through. If you'll do the honors?"

"You want me to *shrink us?*" My voice came out shrill and uneasy. "Jack could do it."

As a conduit, Jack could use supplicant blood to do magic. But he shook his head and held up both hands. "Hell, no. I have *no* training."

Ramsey nudged my arm with his elbow. "You can do it, Char. I know you can."

I'd never tried to make five grown human beings smaller than mice, so my hands shook a little as I closed my eyes and called on my magic. But the power felt...weak. Or to be more accurate, *I* felt weak. I tried to chalk it up to how often, and how furiously, I'd had to use my powers yesterday in the pursuit of finding my father, the madman. But something about the situation didn't sit right in my gut. Something was wrong with me.

I just didn't know what.

And what if I was so broken, I messed this up and hurt one of these men that I cared about?

"Don't overthink it," Ramsey said, his mouth close to my ear. "Remember, get the magic in your hands, then envision us all shrinking. This is a simple manipulation of space. You've got this well in hand."

I hated him for his logical pep talk, especially when I most definitely did *not* feel like I had this well in hand. But we didn't have any other option. Ramsey gave up his powers to save Briar's life, and he'd built his safe haven on Grimoult by utilizing the conduits and supplicants who came to live there.

It was up to me.

"Cut my hand," I told Abram, holding out my palm. "I need a boost."

He grimaced, but unsheathed his small blade and nicked my palm so quickly and efficiently, blood was already welling before I even felt the sting.

Closing my eyes, I tried again. With the added benefit of my blood being *outside* my body, the magic came a bit more swiftly, feeling more normal than it had before. I sent traces of the energy out to wrap around my companions, and when I felt like I'd gotten a grasp on them, I released the spell.

For several moments, magic dipped and swirled around us. I closed my eyes against the disorienting sensation of the world growing larger and fought through a twist of nausea in my gut as the ground rose up to meet me.

Sparkles of magic flowed off my body, and I shook my head, shaking away the last vestiges of the spell. The wooden mouse door was no longer only large enough for a mouse. It stood before me, hanging open to reveal a forested area beyond.

Ramsey appeared next to me and gave me a jovial smile. "We're all here! Let's go!"

So we passed through the door. I expected to feel something magical or strange happen as we crossed into Wonderland, but it was no different than walking through the door of the big house the night before.

On the other side, I waited until all of my tiny companions surrounded me, before I reversed the spell. The ground spun away from me, and my head whirled as gravity rediscovered my normal mass.

As the magic faded away, I gave my arms and legs an experimental shake to find they were in good working order. I glanced around, making sure everyone had grown up and retained their proper body parts. Lucky me, they did, since something was wrong with my magic. At least I hadn't permanently maimed anybody.

I took a deep breath and turned around to get my first glimpse of Wonderland. My jaw dropped as I found a familiar man standing behind me, an amused grin on his ruggedly handsome face.

Huntsman.

CHAPTER 20

"Aren't you a sight for sore eyes, Charisse Bellamy?" Huntsman teased, a big, white grin on his face.

Hunt's dark hair had always been long, but now it was lengthy enough to be tied back with a band. The soft edges of his ponytail brushed over the wooden handle that peeked over his shoulder—his magical axe, I presumed, in some kind of fancy, custom holster. Hunt was classically handsome with a patrician nose, a square jaw, and more muscles beneath his linen shirt than any man should be permitted.

And I was more stunned to see him than I was the night Brad Pitt kissed my cheek at the Met Gala.

I stared at Hunt's familiar face for so long—without moving or speaking—that Abram finally stepped forward and offered the man a hand.

"Good to see you, Hunt," he said gruffly as they shook.

"Likewise, my beastly friend." Hunt's melodic voice held a hint of amusement as he cast a glance my way. "Did I break her?"

Ramsey moved in for his own handshake. "Nobody's been certain of your whereabouts for quite some time, so this is a surprise. For all of us. But clearly for Char more than most."

"I've been laying low," Hunt said, releasing Ramsey's grasp. When my dad stepped in with a smile and a greeting, Hunt's grin widened. "My, oh, my. Archer Bellamy. Last I heard, my brother had you imprisoned."

Dad's smile faded minutely. "Your brother…Darcus? You never told me."

Hunt grimaced. "I assure you, he may have better style, but I'm the nicer one."

I was watching the conversation as if I was outside my own body. It wasn't abnormal for Huntsman to pop up when I least expected it, but his consistency across timelines was eerie. After hearing my father's story about the Oracle and traveling to the future to lay the plans necessary to get me here, I couldn't help but wonder if Huntsman had been one more pawn in our save-the-world scheme. Had he given up fifteen years of his life to get here, too?

Hunt turned to fully face me. "I've been waiting for you, old friend."

"What are you doing here?" I finally managed to ask, all the words rushing from me on one long breath.

"Righting my wrongs, as I told you I would do, many, many years ago." He stepped closer and clasped my shoulders in his hands. "Welcome to my Wonderland."

"*Your* Wonderland?" I asked, but he was already turning me away from him, and I gasped as my gaze fell over the valley beneath us.

We stood on a low cliff with miles upon miles of cerulean sky overhead. The sun shone brightly on a sprawling city much larger, and much more modern, than I'd expected. Roads criss-crossed the plain, lined by houses and businesses no different than those I'd known in the New Haven of the past. A vast area of tents stretched into the horizon to my left, while a thickly wooded area stretched to the right, and just beyond that, the silvery glint of a river winded into the distance. People were everywhere—walking, jogging, biking, and going about their lives as in any other city.

I'd expected *M*A*S*H* and got *Riverdale* instead.

"You're the leader of the rebellion," I breathed, whirling back around to face Hunt.

He shrugged. "We all have our parts to play."

Before I could jam my finger in his chest and demand he tell me what he meant by that, Jack shoved past Ramsey, his blue eyes wild. "You're in charge here? Can you tell me if there's an Alice Carroll in Wonderland?"

Hunt studied the younger man with cool, assessing eyes. "I cannot tell you that off the top of my head, but I'd be happy to check our records for you. If you'll follow me?"

The five of us fell into step with Hunt. As we walked down a twisting path set against the side of the cliff, Abram and I took turns catching him up to speed on everything that had happened since we arrived in this timeline, with Ramsey jumping in to help after we reached Grimoult. It occurred to me just how far we'd already come, but we weren't done. Not by a long shot.

"Did you time travel to get here?" I asked when we were finished with our tale. We were in the city now, passing a strip of businesses as we made our way deeper into the populated area.

"Alas, no," Hunt said. "I knew my brother had a plan. He always does. But I didn't know what that plan would be. I founded this realm between realms not long after your disappearance, Char, and I've been building an army ever since."

"That's a hell of a lot of foresight," Abram remarked.

Huntsman tipped his head in agreement. "You, of all people, would understand how the longer we live, the more of a long game we can play."

He motioned us to follow him up a sidewalk toward what looked like an old church—crisp white clapboard exterior, colorful stained glass windows, and a single steeple with a dysfunctional clock whose minute hand continuously twirled.

"Wonderland headquarters," Hunt explained as he opened the white double doors and ushered us inside.

As busy as the streets had been during our walk, the church was, well, dead. A hush fell over us as we followed Hunt down the central aisle. At one point, there must have been pews, based on the marks in the wooden floor, but they'd long ago been replaced with cubicles that housed computers and silent workers wearing headsets. I peered into one cubicle as we passed, and it looked as if the computer was showing him a video feed of New York City streets.

"Are you running surveillance on the city?" I asked Hunt, impressed.

"Among other things. Through here." He held out a hand to indicate I should walk through a set of open doors.

Hunt's office was large and airy, situated at the back of the church with windows to let in slants of golden sunlight. I plopped into one of the three waiting chairs and immediately realized I was more exhausted than I'd thought. Every muscle in my body gave up the ghost, and I turned into a puddle of ooze, leaning against the back of the chair so that it was the only thing holding me upright.

Hunt sat down behind the desk and booted up the computer. "Alice…what was the last name?"

"Carroll," Jack said quickly from behind my seat.

Ramsey and my father had sat in the other two chairs, while Abram hovered near the door, always on the lookout.

Hunt tapped at his keyboard with little skill. It was clear he wasn't a technology guru, but even so, seeing him do something as mundane as run a computer search seemed fundamentally opposite to who he was. Hunt was a skilled warrior, with a magical axe only magical people could see. Not an office drone.

"Alice Carroll *was* here," Hunt said, his eyes scanning the information on his screen. "She went with the last round of spies into the city, but didn't come back."

Jack's fingers gripped my shoulder painfully, and my heart seized in my chest as I asked, "Darcus?"

Hunt turned a sympathetic gaze on us. "I have no way of knowing. It says here two of our soldiers came back with their brains addled. They were unable to tell us anything, and our recon team couldn't figure out what happened."

"Maybe I could," I spoke up, glancing over my shoulder at Jack, who looked pale and stricken. "I could read their memories."

"By all means, you're welcome to try." Hunt stood and shoved back his chair. "They're next door in the medical center."

We took a back door exit and crossed a narrow patch of grass to a red brick building next door. If Hunt hadn't already told us we were going to a medical center, I never would have known what the building actually was. It looked like an office building meant for insurance agencies and tax accountants, not saving people's lives. But the moment we passed inside, the hustle and bustle of a normal hospital came into view.

The two mind-addled soldiers shared a room on the third floor. Neither made any motion to indicate they noticed our appearance. One boy, one girl, both somewhere in their twenties, wearing hospital gowns and tucked beneath layers of blankets. They both stared distantly at a television on the wall that was playing old cartoons.

I walked up to the girl first, and she didn't acknowledge my presence. She was pretty, with dark oval eyes and raven hair that was probably shiny when it was clean. Her skin looked sallow beneath the fluorescents, and I wondered if there was more going on with her than just brain addlement.

"I'm going to touch your head," I told her, keeping my voice low and as non-threatening as possible.

She didn't even blink.

I put a hand on both sides of her forehead, pressing my palms against her temples, and then reached for my magic.

An ache spread behind my eyes, and I winced, fighting past the pain to coat my hands in magic. My right arm turned hot, and a sharp pain lanced up my forearm and into my elbow, but I didn't let go of the soldier, even as my own fear crept into my mind.

This wasn't normal. Every time I used magic, I felt weaker, as if every time I used my power, it drained me a little bit more. I had to work harder to get it to listen to me and do my bidding, which drained me even faster.

But eventually, I managed to delve into the girl's mind and ignore the headache gathering in mine. Her thoughts were disjointed and blurry, some of them segmented into puzzle pieces that alone, didn't make sense, until I pieced them back together. I took my time, gently sliding memories around, filling holes in her memory and repairing the damage that had been done to her.

Then found what I was looking for.

Alice's face. I recognized it from pictures Lulu had shown me back at the apartment. This version looked longer, leaner, and more hardened than the smiling blonde in pictures, but it was definitely her.

The team was in downtown Manhattan at night. I heard gunfire, and Alice was beside me—beside this girl—with an automatic weapon. I had a moment of motherly protest—*You're entirely too young to be carrying an AK, ma'am.*—and then Alice whipped her gun up and returned fire like she'd been carrying a gun her whole life.

For all I knew, she had.

From there, everything fell apart fast. They were vastly outnumbered. Several soldiers fell beneath gunfire, and several more were taken into custody. As Alice was thrown to the ground and slapped into handcuffs, the soldier girl's attention turned to a militiaman coming at her with a small black device that looked like some kind of futuristic gun.

He put the gun to her head, and everything went dark.

~

I DIDN'T NEED to read the boy's memories, since I'd gotten the answers we needed from the girl, but I did my best to fix his addled mind, too. Whatever weapon the militiaman had used on the girl wasn't a gun, because she hadn't been shot, but Hunt's search of her hairline turned up an already healing pinprick that was likely the cause of her addlement. The boy had a similar wound. By the time they were both more cognizant—not fully normal, but functional—I was ready to pass out.

Most importantly, we now knew that Alice was in militia custody. The question remained—why?

Sometime between dinner and retiring to our borrowed rooms for the night, I took advantage of everyone else's food comas and snuck away for some fresh air.

It wasn't that I didn't want company. On the contrary, I hated any amount of space between me and Abram, and I'd have been content to have my father in the same room with me every day for the next ten years to make up for what we lost. But I was starting to feel stifled. I hadn't had any good time to myself to mull over our situation, so I carved some out the minute I could, despite my overwhelming exhaustion.

Wonderland seemed like a paradise. I found a small park behind the house and set out into a well-manicured garden speckled by trees. The air wasn't too hot, nor was it too cold. There was a hint of something faintly soothing on the air— honeysuckle or lavender. It was the kind of weather that brought people together for barbecues.

Speaking of bringing people together…

I sighed and scrubbed at the knot between my eyebrows. I

was no closer to figuring out how to bring Conduits and Supplicants together to defeat Darcus.

What kept the two at odds against one another? That answer was easy—the fact that Conduits used Supplicants like tools to produce their magic. If a Conduit could do magic without needing a Supplicant, they'd have no reason to be enemies. Supplicants, on the other hand, couldn't do magic at all—they would need to team up with a Conduit for that.

So the answer maybe didn't lie in just bringing them together. Maybe I could discover a way to bridge both sides of the magic—to find a way for Conduits and Supplicants to unlock the *full* power of magic within themselves so they didn't have to use each other.

Not that the idea was any more helpful than the "bridge the gap" idea, since I had no clue how to accomplish either. Now, on top of figuring out how to stop this war, I had to save Stacey and Alice, both of whom were prisoners of the enemy.

It just kept getting worse, like I snapped a heel halfway down the runway and had to make it to the end and back without anybody noticing.

"Charisse Bellamy," a disembodied voice cooed from high over my head. "I see you made it to your destination."

I stopped walking on the path and looked up for the source of the voice. The cat was lounging on a low hanging branch, idly scratching at the tree trunk with a single, razor-sharp claw. He bared his teeth in that hideously strange smile of his.

"You could access this realm and you didn't help me?" I accused, crossing my arms over my chest.

He sighed, the smile dropping from his face. "The gods do not interfere. Must I keep reminding you?"

"You're useless, you know that?"

"I often feel as such. Perhaps you would, as well, were you a goddess whose followers had long since forgotten her." He scratched at the bark, chipping away bits to reveal the smooth, pale wood underneath.

For a brief moment, I *did* feel sorry for him. I'd become a model nobody wanted to hire, and yeah, that wasn't quite the same as being a forgotten god, but still. I could see what he was saying.

"You can't perhaps tell me how to unlock solo magic within Conduits and Supplicants, can you?"

The cat flicked a lazy gaze my way, then returned to his scratching.

"I'm trying to come up with a plan," I said pointedly. "Are you here to help or just to annoy me?"

The cat's paw fell away from the trunk, and in an instant, he'd faded away. I stared at the empty branch, feeling somewhat shitty that I'd pissed him off so much he'd left without saying goodbye. I liked the talking cat, now that I'd overcome my squeamishness about the whole unnatural, cats-don't-speak thing. I'd gotten too harsh with him because I was lost in a cloud of worries.

My gaze slid sideways to the trunk where he'd been sharpening his claws. But that wasn't what he'd been doing—he'd been carving my name in the bark.

I stared at the four letters: *C H A R*. I flashed back to the trees in Central Park, ribbons swirling on the breeze, stuffed animals resting dead-eyed among the roots, and names carved by an unseen hand. Alice's name among the many.

Jack had insisted the trees were trying to tell us something.

I leaned over and put my palm against the wood, my memories shifting from Central Park to the sentient forest where we'd had to run from the Mother and Child. Those trees, according to Ramsey, were in the Mother's power. She could control them with her mind, send branches after us, pin us to the ground with roots.

If trees were sentient…did they have memories?

Feeling as stupid as that time I'd walked a runway in

aluminium foil, I closed my eyes and reached into the tree as if I were reaching for a brain.

My exhaustion, and the headache that I'd been carrying since healing the two soldiers, vanished immediately. I was hit by a surge of natural energy, like I'd dipped into the earth's reserves of strength and gorged myself on it. Visions came hot and fast, disconnected, blurry. I felt like I was racing through an entire history of the world according to trees.

Suddenly, the disorienting rush halted, and I stood in a decadent garden. High stone walls encircled the oasis of lush, green grass and beds full of rose bushes. I was the centerpiece —a tall, healthy tree with a large span of branches that cast dappled shade on the roses.

Two men in jumpsuits stood in front of me, both of them bending over a rosebush. The roses were huge and open, white as snow. I glanced around, noting that most of the roses were red.

It didn't take me long to recognize why. The two men were *painting* the white roses a deep, dark burgundy. I looked closer at the garden around me, and I could see where paint had dripped on the ground and the leaves, like drops of blood.

The men finished their job and moved on to another bush. Red paint dripped freely from the now-painted roses, turning into rivers of bright red on the dirt beneath the bush. As I watched, the rivers began to twist and turn, and letters began to form.

A L I C E.

CHAPTER 21

I HADN'T BEEN GONE LONG, SO I found my entire party still sitting at the dining room table in our borrowed house where I'd left them. I crashed through the door, my heart pounding, and skidded to a stop on the shiny wooden floor just shy of colliding with the table. Both Abram and Hunt jumped to their feet as if ready to draw their weapons and race into battle.

"What's wrong?" Abram said, at the same time Hunt barked, "Char? What is it?"

"Roses!" I said breathlessly, and slouched into my vacated chair to catch my breath. I'd run all the way back from the park, and the stitch in my side told me that had been a terrible idea. The tree might have given me a boost, energy-wise, but I was still a curvy girl who had a better relationship with red wine on the couch than a marathon track. "I had a vision. From the trees. Two men painting white roses red."

Abram and Ramsey exchanged glances, like I'd somehow lost my mind, but before either of them could question me, my father spoke up.

"Darcus's rose garden," he said matter-of-factly. "At his high rise in downtown Manhattan."

"How do you know?" Jack asked.

"Two men painting roses?" My dad laughed humorlessly. "Something about Darcus's presence causes all flowers in his vicinity to bloom white. Colorless. So his janitorial team paints all white blooming flowers to appease his insanity. No offense," Dad said to Hunt.

"None taken," Hunt said with a shrug. "My brother *is* insane. He loves roses with an almost maniacal bent."

"Why would flowers bloom without color around him?" I asked.

"Constant magic use," Ramsey offered, tapping his chin in thought. "Magic comes from inside you, of course, but you also draw on the world around you to replenish yourself when your reserves get low. Perhaps Darcus is over-extending his innate abilities, and thus drawing on the landscape around him, which in turn is affecting the plants."

"My brother would need to expend a *lot* of power to do that," Hunt said softly, his gaze going unfocused on the wall. "What's he up to?"

I had the same damn question, but opted to voice another one. "What about Alice's name? I saw it in the paint beneath the roses. Does it mean she's at Darcus's compound?"

Abram leaned forward and caught my eye. "What if it means she *is* the white rose?"

All occupants of the table turned to look at him like he'd lost his mind, which was a nice change of pace for me, considering I was often on the receiving end of that look.

Ramsey's eyes lit up. "I'm following."

"I'm not," I pointed out. "How could a person be a rose?"

Abram clarified. "If you witnessed this vision through the trees' so-called memories, then likely what you've done is tapped into a kind of plant hive-mind network."

"All plants are connected via their root systems and the electromagnetic pulses of the ground," Ramsey added. "You saw exactly what the tree 'saw.' The tree is telling us that Alice is a part of that rose bush."

"Not just Alice," Jack said, a note of excitement entering his voice. "All of the victims. The trees in Central Park are trying to tell us they're *all* a part of the plant system."

"So what...he turns his prisoners into roses?" I asked skeptically. "Isn't that a little off-brand for a villain in an Armani suit?"

"No, it isn't," Hunt said with a soft sigh. "He's always had a soft spot for roses. It makes perfect sense that he'd use a rose garden as his own personal prison."

"We also know Stacey is in Darcus's custody," Ramsey said. "So it seems likely both she and Alice are in that garden."

Dad spoke again, this time, his voice urgent. "What month is it?"

"Three days until April," Jack replied, pressing a button on his watch to check. "Why?"

My father cursed under his breath. "Darcus purges his rose garden once a year. On April 1st."

"Purges...how?" I asked, horror dawning inside me.

Dad turned an apologetic face to me. "He burns it to the ground and starts fresh."

"Son of a—" I rested my elbows on the table and pressed the heels of my hands into my eyes. "That's some pretty sucky timing."

"Or serendipitous," Ramsey said, while I remained firmly in the darkness behind my eyelids. "If you hadn't delved into that tree's memories, we wouldn't know where Alice and Stacey are being held, and without Archer, we wouldn't know how imperative it is to retrieve them ASAP."

Ramsey's optimism never ceased. I took a deep breath and sat up, peeling my hands away from my face so I could look around the table. "Okay. So we need to sneak into Darcus's compound, get to the rose garden, and save Alice and Stacey before it's too late."

"I can send a team with you," Hunt said. "They can help with distraction and be on hand in case anything goes wrong."

"In case Darcus finds us, you mean," I said with a shudder. "Considering we're in no way prepared to take him on at the moment, you could send a hundred armies and we'd still be outmatched."

"In the event that Darcus discovers you, we'll be ready," Hunt said grimly. "I cannot go with you, but I'll be prepared to come in, guns blazing, if the worst happens."

"Why can't you go?" Jack asked suspiciously.

"I was created to be my brother's supplicant," Hunt said ominously. "My presence would only charge him, make him stronger. Considering what Archer said about my brother possibly overextending himself, it's safe to say we don't want to give him more power than he already has. Not unless we all have a death wish."

We disbanded well ahead of sundown to get a good night's sleep and prepare to roll out bright and early the next day. As soon as Abram and I walked into our bedroom, he began to gather up the few belongings he'd unpacked earlier upon arrival.

"What are you doing?"

He raised an eyebrow at me. "Packing."

"You're not coming."

"The hell I'm not," he snarled, whirling on me with a t-shirt clutched in his fist. "You're not walking into Darcus's compound without me by your side."

"Trust me, I don't *want* to, but need I remind you, they're tracking you through that chip in your wrist." I tapped his arm to punctuate my point. "As soon as you pop back into the real world, you'll show up on their radar and lead the militia right for us."

Abram scowled and ripped open his backpack, extracting a dagger. "Fine. I'll cut it out."

"Don't be ridiculous!" I grabbed the dagger and yanked it out of his hand before he could slice his skin. "Jack said not having a tracker in your wrist in the City is an automatic death sentence. If the militia find out, they'll shoot you, no questions asked. I'm not taking that risk."

"And I'm not letting you go without me. My goal has always been to keep you safe. I'd rather die than let you walk into that viper's nest without me."

"It may be your goal, but it's not your *job*, Abram," I told him, trying to keep my voice calm. I didn't want this to spiral into another fight where he refused to talk, no matter how hard I begged. "I don't need you to keep me safe. I just want you to love me and for us to be happy together, like we were before..." I trailed off. The last few times I'd brought up our time apart, he'd shut down completely.

"Before that thing took over my body," Abram finished, his shoulders sagging. He sank to the edge of the bed and let out a long breath, his elbows resting on his knees so that he was staring at the floor.

I sat down beside him, then tentatively reached out to rub his back. His muscles shifted beneath my hand as he breathed. "Abram, you had no control over what happened."

"Right. I had no control," he said bitterly. "For a year, I was trapped inside my own body. I couldn't fight back. I just had to let him do whatever he wanted. All I could do was watch."

"That sounds horrible."

"You're the only thing that got me through it." He sat up and turned to face me, his warm hands trailing up my arms. "The thought of you kept me sane. I could have lost myself inside that thing, and I didn't."

I knew he was harboring some serious baggage over what happened, but he'd always been so strong, it never occurred to me that the situation had damn near destroyed him, the way it did me.

"I'm glad you made it through," I whispered, leaning into him. "And found your way back to me."

His hand cupped my face, and his thumb trailed across my bottom lip. "I have to protect you. Protect us. I can't let that happen again."

Fire spread in the wake of his thumb, and I caught the tip of his finger between my lips. I rounded my mouth and sucked his finger, burying it to the hilt against my tongue. Heat flared in his hooded eyes, and his other hand tightened on my arm.

I released his thumb inch by inch, teasing his skin with my tongue. "You can protect me without depriving me of the real you."

His breaths had come faster, and his jeans looked a little tighter where his cock pressed against the fabric. I thought back to our night in Grimoult, when I'd *almost* drawn out the Abram I knew, the Abram I wanted. I'd made progress then.

He wasn't going to run away tonight.

Slowly, as if he might bolt if I moved too fast, I slid over the space between us and hooked my knee over his lap to straddle him. I draped my arms over his shoulders and lowered myself onto his lap, as his hands rested easily on my hips.

I rotated my hips, pressing into his hard length and arching my back so that my breasts hovered in front of his face. I'd showered and changed earlier when we arrived, and my replacement tank top wasn't as rank as the one I'd worn into Wonderland, after the Mother's trees made off with my sweatshirt. But this tank top clung lower, putting my tits on display, and God and Abram both knew I had incredible tits.

His gaze darkened as it slid down the expanse of my neck to where my chest strained against the fabric.

Leaning forward, I put my lips next to his ear and breathed in my most seductive voice, "If you knew what I've been up to, you'd be furious."

Abram slapped my ass then fisted a handful of flesh, a growl in his voice as he replied, "What did you do?"

"While you were away…" I murmured as I slid one tank top strap down my arm. "I thought of you. Naked. Your hard cock inside me." Pulling the second strap down, I tugged the fabric off and my breasts fell free, nipples pebbling in the cold air. I pressed against Abram, his t-shirt chafing my nipples and sending a thrill straight to my core, then I scraped my teeth along the stubble on his jaw. "While I thought of you, I touched myself."

A sound escaped Abram's throat, and I took one of his hands from my waist, sliding it up my torso to palm my breast. "It's not the same," I said and dipped my other hand between us, walking my fingers up his erection where it strained against his jeans. "Nothing feels as good as *you*."

Abram's body hummed with tension. He was still holding back, still acting hesitant.

I slipped off his lap, stripping my tank top off over my head as I walked away. He didn't move to follow me, but he didn't run away either, which was good. We'd take this one step at a time.

Keeping my back to him, I unbuttoned my jeans, then hooked my thumbs in the waistband and gently shoved them down over my hips. I moved slow, bending with the motion until my bare ass was in the air, pointed right at my boyfriend. I stood just as slowly and stepped out of the pants, putting a little sashay in my hips as I returned to him.

His gaze was everywhere on my bare body. I cocked a knee up on the bed beside him and rolled my nipples between my fingers, letting my head loll back. He made his first move then—the fingers of one hand inched up my thigh where it rested beside him.

My heart pounded in time with the throbbing between my legs. His fingers were so close. I wanted them on my body, *in* my body.

He just needed a little more nudging.

So I leaned in and widened my stance over his leg, whispering in his ear. "I'm so wet. Don't you want to touch me?"

As I pulled away, I caught sight of a familiar, fevered gleam in his eye, and I couldn't stop the grin from crossing my face. I slid my palm down my abdomen, fingers splayed.

"I guess I could take care of it myself," I said. "The way I did when you were gone."

My fingers had barely crested my pelvic bone when Abram moved with the quickness of a viper and snatched my wrist.

"Don't," he growled. Then he stood, his strong hands flipping me around onto the bed.

The mattress bounced beneath me, and I giggled, spreading my legs, watching as his gaze traveled down my body.

"If you aren't going to do it, I will," I said, challenging him.

I reached down between my legs, but not fast enough. He grabbed my arm, then took the other and shoved them into the mattress over my head, holding me down with just one hand.

The position arched my back, and my nipples were pointing straight at him as if I were the arrow and he was the bullseye. He was between my legs, still fully clothed, still *very* visibly hard.

I slid my knee up his side, finding bare skin beneath his t-shirt. "Touch me, Abram. Feel how much I want you."

He bared his teeth at me. "I give the orders in this bedroom."

There's the Abram I remembered.

I moved my knee over the front of his pants, pressing into his cock. "Then tell me what to do."

Abram released me and stepped away, reaching for his belt buckle. "Get on your knees."

Yes. Thank fuck. I rolled over and leveraged onto my knees, spreading my legs as wide as they went. Anticipation turned my skin to flame as I listened to the *snick* of his belt coming undone, and the soft whisper of the leather pulling away from the belt loops.

A moment later, the leather slapped against my ass. Not hard enough to leave a mark or hurt, but enough to jiggle my skin. I felt the blow in my pussy and moaned out loud.

His next blow hit closer to my core—a little harder. I pressed back on my legs and begged, "Abram, please."

His third blow landed at the juncture between my leg and my core. I cried out as little tingles raced through my body.

I heard his belt hit the floor. A split second later, his hand slapped my ass near the place where the belt had last hit. "You are mine, Miss Bellamy. All of you."

Then his finger slipped inside me.

I gasped, shocked by the sudden entry, and rocked back on my heels so that I could take his finger deeper. But he slipped away, leaving me wet and throbbing for more.

I heard his zipper fall. Felt the heat of his body as he kneeled behind me. His cock rubbed against me, but when I leaned into it, he pulled back.

"You shouldn't tempt me. I'm not the man I was before."

"Yes you *are*," I groaned. "If you would stop holding back, you would see that."

He slid his cock higher, this time nudging against my anus, and I bit my lip. "I've always held back with you, Miss Bellamy."

"I can handle it."

He nudged a little more. Gently. Testing. I'd never done *this* before, but Abram had a way of making everything feel unbearably amazing.

"If you don't trust yourself, Abram, at least trust me." I leaned into him a little more, pushing back against the pressure. The slight pain of the stretch caused pressure to build up in my core. "Stop holding back."

His hands reached around to cup my breasts and pinch my nipples as he pressed deeper, slowly, drawing out a long moan. "Tell me to stop," he ordered. "Tell me to stop, and I will."

It was as if he wanted me to stop him. As if this was some kind of test. "I don't want you to stop, Abram. I trust you."

I rocked against him again, taking him deeper, working my ass closer to his hips as the pleasure built up inside of me. I could hear the shift in his breathing behind me, feel his cock straining even harder than before.

When he pulled away, I feared I was losing him again, but instead, strong hands grabbed my hips and tossed me like I weighed nothing more than a doll. I hit my back again, and then Abram gripped my legs and tugged me to the edge of the bed.

"I want to see your face when you come."

All threat of him running away had vanished.

I'd won.

Abram leaned over me, his skin hot against mine, and kissed me.

Every nerve-ending in my body came alive at the satin feeling of his lips on mine. Every synapse in my mind fired like I'd stepped up to the gate and was ready for lift off. And dear God, was I ready for lift off.

Abram broke the kiss and took a deep breath, but I didn't give him a chance to speak.

"Fuck me," I told him, not bothering to hold back the hint of command in my tone. "Fuck me hard. You can't hurt me."

I braced myself for his aggressive, *I'm-in-charge* reply, but none came. Instead, he surged into me.

The cry that fell from my lips was the accumulation of months without him. I gripped his shoulders, fingernails digging into his perfect, naked skin as he buried himself between my legs as deep as he could go. I rocked my hips into him, gasping as he bottomed out and a pleasurable pain spread deep within me.

Abram pulled out with measured slowness, his entire body vibrating with tension. He felt like smooth fire inside me, inching out with such determination I grabbed his ass and lifted my hips to plunge him deeper again.

"Ah, ah," he said, putting one hand on my chest and pressing me into the mattress. He pulled out until just the tip of his cock was nestled inside me, and I wanted to weep with need.

"Don't stop now," I said, my voice high and breathy. "Do you want me to beg? I'll beg, Abram. I'll beg like you've never heard before."

A smile turned up the corner of his lips. Then he surged back into me.

Abram pumped into me until we found a rhythm and our bodies rocked together. Heat rose between us like a third partner, until Abram's skin grew sweaty beneath my fingers, and my skin flushed red with the warmth. My pleasure rose slowly, unfurling like a rose in spring sunshine, until I was panting, gasping his name.

"Abram, I'm going to come," I said breathlessly. "*Please don't stop.*"

Abram picked up the pace, our bodies slamming together. He grabbed one of my knees and pulled it up, widening my body so he could plunge deeper inside me.

"Don't hold back," he said gruffly, and I could tell in the tension in his voice that he was nearing his own pleasure, too.

I dug my nails into his ass, urging him faster, moaning his name, begging him to fuck me harder. Then my orgasm washed over me and I shook beneath him, screaming louder than necessary because I knew he liked it, because I wanted him to come with me. And he did, spilling inside me with a groan that rocked my world.

Abram collapsed over me, our sweat-slickened skin sliding together as he leaned up to kiss my neck. He trailed his lips over my cheek and to my lips, where he proceeded to thoroughly ravish my mouth in such a way that I had no doubt we were about to go again.

I could lose a little sleep for this. I would lose an entire night's sleep if it meant I could have this man in my arms. In my bed. In my heart.

Because at any moment, everything could go wrong again. So I clung to the here and now as we dipped beneath the sheets and kissed until our lips were swollen, until he'd hardened again and we could come together once more.

We had no guarantee for tomorrow. Not as long as Darcus ruled the world.

CHAPTER 22

MY FIRST SURPRISE the next morning was that Hunt had bagels and cream cheese for everybody. They weren't Panera quality, and there wasn't a soy mocha to go along with my meal, but beggars couldn't be choosers during the apocalypse.

My second surprise came in the form of a magical mouse door that didn't just transport the user *to* Wonderland, but could transport the user back to the real world at any desired point.

That's how Jack, Ramsey, and I, along with a team of Hunt's Wonderland rebels, passed from the front yard of the Wonderland headquarters into the early morning shadows of Central Park.

Miniaturizing and then regrowing twenty-plus people was a harrowing experience, especially with my magic being as haywire as it had been lately. By the time I had everyone back in the size and shape they wore naturally, my right arm hurt and my head swam from the effort. I took a few deep breaths of the crisp morning air, wondering to myself if traveling forward in time had somehow affected my magic.

When I had a clearer head, I unfolded the map my father had drawn us and held it out for Jack and Ramsey. "The garden is here," I told them, pointing to the Crayon-drawn square jutting off the side of the building. "Dad says the walls are ten feet tall and solid. We can't use magic unless we want to get caught, so that's why we have those things." I pointed to the metal climbing ladders dangling from Jack's pack. They hardly looked sturdy enough to support the weight of a fully grown human being, but they were our only option.

Jack glanced around at the team Hunt had sent with us. "Listen up, people. The compound is locked up tight and secured by a rotating armed guard. Your job—blow up an exterior wall on the opposite side of the high rise. Fight if you must, but this is *not* the mission you need to die for, all right? Run, if given the chance."

More than a dozen voices murmured their consent. The crowd rustled with pent-up energy, seemingly ready to go on the job. Hunt had done a pretty damn good job gathering people who *wanted* to fight against Darcus's regime.

Where Jack seemed in control and ready to rock, Ramsey looked a bit green around the gills. As Jack continued giving instructions to the worker bees, I nudged Ramsey with an arm. "Hey. You gonna make it? I told you to stay back in Wonderland, you know."

"My place is here," he said resolutely. "Especially with Hunt and Abram remaining behind, and your father too valuable to the rebellion to lose. You need me."

I gripped his shoulder and squeezed. "You're right. I always need you, partner. I wouldn't be half the Conduit I am without you."

We exchanged smiles, though mine was probably as strained as his. There was a lot I could say to Ramsey, like how much our year training together had meant to me, or how he'd become one of my best friends, even though I knew —for him, at least—that time had been fifteen years ago. But if I busted out the ooey-gooeys, it would feel too much like a goodbye, or a sappy "We might not make it out alive, but I love you, man," conversation.

Words had power all on their own. If I turned this into a goodbye, it might become one.

As a group, we moved off through the park, then separated into less obvious twos-and-threes as we took to the open street. Darcus's high rise compound was close, only four blocks away from the park, and we split up on predetermined routes with the promise to come back together behind the building and out of sight.

I led two rebels down the sidewalk. They had concealed their weapons inside heavy windbreakers, so that the three of us looked like three young women out for a leisurely stroll. None of us spoke, but I could feel the tension radiating off them, along with an air of excitement.

Darcus's high rise looked less ravaged than most in the downtown area. The building was black, the spaces between tinted windows ribbed with stone buttresses. I counted thirty stories, though I lost count twice, and from this vantage point, I could just barely see the gray garden wall jutting off the side of the building.

As planned, we found pieces of the team down a narrow alley behind the building. Over the course of twenty minutes, our twos-and-threes returned to the pack, surreptitiously joining us down the street until everyone was accounted for.

Jack turned to the explosives expert. "You know what to do."

The man nodded, a little gleefully, and then motioned for his small team to follow him out into the street.

The rest of us waited in silence. Jack stared down at his watch, which he'd synced up to the explosives man. The other rebels fingered their guns, gazes darting between Jack and the high rise.

"Get ready," Jack murmured. "Three. Two. One…"

A massive explosion shook the ground beneath our feet,

followed by the thunder and rain of debris falling. Dust billowed from the side of the building, and Jack cut his hand through the air, motioning the rest of the rebels to take off.

Their boots slapped against the pavement as they raced toward the explosives team and the destruction to enact the second part of their plan—diversion. Raised voices met our ears a moment later, and Jack grabbed my arm, holding me back in the shadows a moment longer. Good thing, too, because several camouflaged militiamen came sprinting around the building, making a beeline for the ruckus.

After they disappeared, Jack tugged the metal ladders free of his pack. "Come on. Time to fly."

He took the lead, with Ramsey and me close on his heels. We raced in the opposite direction of the militiamen, rounding the edge of the building to find the garden walls exactly as my father had described them: ten feet of cinderblocks, painted dark gray, and the thick, bushy apex of a giant tree forming a canopy above the wall.

The same tree who gave me the information about Alice, I presumed.

Jack tossed each of the three ladders high, one after another. The two-pronged hooks latched on to the top of the wall, and the slender metal rungs tinkled audibly as they came to rest against the stones.

Turns out, those dinky ladders *sucked*. I clutched a rung and stepped onto another, and the whole damn thing slipped away beneath me. My feet slammed back to the ground, and I grunted with disgust at my lack of acrobatic ability. Jack was already halfway up the wall, and Ramsey not far behind him, while I hadn't even gotten off the ground.

It took two more tries to get a feel for how the ladder worked, so by the time I was steadily crawling my way up the wall, Jack and Ramsey were already on top of the stones and surveying the garden inside. I noticed in my periphery that the other two ladders were being raised, but I focused on putting one foot over the other.

At the top of the wall, I hooked a leg over the edge and straightened. Jack and Ramsey had already scaled down and into the garden, scouting the area while they waited. I followed Jack's lead and tugged the ladder up, turning the hooks so that I could scale it down the inside of the garden. It would also give us an easy out once we retrieved Alice and Stacey, and I was ashamed to admit, it never would have occurred to me to do that. Subterfuge and rescue missions were clearly not my strong suit.

I was half-way down the ladder, moving easier now that I understood how the damn thing worked, when a man shouted behind me.

"Hey! You can't be in here!"

Shit.

I heard the telltale scrape of Jack's broadsword unsheathing, and I picked up the pace. I couldn't sacrifice time or speed to look back over my shoulder and take stock of the situation, but if there was more than one man barreling into the garden, Jack and Ramsey couldn't fight them alone. Ramsey wasn't capable of killing humans, even to save his own life.

That was the curse of being a mage.

But I missed a step in my haste. My foot slipped past the rung, and I'd already let one hand free to move down the ladder. The jolt of my body sliding sideways, and the ladder pitching the opposite direction beneath me, threw me off, and I lost my grip.

For a brief, weightless moment, I fell as if gravity had claimed my body and was dragging me into the pits of hell. Then I hit the ground on my feet, and my legs crumpled beneath me, one ankle wrenching painfully as I collapsed to my side. I cried out and sucked in a breath, tears pricking my eyes.

Jack's sword hit metal, and a moment later, a gunshot cracked through the garden. My heart skipped a beat, but Jack's sword still clanged. I shoved aside the pain in my ankle. I was the only one of us carrying a gun, a loaner from Hunt, and it sounded like my weapon was needed now. Jack couldn't win a gunfight with a broadsword, and Lulu would have *killed* me if I let him die. So I launched to my feet, ignoring the weakness in my ankle and the way every step felt like things were tearing inside my leg, and ran blindly toward the clang of metal.

Jack stood beneath the giant tree, crossing blades with a uniformed guard. Ramsey was darting from rose bush to rose bush, fleeing another guard who held a small gun in one hand. As I paused for a millisecond to decide my next move, Jack's broadsword slashed over his head, and one of the tree's heavy branches separated from the trunk, falling directly on the guard. The poor man lost his sword and disappeared beneath the heavy branches.

Seeing as Jack had things well in hand—though the tree was probably regretting how it helped me get here—I loped off toward Ramsey and his attacker.

The guard was moving erratically, zigzagging across the garden after Ramsey, so I couldn't get a good shot in from afar. I picked up the pace, limping as I ran to get closer to him without being seen.

Unfortunately, he had better senses than I expected, and he whipped around, his gun leveling on me. I dropped to my knees, agony lancing up my leg, and fired at him before I could give it too much thought.

His return bullet whipped past my shoulder, but my shot landed in his substantial gut. He pinwheeled backward, his weapon falling from his fingers. A moment later, he keeled over and hit the dirt, blood puddling beneath him as he lay still.

Jack offered me a hand and helped me to my feet. As I put weight on my leg and winced, he said, "Are you injured?"

"Fell off the ladder and hurt my ankle." I shoved him away and headed for the central tree. "I'm fine. Let's get Alice and Stacey and get the hell out of here."

Our rebel team's distraction was clearly working. There was a fair amount of commotion coming from down the block, around the other side of the building, but other than the two guards we took down, nobody else had ventured into the garden. For the time being, luck was on our side. And thanks to the big tree, I knew exactly where Alice was imprisoned.

I put my back to the trunk and circled it, looking for the same vantage point I'd had during my vision of the Alice rose.

Bingo.

The moment I laid my hands on Alice's rose, I got an immediate and unbidden vision of Lulu's face—Alice's thoughts, probably, considering I knew Lulu wasn't trapped in one of these things. I didn't even need to use my magic to sense Alice inside there, and I could only assume that had something to do with the spell Darcus used to entrap her.

I closed my eyes and delved into the rose's hive-mind, seeking the source of the spell. For my dad, it had been the top hat sewn to his head, so there was a distinct possibility something tangible was holding Alice in place, too.

I caught glimpses of her arrest, and the days she was held in an actual jail cell. Then Darcus came for her and interrogated her. Even though I couldn't hear the words, I could sense his anger and the threatening tone of his voice. I even got an idea that he was asking about *my* whereabouts, but of course, Alice had never even met me outside of the first few months of her life.

Then the scene changed, and I stood in a dark room. Alice sat on a chair beneath a single spotlight, her blonde hair glowing like a halo. She wore a crown of thorns, and blood trickled down her face from where the crown scratched her skin.

She startled at my sudden appearance and then leapt to her feet, dancing away from me. "Who are you?"

My heart ached for a couple different reasons. Alice didn't know me; she didn't even know my face from pictures, which meant Lulu hadn't done much to tell her about me. I'd missed the girl's whole life so far, and I never, *never*, wanted to be a stranger to Lulu's children. But another part of the ache came from just how much Alice looked like her mom. Blonde instead of dark hair, but they could have been twins in the face.

"I'm Char. A friend of your mom's. And a friend of Jack's," I added. "We're here to save you."

Alice's big blue eyes widened, and then her surprise transformed to something like a warrior's stoicism. "This crown, sealed to my head, somehow. I can't leave with it on, but I can't get it off. I've tried yanking, but nothing works."

"Can I see?"

Alice came to my side and knelt to give me a better view of the thorns. I poked and prodded at the thing, doing my best to not hurt her. Anywhere the thorns rested against her skin and drew blood, they weren't just touching her—they were stuck to her. With my dad's hat, I'd been able to cut the stitches and remove it, but there were no stitches on Alice's head.

But I could snap the thorns off the crown.

Alice held statue-still as I started popping thorns off the crown. One by one, I separated the circlet from the thorns in her skin. After a few moments, the blood would stop trickling, and the separated thorn would fall away from her skin. I worked my way around methodically until she was free.

The moment I tugged the circlet off her golden hair, the world around us dissolved, and we were transported out of the rose and into the garden.

"Alice!" Jack's voice came out hoarse and strangled. I didn't even have a chance to move before his long, lanky form enveloped his sister's.

As the two of them began to talk loudly over one another, both chastising each other for their secrets and declaring how much they'd missed one another, I left them to it. I had a Stacey rose to find.

I moved quickly between rose bushes, touching every rose I could see. Like with Alice's flower, I didn't need to use magic to see the person inside. One touch brought a vision of them to mind, and I was looking for a certain pink-haired pixie.

It stung to walk away from so many people. These were real people, imprisoned by Darcus, and there was a very real threat that they'd be destroyed entirely in a few days. But I didn't have the time—or the magical energy left—to dive into every spell and free them from their crowns. Maybe once I had Stacy and Alice, we could come up with a better plan for everyone else. They might know things from being imprisoned here that could help.

Finally, in a corner of the garden way too close to the interior doors, I got a glimpse of a haunted, familiar face. Her hair was no longer pink, but bright red, and she looked a little bit older than when I'd last seen her.

Stacey.

"She's here!" I called over my shoulder. But before I could call up my magic and sink into her rose, I heard a familiar voice behind me.

"Well, well. Charisse Bellamy. Just what are you doing in my rose garden?"

Darcus.

CHAPTER 23

I TURNED AROUND SLOWLY, letting my hand fall away from the Stacey rose and hoping like hell he didn't realize that was one of my friends in there. My heart fluttered so shallowly inside my chest, I felt certain I was about to keel over dead. This wasn't supposed to happen. This was a rescue mission, not a march against Darcus. We were supposed to grab Alice and Stacey and get the hell out.

Not get caught.

Darcus stood outside the glass doors that led from the high-rise into the garden. He looked out of place surrounded by so much natural beauty, in his expensive navy pinstriped suit, his dark hair slicked back from his face like a mob boss, and a sneer slashing across his too-handsome features.

"Were you unaware I'd be able to sense you unraveling my rose spells?" he said haughtily.

Before I could reply, Jack appeared from behind a row of painted bushes, sprinting toward Darcus with his broadsword held high, while Ramsey stepped into the clearing and lifted his gun. But Darcus just waved a hand, and I caught sight of the glint of red blood on his palm. Then I felt the raw prickle of magic on the air before both Jack and Ramsey collapsed to the ground, out cold.

Thankfully, Alice was nowhere in sight, and I hoped to God she stayed that way.

"I figured you couldn't sense anything under that cloud of Axe body spray," I told him coolly as I inched farther from the Stacey rose.

"Oh, Char. You wound me. As if I'd wear something as gauche as Axe body spray."

"Chanel? Hermés? Clive Christian? What's your poison?" I took a few more steps away from the bush, gaining some semblance of control as his attention remained on me and not Stacey.

"I'm not here to shop colognes," Darcus said, some of the levity fading from his voice. "Where's the prisoner you freed?"

"Gone," I said with a shrug. I motioned vaguely over my shoulder at the narrow metal ladders still clinging to the stone wall. "Got her up and out before you got here. Finders keepers."

"It's darling how you underestimate me." Darcus looked over my shoulder, his gaze landing on the Stacey rose bush, and raised his hand. His sleeve fell away, revealing a circlet of leather around his wrist that dripped blood. He was wearing a supplicant's blood.

He's too strong. We're all going to die.

Then he let loose a fireball that enveloped the bush that held Stacey.

"No!" I screamed, whirling around to make a break for her. I didn't even make it one step before magic encircled me. My body went rigid, and my head swam. Magical restraints, I realized, holding me in place—and cutting me off from my magic.

I couldn't save Stacey. She was going to burn up, and I was helpless to save her.

At least Alice was safe, and surely smart enough to remain

hidden. Lulu and Jack wouldn't have let her grow up any other way.

Darcus motioned in my direction, and the restraints tightened around my body. Then I floated along behind him through the electric glass doors, which shut with a decisive clang behind me.

We passed through a black marble and chrome lobby that looked like it should have housed a modeling and talent agency rather than the headquarters of a dystopian regime. The floor was littered with foot traffic—militiamen in camouflage, uniformed officers in riot gear, all of whom were passing back and forth from the chaos outside. I took a moment to hope none of the rebels who'd instigated the diversion had gotten hurt, and then Darcus grabbed my arm and shoved me into an elevator.

I hovered in the corner as far away from him as possible without leaping from the car and into the elevator shaft. He tapped his foot and whistled low under his breath as the elevator dinged every floor we passed until we reached the thirteenth.

I would have expected Darcus's office to be on the 666th, but I guessed that the building didn't go that high. The thirteenth floor seemed fairly apt, though.

There was less hustle and bustle up here. We passed an empty reception desk, though the steaming mug of coffee and the illuminated computer screen told me its occupant had just stepped away. Darcus maneuvered me through the bindings, my toes hardly dragging the marble floors under his spell. As if we were in some kind of horror movie, his leather bracelet dripped blood intermittently on the floor as we passed down the hallway, leaving a trail that someone else would probably have to clean up.

I wondered then if Darcus was as put together as I'd initially thought. Maybe his own paranoia, and his own desire to be great and powerful, had unhinged him. It wasn't exactly a sane man who turned prisoners into roses and then demanded they be painted red. My father's punishment hadn't exactly been normal, either.

Darcus lifted a finger, stopping my forward momentum outside two plain, wood-paneled doors that had no door knobs. He pressed his palm against the wood, a little bit of his stolen supplicant blood dripping down the surface, and then inside, a lock clicked, and the door creaked open.

A massive room paneled in pale wood with matching, creaking wood floors spread around us. Built-in bookshelves covered the wall behind a large, U-shaped desk, and a marble fireplace and an antique furniture suite sat off to the side, like something out of a *Downton Abbey* set.

"Welcome to my private study," Darcus intoned, sweeping a hand out to indicate our surroundings. "Doesn't it smell nice? Cedar wood, you know."

"Smells like a mad scientist's laboratory." I kept my expression stoic. I refused to let him see my fear, even as my heart ached for Stacey burning to death in the garden.

A fleeting look of irritation crossed his face, but he didn't reply. He circled his desk and sat in the tall-backed rolling chair, then pointed to the two cushioned armchairs sitting before him. "Have a seat."

"I think I'll stand, thanks."

Darcus's face hardened. "I said to sit, Miss Bellamy. It wasn't an invitation. It was an order."

"I don't answer to you," I said hotly, then wondered what the *actual* fuck I was doing. This man was walking around with a supplicant's blood leaking from leather onto his skin. He could incinerate me where I stood, and I'd have no way to fight back with these magical bindings keeping my powers in check.

"You'll find that everyone in this city answers to me," Darcus replied, then lifted his hand and crooked his fingers down.

The restraints around me flared hot and forced me to bend. I fought against the magic, but it was too strong for my body without my own powers to back me up. My ass hit the cushion with a little more speed than necessary, and I winced as a sharp pain shot up my spine from the blow.

"There. That's better." Darcus slid a pile of folders to the corner of his desk before he gave me a slimy smile and his undivided attention. "I've been waiting for you, Miss Bellamy. It's been quite some time since our last meeting, but you're just as lovely as you were fifteen years ago."

"Unfortunately, I can't say the same for you. You're looking a little worse for the wear, you know. That's what happens to dictators." I had no clue where this bravado was coming from. I was *terrified*, literally shaking in my shoes. I didn't have the means or the talent to destroy this man, but he definitely could destroy *me*. And here I was, poking the bear in the Armani suit, like he wouldn't rip my face off and eat it for lunch.

"Just as sassy as I remember," Darcus said fondly. "Well. No matter. I'll shut your crass mouth soon enough." He leaned over and pressed a button on the landline sitting at the corner of his desk. "Mariette? Please bring me the weapon."

A high-pitched, breathy voice replied, "Yes, sir. On the way."

My heart had already fallen into a steady, overactive death knell the moment I turned around and saw Darcus standing in the garden, but the mention of a weapon kicked it up even further.

"What weapon?" I asked, though I wasn't certain he'd bother answering.

"Something of my own creation," Darcus replied, standing smoothly from his desk and straightening his suit jacket. Even his sleeves had sharp, ironed-in edges. "A weapon to defeat the gods themselves."

"You can't kill gods," I scoffed, thinking of the all-seeing, all-knowing Talking Cat. "They're the ultimate beings."

"No!" Darcus snarled, slamming a hand into his desk.

I jumped, but the restraints kept me from bolting.

"No, *I* am the ultimate being," Darcus went on, the snarl fading back into his cultured tones. He walked away, his back to me as he went to the window and looked out over the city. "I didn't want to destroy the world in order to gain power. You must understand that."

I rolled my eyes. "Somehow, I don't believe you."

"I quite like the world," he went on as if I hadn't spoken. "Do you know what I miss? Movie theaters. Hollywood fell beneath my army many years ago, and production halted indefinitely. I miss the cinema."

"You realize it's *your* fault you don't have 'the cinema'," I pointed out.

A knock came at the door, interrupting our conversation, though if looks could kill, Darcus's glare would have pulled every bone from my body and left me a dying puddle of meat. He turned, his hands clasped behind his back as he called, "Come in."

The heavy wood door opened, and a young, pretty blonde woman entered the room. Mariette, I supposed, the owner of the Marilyn Monroe voice on the phone. Her hair was pinned into pin-up style waves, and her maroon skirt suit hugged every curve on her. She was carrying a long, dark object that looked like a cross between a baton and a machine gun.

Darcus smiled at her appreciatively as she lay the weapon on his desk. He reached out, brushing his fingers over her shoulder. "Thank you, Mariette. Perhaps you'd like the rest of the day off?"

Mariette flushed to the roots of her hairline and leaned into his touch. "If you have no...*need* of me."

"I always have need of you," Darcus murmured, grasping

her by the arm and guiding her back to the door. "Take the afternoon off. I'll see you early tomorrow, hmm?"

As they talked in low voices, I stared at the weapon on his desk, trying to make heads or tails of what it was. My initial assessment hadn't been too far off—though it was roughly the length of a machine gun, with a two-handed hilt, the long, round barrel wasn't the barrel of a gun, at all. The end of it didn't have a round hole through where bullets could shoot. So…what did it shoot? Or was it just meant to be used as a battering ram? And how could something *that* simple work on the gods?

The loud click of the door locking behind Mariette pulled me from my musings.

Darcus returned to his desk and strolled back behind it, pushing his chair out of the way. "Ah. There's my lovely. Isn't it beautiful?"

"Your definition clearly doesn't match mine," I said shortly. "An embroidered Oscar de la Renta twill dress is beautiful. That is not."

Darcus ignored me. "I'm calling it the Godkiller."

"Ten points for cleverness," I said, laying on the snark. "You should have been a Ravenclaw."

"Where was your father when he should have been teaching you to keep your mouth shut?" Darcus snapped. Then his face eased into a pleased grin. "Oh, that's right. He was here, under my spell, creating this weapon for me."

"Because you imprisoned him and forced him."

"Indeed I did. Perhaps I should have killed him when I discovered his betrayal. I'm just a romantic at heart, I suppose." Darcus lifted the weapon, holding it lightly across both his palms and staring down at it with something weirdly akin to love. "It runs on supplicant blood. A lot of it, unfortunately, and in order to use it, I go through a lot of prisoners. But if I use *your* blood… That special combination of both supplicant and conduit powers… I'll be invincible.

And now that I have *this*, I don't even need your willing participation for you to help me." He traced his fingers over the long barrel. "A weapon of death strong enough to take revenge on the gods. Can you see it?"

"Sure." I crossed my legs, pleased to find his bindings had loosened just enough for my body to move. "What I'm hearing is that you feel less than a god, and you're so butthurt by not measuring up to *divine beings*, you've decided to throw a temper tantrum and destroy them."

"Watch your tongue," Darcus snarled.

"I hate to break it to you, sweetie, but the desire to be god-like doesn't make you so. In fact, it's kind of pathetic," I added flippantly, my voice—and my nerves—gaining in strength. "You're such an inferior creature, you'd get on your knees and suck a god's dick if it meant you could have their powers."

For a long, silent moment, Darcus didn't move. Didn't blink.

Then he roared, the sound shaking me to my core, and swung the Godkiller around like a deadly baseball bat.

Right at my head.

CHAPTER 24

THE BATON HIT me in the side of the head with a nauseating *crack* along my jaw and ear. Blinding pain exploded in my head, and I momentarily lost the ability to see behind a cloud of white noise that felt like it would drag me into unconsciousness. The force of the blow flung me off the chair and onto the cold floor.

I was too lost in the agony of a baton to my face to notice how much it hurt to land. I hit the floor on my right arm, unable to get my hands free from Darcus's bindings to try to catch myself. My head bounced off the marble, and the white noise grew exponentially. An obnoxiously loud rushing in my ears, and the shock of pain, were the only things that kept me awake.

Blood blossomed in my mouth, the coppery tang so startling that it chased away some of the fuzz in my head. I spit it out before it could drown me, blood and saliva spattering Darcus's clean white floor. I had no clue where the blood was coming from—did the asshole break my jaw? Knock out my teeth? God, that would make for *terrible* pictures.

As the white noise faded, little black specks danced in and

out of my vision to the tune of Darcus's tasseled loafers coming my way.

Fury flooded in on the heels of my agony. I'd done it to myself. I'd purposefully goaded a madman who'd destroyed an entire country to get his seat at the top. Darcus would stop at nothing to harness all the power of the world, to become the supreme ruler to whom everyone bowed. I was one more stepping stone—one more *obstacle*—in his way. Just another tool he could use in his quest to be like a god.

He took his time coming to me, as if he knew I was too hurt to move. I lay on my stomach, my cheek pressed into the floor while the other side of my head felt as if he'd shattered every bone in my face. Despite the overall exhaustion and feeling that if I stood up, I'd collapse back down on shaky legs, I'd survived. Honestly, I considered myself lucky to be alive. A few inches higher, and he might have killed me.

Fucking coward. Hitting a woman who's restrained and can't fight back.

His footsteps stopped by my head. But...maybe I could work his hair-trigger temper to my advantage. If I could get him to lash out at me with *magic*, instead of using the Godkiller like a battering ram, I could attempt to harness his magic and release myself from his bindings. Free from his restraints, and with access to my own powers, at least I could have a fighting chance to get out of this alive.

Possibly.

I rolled over onto my back, breathing hard as my head swam from the pain and darkness threatened to take me over. Darcus stood over me, the Godkiller dangling from one hand and his face twisted into a pleased grin.

"You don't know when to stop talking," he said, voice low and dangerous. "I don't need you alive very long to drain every last drop of blood from your body. Remember yourself, Charisse."

I spat more blood on the floor then returned his sneer,

even though it set fire to the injured half of my face. "Oh? Like how you're meant to be this great and powerful conduit, but you're resorting to physical violence like a common human? Maybe you should remember yourself, Darcus."

The slur in my words from my jacked-up jaw took some of the sting from the words, but it got to him, anyway.

He lunged, his leg pulling back in preparation to kick me. I winced, bracing myself for yet another slew of injuries, but he stopped short of attacking. His loafer slapped back to the marble with a loud *smack*.

"You're right," he said, his voice going colder.

For a beat, neither of us moved. Then Darcus bent down and grabbed my arm bruisingly, then hauled me to my feet. He returned me—still bound by the invisible restraints—to my chair. My back slammed into the cushions and I slipped a few inches, settling into a low, awkward pose and unable to right myself.

"Now that you're here," he said, walking to an enclosed shelf behind his desk, "I'll take what I need. Then I'll kill you. There is no reason to drag this out."

Okay. Not exactly what I was going for.

As he poked around inside the cabinet, I wracked my brain for a plan. Obviously, he wasn't going to use his magic on me right now, and my ventures into goading him had only shut him down and given him more purpose. How could I press him into using his powers without him resorting to violence instead? If he cracked me across the face with the Godkiller again, I had a feeling it *would* kill me.

Darcus returned to my side clutching a small, sharp utility knife and a large ceramic bowl. He set the bowl on my legs, then manipulated my right hand over the edge of the bowl. My arm moved as if I were a poseable rubber doll, and I couldn't do anything to stop him. Before I could even cry out, he'd slashed up my arm, releasing a deluge of my blood.

Fear and fury mingled inside me as the cut burned like fire on my forearm. I latched on to those feelings, watching in disgust while my blood spilled into the bowl. He intended to use my blood for nefarious purposes, and I'd be damned if I'd sit back and let him.

He hadn't tightened the restraints on my legs, so I bucked my knees. It was awkward, considering the rest of my body couldn't move at all, but I had just enough give to jostle the bowl. It toppled sideways and slid off my legs, shattering on the marble floor with such violence that my blood spread out like a busted water balloon on concrete.

And *thank God*, Darcus reacted with magic.

"You bitch!" he roared, throwing out his hand and conjuring up a wave of magic meant to more firmly hold me in place. The blood from his leather strip was drying. I needed to get that damn thing off him, because the one thing I had that Darcus didn't was the ability to use magic without supplicant blood.

I let the wave of his power wash over me, then before it could snap into place like the current restraints, I took control.

He could hold me in place. He could dampen my powers.

But he couldn't get rid of my free will.

I yanked Darcus's spell into myself, gritting my teeth against the discordant feeling of his magic becoming one with mine. As soon as it made itself at home beneath my skin, I turned the energy around and used it to rip through the bonds he'd put on me. His invisible restraints fell away like I'd cut them with knives.

"No!" he roared, and then snatched the Godkiller off his desk.

Before he could swing it like a baseball bat, I leapt behind one of the cushy armchairs and tossed a ball of fire at him. He waved a hand, almost as if he were bored, and the ball glanced off him.

As Darcus's leftover power crackled away from inside me, I felt even weaker than I had before, when I'd unraveled the spell imprisoning Alice. The small amount of energy I used to form the fireball had sapped my strength more than it should have. My hand and arm were burning like they were on fire themselves, as if conjuring and throwing the fireball had set me aflame instead of Darcus. I knelt behind the chair and shook out my hand, fighting back a wave of nausea. *What the hell is wrong with my magic?*

Every time I'd used magic in this timeline, I'd lost more and more energy. Any new exhibitions of my power sapped any remaining strength I had left, and I didn't understand what was happening to me.

The Godkiller smashed into the armchair, and the whole thing toppled sideways to reveal me hiding behind it. Darcus advanced, murder in his eyes and the Godkiller raised like he intended to take my head off with it.

I scrambled back in an awkward crabwalk several inches before I managed to get my feet beneath me and stand. My head was so light it might as well have been filled with helium and hovering nine feet over my body. I could hardly lift my feet to back away, and the burning in my right arm had intensified to blinding pain.

I was broken. Something about this timeline had broken my magic.

Darcus let loose another spell, and I attempted to leap out of the way. Too slow, unfortunately.

A wave of energy crashed into me. I tried to absorb it, rather than letting it take me down, but I was too weak. I flipped around, tottered on my feet for a moment, and then hit the floor on my hands and knees. My joints absorbed the shock of my fall, and I collapsed the rest of the way to the ground, my eyes closing involuntarily.

I couldn't move.

"Fine!" Darcus snarled. "You want to play these games? I don't need you *alive* to take your blood, Charisse Bellamy."

I opened my eyes and blinked past the exhaustion. Darcus was leaning over, his fingers dragging through the drying puddle of my blood on the floor. Then he stood and rubbed the tacky fluid on the barrel of the Godkiller.

No!

But I couldn't even open my mouth to speak the word.

Magic flared hot and painful through the room, and my heart plummeted into my stomach. I rolled to my knees and crawled away, reaching deep into my powers.

They felt like they were just out of reach. Out of sight, covered by a veil I couldn't quite grasp to get off.

The dull heat and ache that I'd felt since I tried to incinerate Darcus had intensified in a specific place in my wrist. As I crawled away from the Godkiller, I barely noticed a sudden beeping in the room, as if an alarm were going off.

Darcus laughed, long and loud and maniacally. "You installed a counterfeit chip," he said, voice moving closer behind me. "It's melting down because you're using magic."

I couldn't seem to keep my legs beneath me. My right knee pitched out from under me and I fell onto my elbows on the floor. I vaguely recognized that the beeping did sound like the tone coming from Abram's wrist the night the militia came for him in the Wal-Mart hell woods.

Abram. Fuck, there's no way I could let myself die. Not when we've barely started our life together. He'd be furious if he knew that we were intercepted by Darcus.

"We do that on purpose, you know," Darcus went on, oblivious to the fact my thoughts were on my boyfriend and not him. "We add a failsafe into the chips that tattle when someone is using magic who shouldn't be."

I used the edge of Darcus's desk to haul myself to my feet. My wrist burned and throbbed, and between that and the beating I'd taken, I felt ready to give up. How could I fight back if the chip in my wrist wouldn't let me?

Suddenly, the Godkiller let out a beep of its own. Darcus raised the weapon and pointed it at me like a gun. "Fully charged by your potent blood, Charisse. Any last words?"

Not that he was going to give me a chance to even be snarky. I ducked below his desk just in time for the Godkiller to let out a hissing, whining screech, and then half of the desk blasted away beside me. The force of the explosion threw me away, and I skidded into a corner with a complete absence of hearing in one ear. Unlucky for Darcus, the kick-back of the gun knocked him on his ass, too. He hit the ground on his back, sailed three feet toward the office door, and remained still.

Shock would have rooted me to the floor if it weren't for the incessant alarm coming from my wrist. I scrambled to my feet, using the shelves on the wall to balance myself, and then rushed back to his desk. The chip had to go. Until I got the damn thing out of my arm, I wouldn't have a chance in hell of subduing Darcus, and there was no way for me to know when he'd come around. I had no weapon but my magic, and it was out of reach.

I hadn't watched closely when he'd put down the utility knife he'd used to cut me open. I rifled through the contents on his desk, digging around in loose papers, knocking all the office supplies on the edge off in my search. I glanced around the floor near my congealing blood and the broken shards of bowl. But the knife was missing. Probably in his pocket.

Second plan. I yanked open drawers in his desk, looking for anything sharp enough to cut skin. I was hoping Darcus was enough of a sociopath to have weapons stashed away in his desk, but the closest I found to a weapon was a sharp letter opener.

It would have to do.

I cast a glance back at Darcus. His hands were twitching,

and a low moan emitted from his lips, but he didn't sit up. The Godkiller had hit him square between the eyes, and the raised bruise gave me a vindictive sort of glow.

Taking a deep breath and sending a prayer to the universe that I wouldn't pass the hell out, I jammed the letter opener into my wrist.

CHAPTER 25

I'D THOUGHT the multiple concussions, cuts, and contusions I'd earned since stepping foot in Darcus's compound were painful, but compared to trying to slice and dice your own wrist with a letter opener, all the aforementioned injuries had just been foreplay.

The dull edges of the letter opener weren't sharp enough alone to cut my skin, so I had to saw at my wrist like I was carving up a Thanksgiving roast. Lucky for me, the chip in meltdown had made my wrist so hot, it had turned the whole area numb and worked as a kind of anesthetic. So even though I could feel every hard slice, some of the pain had been managed for me—for now, anyway. All bets were off later.

If not for the malfunctioning chip, I might have passed out from the agony. I finally bit through my skin, and then had to work on widening the wound. Black faded in at the edges of my sight, and I had tunnel vision on the first spurt of blood from my skin. Nausea rolled over me so fast and furious, I thought I would throw up. I didn't have that luxury.

Working quickly, I got the gash wide enough to be able to move the letter opener around in. Unfortunately, moving the letter opener's sharp edge around under my skin hurt like hell, and I jerked it out and tossed it to the ground, breathing hard.

I flexed my fingers and hissed as torn skin and ragged muscles moved. The chip had to be just beneath the surface of my skin, which meant I should be able to slide a finger inside and find it. But the very idea of doing that sent a fresh wave of nausea rolling over me, and I sank against the desk to give myself a moment.

Then I heard a groan from the other side of the room.

Darcus. Waking up.

God damn it.

I couldn't wait any longer. I clenched my teeth, took a couple of deep breaths so I wouldn't pass out, then jammed my finger inside the wound in my wrist.

Nothing could compare to the alien sensation of a finger probing inside a raw, open wound. I bit back a scream, tears stinging the corners of my eyes, and forced my left hand to keep doing its job, even as my brain screamed for it to stop. My innate self-preservation instincts kicked in, and everything in me wanted to stop causing myself such pain.

The pad of my finger passed over slick muscle wet with blood. I was knuckle deep, digging blindly for something that didn't belong, when I heard the Godkiller power up. It was a nearly inaudible whir, like a ceiling fan powering on, but I recognized it from the first shot.

"I know you're still there, Charisse," Darcus taunted. His voice moved closer as he continued speaking. "I can hear you breathing. I can smell blood. Did my Godkiller hurt you? Poor, poor creature..."

My hand shook so hard I couldn't keep control over my finger. It ripped at the torn edges of my skin, and blood flowed freely down my arm, soaking my shirt, my jeans, my left hand. *Where is this damn thing?*

Then the Godkiller blasted again.

The desk absorbed most of the blow, but not all. A cloud

of launching debris and the force of the concussive blast sent me hurtling away from the desk and into the open near the bookshelves, where I had nothing to hide behind.

"Ah! There you are!" Darcus said.

I played dead to give myself time. I'd landed on my side, my back to Darcus. Even though I was dazed, and I could feel blood trickling down my forehead from yet another injury, I jammed my finger back into my arm, doing my best to hide the movement from Darcus's sight. Nothing mattered more than getting this chip out. I couldn't fight him with brute force. I needed my magic. It was my best shot at not dying.

Or at least going down with a fight.

"Char? You're still breathing..." Darcus crooned. I listened intently to the tap of his expensive loafers on the floor as he moved closer.

Finally, the very tip of my finger brushed against something hard. I reacted on instinct, digging my nail into the object and ripping it back toward the hole in my skin with a hooking motion. The wound released my finger with an awful suction sound and another wave of blood, then a tiny, bloody microchip fell to the floor.

Power flooded me like I'd thrown back the curtains on a window and looked out into full, bright sunshine. My magic crackled over me and through me, filling all the nooks and crannies until I came alive with energy. I harnessed some of the magic to stop the flow of blood in my wounded arm and knit the edges of the jagged cut back together, but before I could do too much damage control, the Godkiller powered on again.

I rolled several times, narrowly missing the blast from the cannon, then threw up my bloodied hand and let loose my own magical blow.

Darcus wasn't expecting it. The ball of energy slammed into his torso like an arrow hitting the bullseye, and he flew backwards into a bookcase. Shelves splintered beneath his broad shoulders, then he collapsed to the floor as everything once held on the shelves fell on top of him. My magic crackled over the whole pile, which remained still as the dust settled.

I hadn't even stood up. My legs were tangled underneath me, and I was laying on my hip, supporting myself with one arm while the other hung in the air. The chip had been keeping me from being able to *fully* access my powers. All the issues I'd been having since coming to this timeline hadn't been from time travel or some kind of failure on my part.

Just that stupid little chip. I never should have agreed to it.

I stood slowly, testing out the sturdiness in my legs. My arm still throbbed, even with the half-hearted healing I'd done, but I could stand on my own. So that was progress.

I took a few hesitant steps toward Darcus. The pile of books and shattered knick-knacks hadn't moved since settling, but I wasn't dumb enough to think he was down for the count. And unfortunately, he hadn't lost his grip on the Godkiller—it had gone under the pile with him.

With the Godkiller, Darcus bested me by a margin I had no chance in hell of closing. Without the Godkiller, I didn't necessarily have great confidence in my abilities to defeat him magic-to-magic, but at least my chances would be better. The most important thing I could do, though, would be to get that bloody leather strip off his wrist.

Without supplicant blood, Darcus was nothing. I just needed to separate him from his supply, get the Godkiller, and end this once and for all.

The pile covering him didn't move as I inched closer. One pale hand poked out from beneath a handful of scattered books, but the fingers remained still. Knocked out, I guessed.

Out enough that I could find that leather strip and relieve him of it?

I could tell at a glance that the visible fingers were from the hand not attached to the bloody strip, because they were too clean. The leather strip made his hand look like it was wounded, streaked with blood, dripping as if it were his own veins laid open. So I circled around to the other side and tentatively reached out to dig into the debris.

I moved three books before Darcus let out an almighty roar, and the pile split open like an atom bomb. He used magic to blast everything off him, and all the fallen goods became missiles.

I took the brunt of a thick, sharp-edged book to the head and dropped to the ground with a hiss of pain, slapping my hand to the free-flowing wound. Darcus stood, still roaring like a maniac, bits and bobs from his shelves falling away from him like water, as if he were rising from the ocean. He still held the Godkiller firmly in his bloody hand.

If I didn't react fast, he'd get the upper hand—again—so I tossed another spell at him before he even had a chance to lock eyes on me.

Tendrils of my magic wrapped around the Godkiller and yanked before he knew what was happening. I tossed the gun as far away as possible, and it skidded beneath the curtains on the opposite side of the room. Darcus leveled his bloody hand on me with a snarl, but I darted away on hands and knees—not the most elegant of escapes. His fiery blast hit the ground where I'd been sitting, cracking the floor tiles.

Using magic, I latched onto what remained of Darcus's desk and lifted the whole mass, throwing it at him. He batted it away with a flippant wave of his fingers, sending the desk hurtling back at me. I threw myself bodily to the floor, and the desk slammed into the wall over my head, shattering into a thousand pieces. I put both my arms over my head to protect it as the pieces rained down on me.

I didn't wait for the debris to stop falling before I called up another blast and threw it at Darcus. The magic carried sharp edges of broken wood from the air, fighting with magic *and* weapons, but Darcus tossed up a shield and deflected the lot of it.

For a moment, we utilized the broken pieces of Darcus's office, attacking and counter-attacking one another. It happened so fast, I could hardly keep up, but for the moment, Darcus wasn't focused on where his Godkiller was still hidden behind the curtains. I kept the thought in the back of my mind that if I could reach the Godkiller, I could figure out how it worked and maybe use it to defeat Darcus.

Getting to it wasn't exactly going to be easy under his assault.

I dodged a flying porcelain vase, but not fast enough. It shattered against my shoulder, and I tossed a counterattack using the pieces. Several managed to get past his shield before he got the magic up, and three long cuts raised on his face beneath the sharp edges. But he didn't even pause his assault and launched another ball of energy at me.

Fuck. As long as he had access to magic, I wasn't going to be strong enough to take him down. He moved too fast, his instincts honed from several thousand years of using his powers. My measly three years of practice couldn't stand up to that, and I was losing energy fast, both magically and physically.

There was no fucking way I could get close enough to him to get that bracelet.

Dodging another blast from him, I tossed out a few tendrils of magic in an attempt to lasso the bracelet and yank it from his wrist, the way I had the Godkiller. I managed to get a tendril around the leather, but then Darcus sliced a hand through my magic and severed the connection. I was so stunned by the way he'd literally cut me off, that I wasn't quick enough to block his next blow.

The full force of his blast hit me mid-torso. I flew backwards, bracing myself to slam into the wall or the bookcases like Darcus himself had done earlier, but instead, my trajectory sent me barreling into the wooden door that led out into the hallway.

Thankfully, the door was much thinner and more easily breakable than a wall. Instead of being stopped by the door, I went right through it, the wood splintering loudly around me. I hit the marble hallway floor on my back and slid all the way into the opposite wall, one arm tossed over my head to catch myself before I cracked my skull open.

I'd absorbed most of the blow through the door with my shoulders, so I wasn't *completely* dazed and confused as I lay on the hallway floor trying to regain my bearings. There was a bit of rotation to my vision from the whole flying through the air thing, and some whooshing in my ears, but I'd managed to make it through with my wits intact.

I knew I needed to sit up and be ready for Darcus to appear in the doorway. Be ready to continue the fight. But I wanted nothing more than to close my eyes and give up.

I couldn't win this battle.

Suddenly, other sounds worked through the whooshing in my ears. First, the ding of an elevator arriving, which sounded so out of place right now, I almost didn't recognize it. A split second later, I heard shouts and heavy footfalls coming toward me. Darcus still hadn't appeared in the doorway, which told me he was up to no good, planning his next attack.

If this was Darcus's personal guard of conduits coming to back him up, I was a goner. Might as well dig my own grave and put up the gravestone right here: *Here Lies Charisse Bellamy. Fierce and Pretty but Not Enough to Stay Alive.*

Abram would be furious when he discovered what happened. I'd kept him from coming with us because of his stupid wrist tracker. I'd refused for him to cut it out of his wrist, then turned around less than twelve hours later and did the exact thing I told him not to do. He could have been here with me. Fighting with me. Maybe, if I'd had Abram, I could have won this.

Instead, I closed my eyes and listened to my fate racing closer.

Then a voice hurtled down the hall. "Char? Oh my God!"

I would have recognized that voice anywhere.

Stacey.

My eyes flew open and shock made my fingers numb. I sat up abruptly, my gaze seeking out the crowd of people racing down the hall. Not Darcus's guard or militia, like I'd expected.

My cavalry had arrived.

Stacey. Jack. Ramsey. Alice, too, and all of them carrying weapons. *Multiple* weapons, like they'd taken the weapons from every single body they'd felled on their way to find me.

I scrambled to my feet and launched myself at Stacey, who reached me first. Her skinny arms wrapped around my neck like vises, and I laughed maniacally into her shaggy, bright red hair.

"You're *alive!*" I gasped the words, barely able to express them through the rush of emotion I felt. "You were burning!"

She stepped back, a machine gun swinging from a sash around her body. She'd always been thin, but she'd lost a lot of weight on this side of time, and the dancing playfulness she used to carry in her eyes had morphed into something harder, flintier. "Let me tell you, it got *real* hot. But Jack and Alice managed to get me out of there."

"Jack and Alice..." I turned to the two kids in question.

They stood side by side, both of them hard-faced but shining with golden good looks and tentative smiles. Jack held up his hands to show me they were soaked in red fluid. "Alice's blood. Her plan, too. She knew how to unravel the spell, thanks to you."

I tossed my arms around both of them and squeezed. These smart, clever, beautiful fucking kids. Lulu was going to be so proud of them, as long as I could get them back to her alive.

And I would, I realized. Just their presence here lightened

the weight on my shoulders and gave me a jumpstart on energy. I'd fight to the death if it meant getting Jack and Alice home to my best friend, like I'd promised her.

Ramsey squeezed my shoulder. His eyes were red, as if he'd been crying. "I thought we'd lost you. Are you all right?"

But before I could respond, another voice joined us.

"Aw. Isn't this just darling?" Darcus cooed.

We turned as a group to find him looming in the office doorway, fresh blood in rivulets down his hand and the Godkiller leveled on us.

Then he pulled the trigger.

CHAPTER 26

Ramsey slammed into me, both arms pinioning me to his body, and the two of us hit the ground as the Godkiller's wave of deadly energy shot into the hallway. The magic hit the wall behind us with the force of a wrecking ball, so that bits of plaster rained down, dusting everything in a fine white powder.

"Jack!" I screamed, shoving Ramsey off my legs. Fear damn near levitated me to my feet as I sought out the kids in the melee, praying to anyone who would listen that they weren't dead.

I promised Lulu.

They weren't. In fact, there wasn't a scratch on them. Jack had his hands up, and a forcefield was visible beyond his fingertips in the cloud of falling dust. He'd used Alice's blood —still coating his hands—to protect his sister and Stacey, who had been closest to him when Darcus fired. The force of the blast on his barrier had shoved all three of them against the wall, and they were pinned between the magic and the wall. Everything around them had been blasted to smithereens, but they were safe. His quick thinking had saved their lives.

Also, holy moly, the kid had some power. I could only imagine what a great conduit he would be after some training with Ramsey.

Assured that my friends were all right, I whirled on Darcus to retaliate. Even though he'd seemed to get used to the powerful kickback on the magical gun after the first couple shots he took at me, he was now teetering precariously, obviously knocked off balance.

I threw a lasso of energy and grabbed the Godkiller, ripping it from his hands. He slashed my magic, like he'd done only moments before in his office, but not quick enough to keep me from sending the Godkiller flying down the hallway.

I ducked magic from him and returned the attack in kind, while my friends opened fire with their guns. I thought I saw several bullets strike gold before Darcus leapt back into his office and disappeared from view.

Jack and Alice followed his movements sideways, their rounds cutting into the walls like they were made of butter, kicking up plaster and wood and leaving inch-wide holes illuminated by sunshine from within.

Getting shot wouldn't have killed him, but it could slow him down. I was hoping for multiple gunshot wounds.

"Coward!" I yelled. "Come out here and fight like a man!"

Ramsey grabbed my elbow and tugged me away from the open doorway. "Or we could run," he told me urgently. "The reason we found you was because Jack could sense your magic up here with Darcus. We're not going to be the only ones. He'll have back up coming."

"It would be safer to get out and get back to Wonderland," Stacey agreed. She was still holding her gun at the ready like some kind of fiery-haired assassin. Like Lulu and Ramsey, the lighthearted, laughing Oracle had had to adapt to Darcus's hell.

I cut my glance to the office doorway, but he was nowhere

to be seen. What if they'd managed to riddle his body with bullet holes? Now might be the *only* chance I'd get to take him down without trying to build an army larger than his. I didn't have a plan. As far as I knew, Huntsman didn't have a plan beyond "get more fighters." If I could take him out here and now…

We couldn't run. Not yet.

Then the elevator dinged again.

Jack, Alice, Ramsey, and Stacey raised their guns on the shiny metal doors opening at the end of the hallway. I helped myself to a spare dangling from Alice's shoulders and did the same, gathering a bit of magic in my hands to turn the bullets to cannons.

Then the doors opened and a mass of militia men spilled from the elevator with a handful of the uniformed conduit guards who served Darcus. They hadn't expected us to be standing so blatantly in the hallway, so we had a moment of surprise on our hands to act.

We let loose a volley of bullets, including my magically enhanced grenades, and managed to take down several soldiers before the conduit guards threw up a barrier. I dropped the gun, and it slid back into place around Alice's shoulders as I pulled up a forcefield of my own and deflected the first few return blows from the conduits.

"You have to teach me how to do that," Jack told me, a gleam of interest in his eye.

"You can do it with your broadsword, too," I replied. "Making your blows stronger and faster."

Stacey butted in, exasperated. "Weapons training *later*. We are way outnumbered. What do we do?"

"We fight," he said with a shrug. "We do our best and go down swinging. Take as many of them with us as possible."

Still holding up my forcefield, I stared at Jack in horror. His matter of fact tone tore me up inside. He was just a *kid*.

Barely an adult, but he'd had to grow up so much faster than any child should have, because Darcus had ruined this world. But for Jack to stand there and sacrifice his life for the cause… that was some dark shit.

"Drop the shield, Char," Jack said, face resolute. He lifted his borrowed gun. "Let's do this."

"No," I snapped, sending another wave of energy into my barrier to strengthen it as yet another conduit tested my skill with his own. Magic flashed over us like lightning. "I'm not letting you die. We'll take the stairs at the other end of the hallway."

"And get out how?" Jack barked. He kept his gun sighted on the crowd racing up the hall, getting closer by the second. "This building is packed with Darcus's cronies. We fight, Char. It's the only way."

I opened my mouth to retort, but paused as the ground moved beneath my feet. I thought I'd imagined it at first—I wasn't exactly in great shape after losing a *lot* of blood and fighting Darcus like these were my last moments on earth. At this point, I figured maybe my body was finally giving out on me and *I'd* been the one moving unbidden. But one glance around, not just at my friends but at the militia on the other side of my forcefield, proved I wasn't alone. Darcus's goons came to an abrupt halt about ten feet down the hallway, looking around at each other in confusion.

The floor moved again. I realized with a start that the floor wasn't *moving*, not really. It was rumbling, like the grumble of an eight-wheeler on an interstate ramp, and the sound was growing in volume. Not an earthquake, because the building didn't sway or shake. More like… Something was coming. Something big.

There was a commotion at the other end of the hall, behind us. A door banged open and slammed into the wall, then dozens of people spilled from the stairwell. The very first face through the door was my most favorite in all the world.

Abram.

He was half-beast, with his arms and hands transformed into those dangerously strong claws. I recognized a few of the faces behind him—members of Wonderland who had helped with the diversion out on the street. My boyfriend's dark gaze swept over the tableau, noting the small Scooby gang up against the larger Darcus army on the other side of my forcefield, and then he roared. Even though the sound wasn't directed at me, it chilled me to the bone and raised goosebumps on my skin.

Abram was here for blood.

As if his roar was a signal, Wonderland raced into action.

For a few moments, everything turned to chaos. A hailstorm of bullets, the flash of conduit magic from both ends of the hall, voices yelling orders. I dropped my forcefield and leapt out of the way as the two forces clashed, then Abram was in front of me, his claws gentle on my arms. His lips crashed to mine, and he gave me a spine-tingling, toe-curling kiss that awakened my body in a way wholly inappropriate for the life-or-death situation.

"What took you so long?" I teased, clutching his shirt in both my hands.

Two militia men edged closer to us, and Abram whirled on them with a beastly snarl. His claws slashed through the air, and he took down one, while I sent a blast of energy into another group of Darcus's soldiers, before throwing up a forcefield to protect us.

"The conduits felt your blood touch the ground," Abram said over the din. "We were ready to roll the moment it happened. Where's Darcus?"

I pointed over Abram's shoulder at the open doorway to Darcus's office. The man still hadn't emerged after Jack and the others had opened fire on him. I hoped he was maimed. Unable to walk. A sitting duck.

Ha. As if. More than likely, he was lying in wait for me to walk through that door.

"Let's end this," Abram said. "Together."

He kissed me fiercely one more time, and I clung to him, drawing it out, refusing to let him pull away from me. The moment it ended, the moment I dropped this barrier and we walked into that office, anything could happen. We could *die*. So I'd be damned if I didn't get one last kiss before I went.

"I love you," I told him as I pulled back, my lips as warm as my eyes.

"And I love you," he replied.

Then we darted across the hall to our fates.

The moment I passed into the office, a sphere of power blindsided me. I caught it on my right side, and it tossed me to the ground like a rag doll, my arms and legs akimbo as I rolled into the wall. Abram roared in response and leapt on Darcus, claws slashing and his snout elongating enough for his knife-like beast teeth to protrude.

Abram opened several vicious wounds in Darcus's face before the man got a hold of himself and countered the attack with a punch, since the two of them were in such close proximity. Before he could let loose his magic, I slapped my palms to the floor and coaxed the marble into a wave. White tiles pitched beneath Darcus's loafers, and he keeled over backwards, the spell he'd called up flying well wide of Abram.

I was on my feet again immediately, tossing a fireball at Darcus's coiffed head as he fell. This wasn't the time for honor or any of that stupid machismo crap—if Darcus was down, he was fair game. His dark hair flamed as he hit the floor, and Abram bent over to stab him in the gut with a dagger-like claw.

Unfortunately for us, that was when Darcus got *furious*. He jammed a hand up into Abram's chest and shoved a massive amount of power into his torso. Abram flew off him, but managed to land on his feet, his eyes twitching as his body filtered Darcus's magic.

While I was busy worrying about Abram, Darcus used my distraction to launch another attack on me. He sent an entire bookshelf hurtling across the room at me, and I fell to the ground out of the way, though I caught the bottom edge against the side of my head. My body rolled with the force, and I came to a stop at Abram's feet.

The air smelled like Darcus's burning hair, and I had the woozy thought, *Good, I hope I burned him bald. Dick.*

I sucked in a breath, trying to blink past the lightheadedness. Without the chip, my power was back and even seemed better than ever, but I still wasn't fast enough and good enough to go one on one with Darcus. Abram had the brute force, and he could slice and dice Darcus all day long, but only magic could best him—and only if we neutered him.

That fucking leather bracelet had to go.

Abram knelt to help me up, then fell into a tuck and roll as Darcus shot a fireball at us. The world dipped and turned as Abram protected me with his body, and then we came to a halt behind the pile of splinters that had once been the desk.

"The leather on his wrist," I hissed, ducking another blast that tore through the vestiges of the desk. "If you can get close enough to cut it off, do it."

Abram nodded and pushed to his feet, then leapt across the room, zig zagging as Darcus tossed things at his head with magic.

I wobbled to my feet and used my power to tilt one of the two remaining bookshelves onto Darcus's back. It landed against him but didn't explode, so he managed to shove it off with another blast of energy, then turned on Abram.

Abram's claw slashed up Darcus's arm, and I watched breathlessly as the bloody leather strip fell to the floor. I threw a fireball at the thing and smiled as it burned white hot, taking away Darcus's last source of supplicant blood.

But it didn't help. Darcus used his magic to add force to his punch, and I heard something crack in Abram's face. He fell sideways, his body limp. His beast arms transformed back into human arms before he slammed into the floor and lay still.

Deadly still.

CHAPTER 27

THE RAW, ragged scream that tore from me was the lament of a woman who had just watched everything in her world fall apart.

Abram lay still on the marble floor, his face settled into the lax, peaceful look of someone sleeping. I didn't know if he was alive or if Darcus's magically-enhanced punch had broken his neck and stolen him from me. But I didn't *need* to know. I knew Darcus had hurt the man I loved, and I'd avenge him with my very last breath.

Fury filled me so completely, I didn't know where I ended and the vengeance began. I wanted to tear Darcus's face off with my bare hands. Eviscerate him and dance in his pieces like some kind of psychopath warrior.

I whirled on him with fire crackling over my fingertips, and if looks could kill, he'd have withered to a decaying corpse. Too bad even magic didn't work that way.

Darcus eyed me warily as he conjured up a sphere of energy, but I was quicker. I blasted a shield of magic at him that barreled into his body like a moving concrete wall. His expensive loafers slid uselessly across the floor as I pressed the shield into him and shoved him back against the broken remnants of his shelves.

My hands shook as I held the forcefield in place and advanced on Darcus. He slammed his palms into the magic, his own energy sparking against mine with a strange, tingling sensation that I could feel in my core. No matter how hard he punched and kicked, no matter how much magic he threw at the shield, nothing worked.

I had him pinned, the way Jack had pinned Alice and Stacey to the wall to save their lives.

Points for defensive magic, I thought. I was barely breaking a sweat holding him in place. But I couldn't do anything against him like this. I couldn't get through my own shield to take him down. Bullets, magic, none of it. As long as I was safe on this side, he was safe on that one.

If we were to fight, to end this shit once and for all, I'd have to let him go.

Glancing back over my shoulder, I eyed Abram's fallen form. I thought I could see him breathing, his sides expanding and contracting shallowly. Maybe that was wishful thinking, or maybe Darcus hadn't broken his neck.

"You can't hold me here forever," Darcus called. His voice came through the shield strangely muffled.

"Sure I can." I took another two steps forward, closing the space between us. "I could hold you here for hours. Wait for the supplicant blood on your hands to dry so that you can't use it anymore."

"What about your friends?"

As if his words had broken a spell, the sounds of fighting from the hall leaked into the room. A pang of fear hit me in the chest, and I turned my gaze on the door. The fight hadn't spilled into this room yet. I probably could thank Darcus for that—a spell over the room or the door, something like a hex I couldn't see. But somewhere out there, Jack, Alice, Stacey, and Ramsey were fighting for their lives.

Darcus seemed to know he'd touched a nerve. He stopped beating on the shield and leaned into it, sneering at me. "Ah. Bound by the love of other people. How sweet. As I've told you, Charisse, that's what makes you weak."

I rolled my eyes. "Am I the one pinned right now?"

His face twisted in fury, and he slammed another crackling palm to the shield. "Release me at once, woman! Fight me like—"

"Like a man?" I laughed and crossed my arms. "Or did you forget how you hid behind your office wall like a coward while I was ready to fight? You're such a hypocritical jackass. You play dirty. You use other people to get where you want to be. You're just a garbage person that no one will ever love."

Darcus roared and renewed his efforts to free himself from my shield. He looked like a madman, his limbs thrashing, fingers clawing at the magic like he could dig his way out. I watched his struggles with a smile on my face. I didn't have a plan, but this was a nice change of pace, being the one in charge.

Someone behind me chuckled. "You've always been good at poking the beast."

I froze, and behind the shield, Darcus did, too. He locked his gaze on the person behind me, slamming both palms into the shield one more time for drama. If I thought the venom in Darcus's gaze towards me could sting, it was nothing compared to the hatred there now.

"Brother," Huntsman said as he stepped up to stand beside me. "Long time no see."

"What the actual living hell are you doing here?" I hissed at him, turning my back on Darcus. "You're his *literal* battery pack, Hunt. You're going to lose me this battle."

Hunt placed a calming hand on my arm. "Righting wrongs, Char. What I'm always doing."

"If he gets control of you, we lose the war before it even begins."

Hunt swung his other hand up, and the Godkiller landed in my arms. "Do you trust me?"

I wrapped my fingers around the cool hilt and took the weight of the weapon from him. Meeting his gaze, I thought I saw sadness there, and I wished I could see into his mind to figure out what game he was playing at. Instead, I nodded and assured him, "I trust you."

Hunt tore his gaze away from mine and smiled at Darcus. "Two Brothers, the bane and the answer. One cannot exist without the other, but both survive if they survive together."

"Shut *up*, Huntsman!" Darcus snarled.

"Is that a song?" I joked, glancing sideways at my partner.

"A prophecy," Hunt corrected. He clasped his hands behind his back, his gaze still on Darcus. "Arcane knowledge, so ancient only the gods and the Brothers know it."

"You're a fool!" Darcus screeched, slamming his shoulder into the forcefield. "Let me out, and I'll kill you with my bare hands."

"You can't do that without killing yourself, and you know it," Hunt said coolly. He looked at me. "Do you remember Stacey predicting that I would be an integral part of defeating the Brothers?"

I nodded. My heart pounded so hard, I thought I'd choke on it.

Hunt tapped the Godkiller on the barrel. "Use it when I tell you to. Drop the shield."

"But—"

Hunt grinned wryly. "My brother is a pain in the ass, but he's also right in that you can't hold him forever. Drop the shield, Char."

The bottom fell out of my stomach. I'd fought alongside Hunt many times since I first met him, and I'd never seen him look so serious. I had a feeling if I didn't obey, he'd find a way to drop my magic himself, even if it meant knocking me out cold.

I shifted the weight of the Godkiller to one arm, and my hand shook as I cut the connection to the shield.

Darcus burst away from the wall with a high-pitched shriek, magic already gathering at his palms. He headed straight for his brother, as if I no longer existed.

Hunt unsheathed his axe and whipped it around, spinning it in an impressive circle that slowed Darcus's race forward. I was sure he didn't want to become a human filet. Hunt didn't have magic to fight with, which made this whole situation feel like a suicide mission. But he had his axe, and he had me, and that would have to be enough.

I trusted him. I trusted that he had a plan. I just wished he'd shared it with me so I wasn't going in blind.

Darcus shot a fiery ball at his brother, and I batted it away with another shield before returning fire. While Darcus was distracted by my small, gunshot fire balls, Hunt leapt forward and swung his axe. The metal rang in the air like a melody, and Darcus wasn't quick enough to keep the broad side of the axe from slamming into his head.

I threw a lasso around his legs and tugged so that Darcus slammed shoulder-first into the ground, all the breath expelling from his lungs. For the first time, I thought maybe Hunt and I would be strong enough together to defeat Darcus. We could wear him down, just like this, physical and magical violence until his body gave out.

But then Darcus levitated bits of sharp debris from the destroyed desk and turned them into shrapnel. A cloud of deadly missiles hurtled at me and Hunt, and I couldn't get up a shield fast enough to protect us both. My moment of indecision kept me from protecting either of us.

I took large wooden splinters to the right leg, crying out as they sliced into me like knives. The pain made me drop the Godkiller, and it skidded away on the slick floor. Hunt got a few splinters to the arms, and his bright, red blood welled up on his skin, soaking through his t-shirt. Supplicant blood.

Blood that Darcus could use against us.

A maniacal gleam came into Darcus's eye, and he rushed toward Hunt.

But Hunt danced away from Darcus's grip. "Ah, ah. No blood for you, dear brother."

Darcus threw energy at Hunt, pulling him toward him, but Hunt lashed out with his axe, using the flat side of the metal. I didn't understand why he didn't just use the sharp end. Lop Darcus's head off. But I knew the Brothers were eternal, so maybe even losing a head couldn't slow him down.

I lashed out with my own magic, severing the strands holding Hunt. For several moments, things moved quickly—almost too quickly for me to keep up. I shielded and returned a magical assault on Darcus, while Hunt used his axe. The Brothers both moved so fast, just blurs darting in and out, metal flashing, magic crackling. I did my best to keep up and help, but it got to the point the fight became too much and I couldn't be sure I wouldn't hit Hunt.

Then suddenly, Hunt broke away from the battle. He darted across the room and kicked the Godkiller toward me. The weapon skated across the floor and slammed into my feet. I'd clearly forgotten about it, but now the sight of the damn thing sitting below me felt like the end.

Hunt leapt back at his brother, axe flashing. Darcus's head rang from the blow, and he slumped to the floor. Now that he was still, I could see all the tiny wounds on his body from Hunt's assault.

Hunt picked up his brother in a headlock and turned to face me. "Now, Char. Use the Godkiller on us both."

Cold dread trickled through me. "On you...both."

Darcus struggled vainly against Hunt's grip, but he'd taken a few too many shots to the head. His eyes were glazed and unfocused, and he couldn't even grip his brother's arm.

"If both Brothers are alive, both are safe," Hunt told me,

his voice deadly calm. "But to kill one, you must kill both. This is the only way to rid the world of Darcus, once and for all."

"By getting rid of you, too."

He inclined his head. "I knew this day would come, Char. Wonderland was my vessel to help me get here. To fight my way into Darcus's compound and destroy him. I cannot kill him myself, just as he cannot kill me. But you…"

"No. There has to be another way."

"This is the only way," Hunt said softly. "I promise you, the world will go on turning. The human race will heal and come out of this stronger than ever. The good fight against evil and injustice will be continued by the men and women who are meant to continue it. I am but flesh and blood, Char. Let me right the wrongs. Give me this."

I thought of Jack standing in the hallway with a gun and a sword, ready to give his life to the cause. Jesus, I was just a plus-sized model with great hair and a life full of guilty pleasures. Wine and reality TV and clothes so expensive you could put a down payment on a car with the money spent. But my friends had taught me over the years that some things were bigger than us. Some things were worth fighting for. Worth dying for.

I looked over at Abram, still laying on the floor where he'd fallen. I thought of Jack and Alice. Stacey and Ramsey. Lulu and Briar. All the people I would fight for. Die for.

Then I leaned over and dragged the Godkiller through the blood flowing down my leg. Hefting the weapon up to my shoulder, I braced my feet wide and took aim at Darcus's face.

"Goodbye, Char," Hunt said, voice thick with emotion. "Keep up the good fight."

I let out a single sob and pulled the trigger.

CHAPTER 28

I'D NEVER GIVEN THOUGHT to the potency of a supplicant's blood. Most of the time that I'd seen a conduit use it, they'd take it right from the vein and do the magic immediately. I'd never seen anyone have any reason to hold on to old blood.

Darcus had charged the Godkiller in my blood—my spilled blood, that had grown tacky and oxygenated. He'd done some damage with the weapon under those circumstances, but it was nothing compared to having my fresh blood.

The wave of power that shot out of the end of the pseudo-gun was blinding, like an atomic bomb dropped in a desert in those old films from the war. The gun kicked back painfully into my shoulder which threw me backward onto the ground, even as I still clutched the damn thing.

The air fell staticky and silent before the blast hit its intended target. Then the explosion was deafening, swallowing all sound into a roar that didn't end.

I sat up on my elbows to see Hunt one last time, but he and Darcus were nothing but silhouettes inside a sphere of radiant energy. Then that sphere exploded.

Throwing myself onto the floor, I covered my head and

neck with my arms as the room fell apart around me. I caught sight of Abram, still laying where he'd fallen, and tried to crawl to him.

But something heavy slammed into the back of my head. I knew nothing else.

$$\backsim$$

SOMETHING SCRATCHED at the edges of my awareness. Sounded like mice in the floorboards, which had been a legitimate problem in my first New York apartment. My landlord got quite a few middle of the night phone calls in which I screeched like a banshee and demanded he come do something about it.

So my immediate reaction was to pull my feet up off the ground. That's where the mice were, after all. They couldn't fly. Although, I guess in New York City, anything was possible.

But my knees couldn't budge. I was wedged between something heavy and the floor, my knees curled up in the fetal position and my arms uncomfortably wrapped around my head. I couldn't move anything but my fingers. Then I remembered the Godkiller. The explosion. Hunt.

Terror kicked in.

"Help!" I screamed, attempting to kick at the debris laying over me. "I'm stuck!"

Tiny slants of light pierced the darkness nearby, the air thick with dust. So at least I wasn't in some kind of airless tomb. But not being able to move was a horrifying sensation. All of a sudden, I wanted nothing more than to stretch out my legs, to stand up, to feel light on my face, and that sudden, completely illogical need filled me with stark terror. What if I could never do those things again? Maybe the entire building had collapsed on top of me and this would be my final resting place.

Then some of the weight on top of me shifted and Jack called, "Char? Are you there?"

His voice sounded as if it came from far away. Could have been the inches of debris between us, or the ringing in my ears from the Godkiller.

Relief chased away the terror, and I had to speak past a lump in my throat. "Yeah. It's me."

"Don't move. I'm going to get this stuff off you."

The scratching intensified, and I realized it hadn't been mice, like my waking brain had conjured up, but rather, Jack searching for me. And others, by the sound of it, since I could hear more rubble shifting and moving farther away.

While I waited on Jack to break through to me, I focused on my breathing. In and out, a reminder that I was alive. Somewhere close by, Abram would be alive, too. I just knew it. He'd come out of much worse before thanks to his beast, and he would this, as well. I clung to that as the heaviness above me lightened, then as objects began to shift, then as gray sunshine filtered in around Jack's smudged, worried face.

"Oh thank fuck," Jack muttered, leaning into the hole he'd made. "Is anything else stuck? Can you stand up?"

I tentatively pulled my arms down to my sides, groaning as all the blood rushed into my fingers and made everything tingle. I had just enough room in my womb-like hole to sit up and reach Jack's arms.

He pulled me out of the rubble, and I blinked into an abnormal amount of gray sunlight. Darcus's office had *not* been this bright, but that was because prior to the Godkiller blast, there had been an exterior wall.

The whole of New York City stretched out beyond the open hole, the sky now a gunpowder gray and spitting rain. Overhead, another hole opened onto the floor above, where the Godkiller had decimated the ceiling and sent loads of plaster, wood, and rebar crashing down into Darcus's office. I sat on my ass for a long moment, staring at the city and the destroyed floor above, understanding just how close I'd come to death.

Jack sat with me in silence, his hand on my shoulder. I appreciated his willingness to just *be* there, because I needed it.

"Abram," I finally said, getting to my knees and trying to find a path not littered with debris. "Abram's under here somewhere."

Jack leapt to his feet and helped me down off the giant pile that had once covered me. "Can you sense him?"

"Maybe," I replied, glancing down at my half-healed wrist, where I'd torn out the microchip. Closing my eyes, I called on my power and cast my senses out, looking for Abram's magical signature. As a beast, he burned hotter and brighter than a normal human life, so I knew I could find him.

If he'd survived.

I turned a slow circle, scanning the area with my heart in my throat. What if he hadn't? Darcus could have killed him with that magically-enhanced punch. The explosion and subsequent fall out could have left him dead. And the longer I scanned the room looking for him, the more it looked like he wasn't there.

No. I refused to believe it. I picked my way around the room, moving as quickly as I could, considering the amount of obstacles in my path. I knew where Abram had lay in reference to the office door, which was still intact, surprisingly. After I located where I thought he should be, I touched piles of detritus, sending a kind of pulse into everything I could touch that would search for an organic body.

And I found one.

"He's here," I told Jack, my heartbeat choking me as I began to yank at the shit covering the man I loved.

"Hey, wait. Calm down," Jack said soothingly, pulling me away from the pile. "We have to be careful. If we pull out the wrong thing, the whole pile could collapse and suffocate him. We have to take it slow, okay?"

I nodded. "What about magic? Could I use magic?"

Jack shrugged and reached for a broken chunk of ceiling. "I'm not sure. We can't see him under here to make sure we don't hurt him. Maybe just be on standby in case something goes wrong."

So against my better judgement, I stood off to the side and let Jack take the lead. He worked slowly but efficiently, calculating whatever physics existed in his clever brain before he chose what to move or shift next.

"What happened?" I asked as he worked.

"You blew up the side of the building, and the conduits in charge of Darcus's army just...stopped fighting." Jack tugged a wicked long piece of rebar off the pile and huffed with exertion as he pushed it aside. "They were under some kind of curse. Darcus's death ended it. They weren't fighting for him by their own will. He'd forced them. At least, that's what they told us."

"That makes a little more sense. Who would have wanted to work for that nutjob?" I took a deep breath and asked, "So they confirmed Darcus is dead?"

Jack nodded and gestured over the rubble. "I'm guessing we'll find his body somewhere in here, too."

"His and Hunt's," I said softly, then gave him a quick and dirty of what went down before I pulled the trigger.

Jack whistled, his gaze still on the slowly lowering pile and sweat dotting his pale hairline. "Wow. Hunt knew what he was doing."

"Yeah. It was his plan from the beginning, I think." I reached out to take a hunk of ceiling tile from him and tossed it aside. "What about Ramsey, Alice, and Stacey?"

"All safe and accounted for," Jack assured me. "They went downstairs to help free the prisoners in Darcus's rose garden. And a few of the commanders of Wonderland are working out negotiations with Darcus's army."

"So it's really over?"

"Looks that way." He yanked a solid piece of plaster off the pile, and as it slid away, Abram's face was revealed below.

My heart stopped in my chest. He looked pale. Ghostly.

Then he opened his eyes and said, "I think there's something in my leg, if you'd be so kind as to yank it out."

I burst out laughing, with a little bit of tears to go along with it, so that I sounded slightly hysterical as we finished pulling my boyfriend out of the rubble.

Sure enough, a hunk of twisted metal had embedded in his thigh. It was thick enough, and precariously jammed near his main artery, so that I didn't feel comfortable pulling it out and trying to heal it on my own.

"There's a medical center on the fourth floor," Jack said. "I'll grab a team with a stretcher and be right back."

After Jack left the room, I lay down on Abram's uninjured side and put my head on his chest. His heartbeat was strong and steady.

"I thought you might have died."

"If I wasn't a beast, I probably would have," he said, tightening his arm around my back. "I'm a lot harder to kill than most."

Lifting my head to look up at him, I murmured, "Thank God for that."

Then I kissed him. All of my worries faded away with the satin feel of his lips on mine. He cupped my face in one hand, his thumb tracing lightly over my cheek as he deepened the kiss. I would have stayed there, holding him, just to touch him and know he was alive, if Jack hadn't returned with help.

A couple of big burly Wonderland guys managed to shift Abram, and his metal spear, onto the stretcher without hurting him too much. As they lifted him, I took his hand and said, "I'm going to stay behind with Jack and dig out Darcus and Hunt. Are you going to be okay?"

Abram grinned, though it was just a little pained. "I'll be better the next time you see me."

"I'll be down ASAP," I promised, then watched as the Wonderland team carried him from the room and disappeared into the dark hallway.

"I want to see Darcus's body," I told Jack, squaring my shoulders. "To be sure he's gone. And I want to retrieve Hunt to give him a hero's burial."

Jack nodded. "I agree on both counts. Do that thing you did to find Abram?"

We walked around the room as I sent pulses into piles of debris. I was hesitant to walk too close to the wide-open exterior wall, in case the floor was compromised and our weight would just send us crashing into the floor beneath. Or out of the building entirely.

But it wasn't until we got close to the edge, when I finally felt bodies—or more so, a void where bodies could be— beneath the rubble. No heat pulse, which was both promising and heartbreaking at the same time.

We didn't bother being careful this time. If Darcus's cronies said he was dead, then more than likely, both the Brothers were beyond help now. And it was true, because we found...pieces.

I stumbled away and retched over the floor, though nothing came out. My last meal felt like a hundred years ago.

"Their faces are almost untouched," Jack said. He was still staring down, lifting up pieces of debris and eyeing the decimated bodies. "But their parts are burned nearly beyond recognition. Whatever that Godkiller weapon does, it does it well."

My legs felt weak. I dropped to my knees and wrapped my arms around my stomach, trying not to remember Hunt's face. *"Goodbye, Char. Keep up the good fight."*

I'd killed him. It didn't matter that he'd told me to. It didn't matter that he'd come here willing to die if it meant ending his brother's reign of terror.

I'd killed my friend, and I would have to carry that weight the rest of my life.

"Hey, what's this?" Jack said, tearing me from my lost and lonely thoughts.

I glanced over at him. He stood silhouetted by gray daylight, his form wavy with the tears in my eyes. He bent down and pulled something shiny from the wreckage.

Huntsman's axe.

Jack hefted the weight of the weapon, staring at it with a strange look on his face. "It tingles. It almost feels like…"

He didn't finish his statement. There was a flash of light and magic, and tendrils of orange magic wrapped around Jack's arm, then around the axe. With another flash, the magic sank into them both, connecting them.

The ax had chosen its new huntsman.

Lulu was going to kill me.

CHAPTER 29

FOR THE FIRST time in my life, I had no desire to live in the city.

It would be years before New York City became anything like its old self again. The poverty, the destruction, the decay —it had taken its toll under Darcus's leadership, and none of those things could be rectified overnight.

So Jack and Alice moved their mother to Wonderland, where they would be comparably safer while the world found its new balance. Jack was welcomed as a hero—their new leader, the man who carried the magical axe, the new huntsman, though he refused to use the name.

Just because Darcus was gone didn't mean some of his more maniacal cronies weren't still around, trying to cause problems. Apparently, not all of them were only doing it because of some curse. And that meant Wonderland still had a purpose of bringing peace to the world and rebuilding the dystopian society that had subsisted for so long.

And boy, did they have their work cut out for them. The human race could be crooked and evil, just as easily as it could be kind. Luckily, I thought Jack, and Alice too, were equal to the task.

Two weeks after the events in Darcus's compound, we laid Hunt to rest in a Wonderland tomb with a beautiful service where we each took turns talking about him. Stacey could hardly speak through her tears—apparently, in the fifteen years I'd been absent, they'd built a stalwart friendship. When it came my turn, I wasn't much better, blubbering about friendship and sacrifice and damn good people like I was drunk on a karaoke mic.

After Hunt's funeral, I headed into the park behind headquarters for some fresh air. I needed to breathe, to be alone with my thoughts and not be expected to share them. Being surrounded by all the friends I loved meant I had very little time alone. Especially with the weight of Hunt's funeral sitting on my shoulders, I just needed some peace.

But the park wasn't empty, despite the late evening hour. I found Alice sitting on a bench, watching flames dance atop her fingertips. In a world of magic, burning fingers aren't really startling.

Unless it's a supplicant doing it.

I sank to the bench beside her, stunned at this new development. A supplicant shouldn't have access to magic. They were the battery for the conduits, who had the magic but not the charge. Two halves of one whole to perform magic. Except for me, of course, and my dual blood.

But Alice wasn't dual. Yet...

"It started after the battle," Alice said without prompting. She didn't look at me, choosing instead to keep staring at the flames. "Jack pissed me off. I don't even remember what he did. Something insensitive, like he always does."

"Big brothers," I scoffed.

She finally looked up at me and smiled. The flames reflected in her blue eyes, and I could see Lulu in her face. "Yeah. Anyway, something came over me and I just...did it. Shot a fireball at him."

"Whoa. What did he say?"

"He can do it, too."

My mouth dropped open. "So a conduit and a supplicant both now have the ability to do magic without each other."

Alice extinguished the flames and rubbed her palms up and down her black jeans. "I guess. A few other people are muttering about it, too. Like something shifted when Darcus and Hunt died. The magic is just suddenly...*there*. Open for the taking."

A few minutes later, she bid me goodnight and left me sitting on the bench, my head going over and over what I'd just seen and heard. Something, presumably the death of the Brothers, had blurred the line between supplicants and conduits. The rules of magic were dictated by the gods before the beginning of time, but now the rules had changed. Because the Brothers died?

I knew innately that supplicants and conduits wouldn't become besties overnight. It would be a process, one that took time and trust and a world without an evil dictator. But despite that, this new revelation gave me hope. Nobody needed to "use" one another anymore. Both conduits and supplicants could be self-sufficient. That would go a long way to mending old bridges.

But would it be enough? It still allowed for magic to fall into the wrong hands, afterall.

"For never was a story of more woe than this of Juliet and her Romeo."

I startled at the sudden voice and turned around to see the talking cat where Alice had been just moments before. "What's that supposed to mean? Abram and I got our happily ever after."

If a cat could raise an eyebrow, that is what this one did. "I wasn't talking about you, Char."

"Then who?"

"Why, Darcus, of course."

I throttled to my feet. "Darcus was no Romeo."

"Ah, he was not a good man, but was he not just as much a star-crossed lover?"

"What's that supposed to mean?"

But the cat was already fading away.

"Wait. Get back here! What's that supposed to mean?"

Too late. Of course that stupid cat wasn't going to tell me anything. I plopped back down on the bench and crossed my arms, completely distracted by the new riddle.

I felt Abram approaching before I saw him, and some of my nerves eased.

"There she is," he said, and my cheeks warmed as I gazed up at Abram in the fading sunlight.

He filled out his suit nicely, looking somewhat like the man I'd met so long ago in that basement nightclub, who had let me weasel my way into management and then stolen my heart. But he was different, too. Changed, somehow, in the way that hardship could mold people into better, stronger versions of themselves.

"Briar and Ramsey are waiting for us," Abram said, offering me a hand. He stepped back to draw me to my feet, and his limp wasn't quite as pronounced as it was a few days ago. A few more transformations to beast, and the internal damage would be gone for good.

As we walked, I told him about the cat and he nodded, silent for a moment before offering, "Do you think that means he was in love with a goddess?"

My eyes went wide. "I don't know, but that piece fits the puzzle and makes my brain stop hurting, so I'm gonna go with that."

He wrapped his arm around my shoulder. "Love can make people do crazy things," he muttered.

"Sacrificing an entire planet maybe takes it a *little* too far, don't you think?"

Abram didn't answer. Somewhere in there was a beast who thought there were no lengths he wouldn't go to. But I knew, deep down, the man I loved would always overcome the beast. One day, I'd get him to see it, too.

I stopped by headquarters to give my dad a hug. He'd already hooked up with a couple of his old scientist pals, and the group of them were working on new tech to get the future back in motion. He gave me an absentminded kiss on the cheek, but before I could walk out the door, he stood up and yelled, "I love you!" so loud the whole room laughed.

It was my favorite part of the night. I'd gone from an orphan to having my dad again. What girl could say that?

In the two weeks we'd been staying in Wonderland, Ramsey and my dad's team had worked round the clock to build a portal between Grimoult and Wonderland. That's where we found Briar, tapping the toe of her elegant rope sandal and glancing at her watch like we were holding her back from afternoon tea.

"Rose has dance rehearsal," Ramsey explained when I gave him a *what-is-wrong-with-her-now* look. "And apparently the other moms think Briar isn't involved enough."

"The other moms know nothing," I assured her, tossing an arm around her skinny shoulders. "You do you, girl. The rest will fall into place."

I'd thought we'd be staying at Briar and Ramsey's palace —it was certainly big enough for all of us. But on the other side of the portal, beneath a late night sky filled with stars, Abram took hold of my arm and said, "I have a surprise for you."

We said our goodbyes, and I promised Ramsey I'd see him bright and early to head back to Wonderland and set up our schedule for teaching budding magic users. It reminded me of my conversation with Alice, and with a little thrill, I realized our students were going to double.

I laced my arm through Abram's elbow and leaned into him, letting him take the lead. "What do you think about starting a new bar?"

He glanced over at me, one dark brow raised. "A bar?"

"Yeah. Like The Castle, Part Two."

"You realize our first foray into running a bar didn't end well," Abram pointed out.

"I'm going to go ahead and blame your curse for that fuck up. Because I was running the show *like a boss*." I flexed my other arm, pretending I had muscles.

I had strength. On the inside.

Abram chuckled. "You did your best, I'll give you that."

"Come on. It'll be fun."

"Let's talk about it after we find our new normal. Promise," he added when I opened my mouth to argue. "Let's just be together for a while. You and me."

"That sounds wonderful."

The path we walked was free from streetlights and illuminated only by the moon. We passed sleeping cottages set back into trees, and in the distance, I could hear revelers partying, music playing, the rhythmic crash of ocean waves. For the first time in what felt like ages, everything was all right.

Not only that, but everything was all right—and I had the love of my life strolling by my side.

I was too busy mooning over Abram's face in the twilight to realize he'd come to a stop and was looking at me expectantly. I snapped out of my sappy reverie and said, "What?"

He cut his dark gaze to my right, and I followed his lead, glancing in that direction. We were at the edge of a short cliff covered in trees surrounding a cottage. The stucco walls were so white they glowed pale in the night, and the shutters were a deep red that looked nearly purple in the dark. Flowers danced on the breeze in the mulched bed on either side of the front stoop.

"What...I don't understand?" I looked between him and the little cottage. "Is it a hotel?"

Abram laughed and dug out a key ring from his pocket. "No. It's ours."

"You bought a house? For *us?*" My heart swelled like a balloon, and I clung tighter to him, lest I float away.

"Yes. For us," he said gruffly. "Might I carry you over the threshold?"

I threw my arm around his neck and jumped into his arms, trusting that he'd catch me. He did, of course, as he always would. His arm clamped firmly under my knees, and I threw my head back dramatically. "Take me home, baby!"

I thought I caught sight of an eye roll at my theatrics, but come on. The man knew what he was getting into.

A short, narrow front walk flanked by flowers led to a small stoop that was barely big enough for the both of us. Abram reached under my bottom and unlocked the door, then kicked it open with his shoe to carry me inside.

The moment he put me down, I raced off through the house. It was adorable—not at all like any place I'd ever expected to live in my past life, but I was a different person now, too. I could see Abram and I cooking at the gas stove, watching television with a view of the ocean out the window, walking these halls, decorating these rooms. It was perfect.

And I could definitely see him naked on the king size bed.

A cool, salty breeze rushed in off the ocean through the open window as I turned to eye Abram standing in the shadows. I hadn't turned on the light—it wasn't necessary, with the way the moon illuminated the room.

I reached behind my back for the zipper on my dress. "Seems we have a new bed to break in."

Abram's eyes glittered, and he stalked forward, shedding his suit jacket that he then tossed over the armchair in the corner. He unbuttoned his sleeves and licked his lips. "It's imperative we test it out. We want only the best."

Turning around, I purred, "Can you unzip me the rest of the way?"

Warmth poured off his body as he grasped the zipper and tugged. The fabric parted, letting in the cool breeze, and then his fingers trailed down my spine with aching slowness. He reached up and unhooked both sleeves, sliding them deliberately off my arms before he placed a kiss to my bare shoulder. He kept tugging, until the dress fell away from my breasts, rolled past my hips, and then fell to the floor.

"Naughty girl," Abram whispered, both hands sliding up my belly to cup my bare breasts. "Why didn't you tell me you were naked under there?"

I leaned back against his chest, arching my back as his fingers pinched and rolled my nipples to hard nubs. "To be fair, I just don't have any underwear right now. The apocalypse has not been kind to my wardrobe."

Abram laughed, and I felt the rumble of it through his chest. "We'll replace your closet in no time. But for now… clothes are simply unnecessary."

He guided me forward, then took me by the hand and twirled me to face him at the edge of the mattress. Our bodies melded together and our lips met in a slow, sensuous kiss that awakened every nerve ending in my body. My nipples chafed across the cotton of his shirt as I pressed harder against him, deepening the kiss, wrapping one leg around my waist until his hard cock was pressed against my core.

Abram slipped his hands beneath my legs and lifted me, then both of us tumbled to the mattress in a tangle of limbs. His hips ground into me, teasing small gasps from me that he caught with his lips. Then he broke the kiss and straightened, ripping his shirt off his body in a ridiculous show of machismo. And let me tell you—it did it for me.

Then Abram's lips moved lower, lower, lower, until his mouth closed over my clit and his tongue danced up the seam of me like a stroke of fire on sensitive skin. I moaned, and he glanced up at me, mouth working my folds with languid sensuousness, and the sight of his face between my legs was so damn hot, an orgasm rose with ferocity.

"I'm going to come," I gasped out, moving my hips against his mouth. I didn't know what I wanted more—to feel his tongue and ride out my pleasure on his face, or for him to whip off those pants and sink into me before the orgasm came.

But he sure knew what he wanted. The moment I told him it was coming, his tongue flicked across my clit and he sank two fingers deep inside me, where he massaged the sensitive spot inside and worked my orgasm out in a matter of seconds. I writhed as pleasure washed over me, gasping his name like a prayer.

His warmth moved away, and I stared at him through satisfied, heavy-lidded eyes as he shucked his pants. His cock sprang free of its trappings, and I reached for it, wrapping my fingers around his shaft and squeezing. He swallowed visibly, leaning into my grip as he dipped a hand back between my legs, testing me. His fingers slid in and out, slowly, torturously. Then he lunged, his thick length spearing me with a kind of possessiveness that sent tingles down my spine.

Our bodies moved together in tandem, slowly at first, but building in intensity until Abram pounded into me, taking me like the alpha male I knew and loved. He grasped my ass, lifting me up, spreading me wide until his cock bottomed out inside me. Another orgasm unfurled inside me, and I urged him faster, harder, until we rode the crest of the wave together, our breaths mingling and our lips touching.

In the aftermath, laying sweaty with his arms around me and his lips pressing lazily against my shoulder, I thanked every god, deva, and angel of every religion for bringing this man back to me.

~

"HONEY, YOU STOCKED THE FRIDGE!" I crowed, closing the door to open the freezer. Gasping, I pulled out a quart of double fudge cookie dough and turned wide eyes on him. "You got me ice cream."

Abram stepped close and planted a kiss on my forehead. "I did. And I'll have some with you."

I filled our bowls with ice cream while Abram sliced strawberries to throw on top, then we grabbed fresh spoons from the drawer and headed out onto the back veranda.

The view was spectacular—not so high that my innate fear of falling made me want to crawl on the ground instead of walking, but high enough to give us a one hundred eighty degree view of the ocean and the white sand below the cliff. A bright blue patio table and two matching chairs waited for us, angled toward the ocean and a sky full of tiny stars.

"How on earth did you have time to not only track down and buy a house, but to get it fully stocked and furnished." I held up my spoon and waved it at him. "We have spoons!"

"Magic," he said with a wink.

We didn't talk for a while. We just ate our ice cream in companionable silence with the cool ocean breeze keeping us company. All the terror and the near-death experiences, all the loss and worry, everything had led to this moment. We had no enemy banging down our new door. No ghost of a long-dead Conduit breathing down our necks about our next big task in the quest to save the world.

Just me and Abram and the rest of our life spread out before us like the ocean.

After I ate my last spoonful of chocolate and strawberries, I sank back in my seat and sighed contentedly.

"Do you like it?" Abram asked, his voice so low it was nearly whisked away on the breeze.

"Love it," I murmured, mesmerized by the tiny white caps playing across the dark surface of the sea. "It's perfect. Couldn't be more perfect."

"There is one way it could be. At least, for me."

I glanced over at him, confused, and found him on one knee. He held a red velvet ring box between his hands, opened to reveal a delicate silver band set with a perfect sweetheart diamond.

Shock rendered me deaf and mute for several moments, before I shot straight up in my seat. My heart resumed its regularly scheduled beating, albeit a little faster.

"Charisse Bellamy," Abram said softly. "Would you do me the honor of becoming my wife?"

I stood, accidentally knocking over my chair in my haste. I wanted to be closer to him and not have the arm of a chair between us when I said, "Are you fucking kidding me? *Yes!* Yes, I'll marry you!"

A grin broke out across his handsome face, and he stood, already tugging the ring out of the box to place it on my finger. It slid into place like it had been made for me and only me. Then he leaned down and gathered me in his arms, kissing me senseless.

"I should have thought to bring champagne for this surprise," Abram murmured against my lips.

I pulled away at his mention of champagne, and realized now was the perfect time for me to reveal what I'd been holding in. "So here's the thing," I said, my heart pounding faster. "I have a surprise for you, too."

"Oh? How'd you have time for that?" he teased.

"Well, the thing about this surprise is it only takes one good try." I reached out and took his hand, gently tugging it to rest against my belly. I saw the recognition in his eye before I even spoke. "We're pregnant."

The cheers that came out of him as he lifted me in the air and swung me around the veranda could probably be heard all the way back at Briar and Ramsey's castle. I heard answering cheers from off in the distance from people celebrating their freedom from Darcus's tyranny. Then Abram was kissing me, and my cheeks were wet with tears that could have belonged to me or him.

But at least, for now, they were tears of joy, for the new life we'd been given—both here in this little cottage on Grimoult and the one growing inside me.

Our happily ever after had only just begun.

Want more books in this world? Subscribe at https://rebeccahamilton.com/newsletter/ to receive alerts on any upcoming spin off series! For another high-heat paranormal romance, you can also read Rebecca's standalone novel, Origin.

ABOUT THE AUTHORS

ABOUT REBECCA HAMILTON

New York Times bestselling author Rebecca Hamilton writes urban fantasy and paranormal romance for Harlequin, Baste Lübbe, and Evershade. A book addict, registered bone marrow donor, and indian food enthusiast, she often takes to fictional worlds to see what perilous situations her characters will find themselves in next.

Rebecca's Books

CONNER KRESSLEY

USA TODAY bestselling author Conner Kressley is an avid reader and all around lover of storytelling. He's been obsessed with mythology, magic, and all the things that go bump in the night since he could remember. Also, pizza. But who isn't obsessed with pizza?

Conner's Books